The

# The Long Shot

Michael Atherton

© Mike Atherton, 2014

Published by Michael Atherton

A CIP catalogue record for this book is available from the British Library.

ISBN 978-0-9930645-0-0

Book layout and design by Clare Brayshaw

Prepared and printed by:

York Publishing Services Ltd
64 Hallfield Road
Layerthorpe
York YO31 7ZQ

Tel: 01904 431213

Website: www.yps-publishing.co.uk

For Charles, Eric and Phil

# Acknowledgments

Writing 'The Long Shot' was a joy, having the support from my wife and family made it so.

So special thanks go to Di, she gave me the time to sit and write when really other things needed doing.

A heart felt thank you also goes to Jonathan Ferguson at the Royal Armoury in Leeds for guiding me through the more technical aspects of weaponry in the First World War

On an historical note, the characters in 'The Long Shot' are mainly fiction but the soldiers they represent are very real, the battles and conditions are as they were. With that in mind spare a thought for the men who stood and fought and the thousands who are still there.

This book is for them.

Mike Atherton

# CHAPTER 1

# Jack

**August 22, 1916**

The Somme offensive is in its seventh week, six weeks longer than planned.

Sergeant Jack Adams coughed, part of his morning routine after a breakfast of fags and phlegm. The tea he had in his mess tin stank, but worse than the smell was the taste, tainted with petrol and an oily film that floated on top.

Jack rubbed his hands together to try and get some movement into his stiff fingers. It had been a cold night, but the day promised to be warm and balmy. At home, the harvest would be starting, the rabbits running wild without anyone to stop them.

Something had changed; it had been two days since that shot, the one that had had his name on it and which had missed by less than an inch. Clearly, his name had been spelled incorrectly. The bullet had thumped into the sandbag that he'd been resting his head and rifle on. It had been heading straight for the centre of his head and but for a splendid rat that had caught his eye and made him turn his head. It would have killed him outright.

A sharpshooter, like him, trained to hit first time every time, had been watching Jack for about an hour, waiting.

There was something personal about snipers, not random – like with shrapnel or machine gun fire – but carefully aimed.

Loathed by the enemy and loved by his own, Jack was an excellent shot but he had a human failing: compassion. He never released the key to eternal rest (or bullet to most people) until he was absolutely certain he would kill his target, quickly and efficiently like the rabbits he shot for the pot back home.

The realisation that he would very probably die here in France, far from home, had hit him hard. He didn't want to die; he had everything to live for. He did know, however, that it would be quick: a sniper's shot to kill a sniper.

He walked, hunched over, down along the trench. His watch was due to start in an hour but he had to find a new place today. News was that the Bavarians had moved into the trench system opposite. No one liked the Bavarians, and killing their officers was easy – they were like proud peacocks strutting around.

Brave or just stupid, Jack didn't really care. As a gamekeeper on the estate back home, he had seen enough of the upper classes to be satisfied when he saw one drop, and if he was honest with himself, he didn't much mind which side the toffs were on, they were all the same: strutting, and cock sure.

He did, however, like one: Captain Alcot – known as Master Tim back home – was the son of his employer, Colonel Alcot. The Colonel was an old man now, too old to join in this war. He had been too old for the last one but had gone anyway, and he'd come back with shrapnel in his back after only a few weeks, invalided out of the Army with little more than his pride injured, but redundant nevertheless.

Master Tim was a good lad, honest and hardworking and what he lacked in handsome he made up for in grace. He was never far from the thick of it back home and even closer to it here in France. Jack had watched him grow from a lad, teaching him to shoot, catch rabbits and to fish in the stream. Jack was only five years older than Tim but had aged like an old ham compared to him.

"Morning Adams."

"Morning Sir." It was a show for the others – the new boys – for there were precious few of the old ones left. Most had fallen on that first day six weeks ago, felled like so many trees. The awfulness of it still made Jack shiver, but for Captain Alcot, it must have been much worse. A Lieutenant then, as Company Commander he had seen all but two of his men fall that day. All gone, many still out there, some no more than twenty feet from where they'd started.

Jack felt his stomach churn, not sure if it was the tea, the guilt or the anger. He took a deep drag of his last Woodbine for the day and with a hearty cough spat phlegm onto the muddy floor. Time to move on; there was work to do.

His job today was to kill Germans, officers preferably but any German would do. He dropped all but the essentials: his Lee-Enfield with sniper scope and 50 rounds of ammunition in pouches, tucked inside his heavy woollen trousers. Despite the heat he was glad of his lice-ridden ghillie suit; the mud that clung to its weave made the legs of his trousers almost impervious to the many sharp hazards he would encounter today on his way to his lair.

He crawled his way along the slip trench, heading for the most obvious tree for ten miles. Why they had asked him to look at that particular site wasn't for him to question really,

3

but he knew for a fact that every tree was used by the artillery for range finding, and every forward observation officer knew the exact distances to everything above five feet high.

He shook his head as he crawled. He would give the tree a miss today; he still had high hopes for his hide in no-man's land, despite the shot the other day. It was the best hide he had ever built, and besides, no one would expect him to return to that site so soon after such a close shave.

As he clawed his way forward, the trench slope got shallower; this was a good place to keep your head down. He went past "Fritz" who was part of the trench, having been laid to rest there last year following a very close call. He had died like so many, but unable to be buried, he was pushed over the top of the shooting line and there he lay until the shells dug him a new grave.

He no longer had a face, nor indeed any features apart from a constant snarl on his dull grey skull, and Jack had seen him many times since he'd been in this hell-hole people called home. Some days – if it had been raining – the skull would shine bright white when the sun shone through, but today, he was still wearing splashes from the wet mudpack of a few shells that had burst around him.

Jack smiled; surely Fritz had it better than anyone else around here. As he always did, Jack touched the skull on the forehead and said a quiet prayer. "Sleep now, Fritz, it's over." For some strange reason, Jack always felt better for saying this, as if compassion had any place here!

The lone standing tree was some sixty yards out of the trench system along a belly rut worn by previous lone gunmen over the past year. Dear God, did nothing ever change here? How had this tree survived when all its wooden

4

comrades had fallen? Much like Jack's story and his battalion, he supposed. The truth was that neither the Germans nor the British wanted to destroy this lone tree; it was much in demand by observers and snipers.

He veered off to the left and crawled into the first of many shell holes that would afford him the cover he needed to get to his camouflaged sniper's lair. It was quiet today; nothing was crashing and shell bursts were rare, a brief respite from the madness. This was a dangerous time of day for everyone, not least because it allowed men time to think.

Thinking led to questioning and nobody liked to be asked questions because no one liked to answer them. The question was always the same: why? The truth was, no one knew why, and most of the time no one really cared. The best any man could hope for was a "Blighty one" – a wound that would take him home, or failing that, take him to the promised land, and quickly.

Most men thought they were invincible and that it would never be them. Indeed, that had been Jack's exact thought until two days ago, but now he knew: invincibility was the dream of fools.

The realisation that he could and probably would die here in France was a hard lesson to take. He knew he wouldn't be blessed with a Blighty; snipers were vermin and had to be shot dead. He crawled along towards his nest, where the only company for the next twelve hours would be his new best friends, the rats. He let his mind drift back to happier times, back home with Alice.

# CHAPTER 2

# Alice

Jack had met Alice again in early spring 1915; she was a local girl from the village who had lost her husband in the first days of the war. He had been a local huntsman who joined the cavalry in July 1914, just a month before the dreadful war had started. He fell, along with most of his comrades, at the heroic retreat from Mons.

Alice wore her grief like a heavy winter coat. Her pale complexion was clear through her mourning veil. Jack had known Alice for most of his life; she was a girl he'd gone to church with on Sundays. She was the daughter of Harry Barber, the local butcher, and she had met her future husband at the hunt kennels where her father was delivering meat for the hunt hounds.

At the age of 18, Alice had married Tom Kelly and by the age of 20, she was a widow. Jack had high hopes for Alice, and before he'd left to join the Army, they had walked out arm in arm.

Jack had spoken to Alice in church on the first Sunday after the post lad had delivered the dreadful news about Tom's death. She was dignified but shattered, a delicate crystal vase dropped and caught as she hit the floor. She had maintained her form but had cracked into a thousand frosted pieces in the catcher's hand, beautiful but damaged.

Jack thought she was the most beautiful woman he had ever seen. In all honesty, he hadn't seen many women outside the village, but whenever he saw Alice she was happy and laughing. Now, she was wearing her black dress. Jack had waited until after the service to talk to her, clutching his hat in his hands. He wasn't the only parishioner who wanted to pass on his condolences: there was a long line, a very long line indeed.

# CHAPTER 3

# Home

The summer of 1913 had been hot – the harvest this year was going to be a good one – and there was a sense of bounty all around the estate.

Colonel Alcot was both a generous and canny gentleman, very popular as a land owner who looked after all his tenants and farm staff. It was he who had recognised Jacks uncanny ability with a rifle. Indeed, he had let Jack use his James Purdy SMLE Mk 3 sniper rifle, with a set of Aldis sights, to shoot a wild boar that had gored some of the hounds whilst cornered.

Jack and the gamekeeper, Jim Cunningham, had accompanied the Colonel. They had found the boar but it was quickly out of sight and way too far away for the Colonel to shoot. Cunningham couldn't use the rifle because he was a left-hander so the Colonel had asked Jack if he fancied a pop, handing him the rifle.

It was a marriage made in shooting heaven. Jack took careful aim. Whilst resting the rifle on a log which lay on the ground, he took aim and sighted the boar about two inches above its head. Taking a long breath, he slowly breathed out, feeling the trigger and gently, oh so gently, he squeezed.

He never even heard the crack; he just watched as the boar lifted its head and fell dead to the ground. Both the

Colonel and Jim shook their heads in disbelief – neither had ever seen a shot like that. They walked over 600 yards to find the hog lying exactly where it had fallen. The bullet had entered the boar's mighty head just behind the ear and he had died instantly.

Over the next few weeks, they tested Jack again and again but he never missed, resulting in the Colonel giving Jack a position with Jim Cunningham in the shooting lodge. Jack was a willing and more than able student, and under Jim's tutelage, he became a phenomenal shot.

It didn't take long for Jack and Jim to become friends. Jim was an easy-going master at arms; his knowledge of shooting seemed endless. The Colonel sponsored Jack in both County and National shooting meets at Bisley near Aldershot. For Jack these trips were full of adventure, and he was sure that somewhere, the local yeomanry would notice his skills.

War was on the horizon and men like Jack Adams would soon be needed and in great demand.

# CHAPTER 4

# *Spring* 1915

Jack had asked Alice to walk after church. If she was honest, she was glad of the company; things had been hard since the news of Tom's death had arrived. First there had been sympathy, then pity. Within days there were more widows with life-changing letters, the post boy had a new bag to deliver the mail, bigger and getting fuller on a daily basis.

Mrs David had had one and so too had Elizabeth Corby, her husband listed missing. Mrs David wore a black veil and red eyes that told everyone her son William had fallen, shrapnel apparently but no one was really sure what that was. Jack had heard of a shell called a Jack Johnson named because it carried a punch like the heavyweight boxer over the sea in America.

Alice looked shy, almost coy, barely able to look at Jack who in turn stuttered his way through his words. It was awkward. People would talk, it was natural. Both Jack and Alice were thought of highly within Langwith, the small country village in which they lived – Jack on the outskirts and Alice in the centre, no more than a good walk or a cycle ride apart.

Harry Barber's shop was full of the womenfolk of Langwith, all chattering like chicks in a pheasant pen. Outside, the shop front was decked in rabbits: there must have been two hundred hanging there, their partners, the ducks and three huge hares, all staring through dead eyes.

The shop quieted to a hush when Alice came out of the back room, still wearing her black dress and hat. Balanced precariously on her head, it was held with a large pin, her Mother's 'Sunday hat' pin. On her lapel she wore an emerald green brooch given to her by her late husband as a wedding present. It stood out and reflected her steely look of determination to carry on as strong and proud as any woman.

Jack waited at the door; he couldn't help but notice the looks some of the local gossips cast his way. 'How could he?' they asked, she's not been widowed for a year yet and here he was courting her affections; the gall of the pair of them!

In truth, their accusations were wide of any mark. There was no plan of romance or indeed any liaison other than that offered to a long standing friend, who due to the awful ghastly business of war had made her young face seem so much older.

Yes, it was true that Jack was sweet on Alice but decency demanded he could only offer a kindness he would have offered any widow. Not many widows in this village could walk out, most of the widows like Agnes Cunliffe were old and had enjoyed the joys of a long marriage to husbands who fathered the children whom Jack and Alice had grown and played with. There were more widowers than widows in Langwith, but the next few years would change all that.

In time, the lads from the pit would go to war and many would never return.

Jack took Alice's offered hand on his arm. It was a beautiful day, warm with a gentle breeze. The river would be alive with the hatch of summer mayflies later but Jack would have Alice back in plenty of time before he would cast a line that evening. There was a huge trout he had spotted lurking behind a large boulder in the middle and he thought it would make a fine meal for his mother and father, with plenty left for him.

He smiled at Alice, who was ignoring the whispers behind her, and shouted to Harry that he would have her back in time for dinner. Harry looked at Jack with old eyes, kindly eyes that had shed many tears for his beloved wife and daughter's grief, but quiet and strong was Harry's way; he showed little emotion to the outside world. He could dispatch an animal in seconds, but inside he felt each one.

He called back, "Look after her, Jack!" There was no need for him to say anything but he wanted the gossips to know he held Jack Adams in high regard, and trusted him to protect his Alice from any harm or hurt.

Alice found her time in Jack's company a blissful escape from the pain and emptiness she felt when she was alone. She had moved back in with her parents shortly after the news of Tom's death. There would be no funeral to attend; Tom had already been buried by the time she had been informed.

Mister Graham, the master of hounds and Tom's employer, had said she could stay in the hunt cottage for as long as she needed, but Alice knew they would need it before the autumn and "cubbing" and that a new huntsman would soon be appointed; it was the country way and Alice was a country girl so she understood.

The rumour was that there would be no hunting until the war was over but no one really worried because it would surely be over by Christmas. It did cause some concern that the Army had commandeered a lot of the horses from both the estate and the hunt; most of the best horses had already gone as gifts for the hunt staff that had joined up the day the war started. There was no shortage of horses for the Army.

Alice was pleased that her parents had offered her some escape from the home she had made with Tom. It was a simple life. A whirlwind of a romance had ended with a proposal. Tom was a good man, honest and kind, and well known to everyone in the village. He was a master on a horse and had won the last two point to points; he was born to ride and hunting was his natural environment.

It all seemed a long time ago but it was only two years past, and Jack had been a constant comfort since the memorial service held for Tom. It was a friendship born from pain and sadness rekindled from a childhood spent laughing and playing in the wide expanse of rolling farmland.

Tom and Jack had known each other from the estate but only in passing; their paths rarely crossed but they liked each other, sharing many traits. Both were simple, honest men with good minds and hearts. Both had a passion about the countryside, and at times when they did meet, they were doing work on the land, either preparing it for the chosen sport or working to ensure that the game they hunted was in the very best condition.

Foxes were a perpetual problem; they were controlled by the hunt, but never hunted to oblivion. Only the best animals escaped. No one could really have foreseen the terrible events that would be served on them in the next couple of years, and life was hard but happy.

Tom had been keen to join up; he had met the recruiting team from the 20th Hussars and was totally beguiled by the fine horses and wonderful tunics. There had been problems in Europe between the French and, well, just about everyone, but no one thought it would involve the English.

Tom had spoken to Alice and to Mr Graham about a short stint in the Army and both had been supportive. Alice, however, had been less so because life with Tom had a settled calmness she enjoyed, but she knew Tom wanted more.

# CHAPTER 5

# *Tom*

The Army Sergeant had said that Tom would fit in very well; his riding skills would ensure he earned promotion and a wage that he could send home. Show jumping, polo, and point to point were the breakfast, lunch and dinner of the Hussars.

Mr Graham had said he would hold a position for Tom as long as he was only away for three years; the house would be available to Alice until he came back, and when he did, it would be time to start a family. Everyone was so positive about Tom doing his bit.

He had signed the allegiance form and within a month was away to join the Army. His training had been hard; he gained weight and filled out his manly frame despite working 18 hours a day. He was at home with all things equine, cleaning leather was second nature to him, and sitting on a horse was more natural than walking to Tom; he was an exceptional soldier and very popular within his Squadron. He won the best recruit award and was promoted from Trooper to Lance Corporal within months of finishing his training.

Alice felt a tear run down her cheek. She hadn't even realised she was crying. She remembered how proud she felt the day he had come home on leave, how handsome he was in his Hussars uniform.

Mr. Graham had invited them to attend the hunt ball as his guests, Tom in all his finery and Alice in a long frock she had borrowed from her mother. They were indeed a beautiful couple and danced the night away, Tom a little bit drunk and Alice drinking wine. It was the first time she had sampled wine and after just two glasses she felt her head spin. She wasn't sure if it was the wine or the tight bodice or maybe she was just ecstatically in love.

She felt a familiar ache in her chest; her grief at the loss weighed heavy in her heart. They had been such happy times. She felt Jack's hand on her arm and patted his hand, the tears running freely now.

"Oh Jack, I miss him so."

War was on everyone's mind now; it wouldn't be long before Jack marched away to join his pals, and Alice knew it. He would leave her to go and do his duty soon, maybe before he knew how she felt, but she was helpless to tell Jack. It was too soon, too painful and indeed too forward, but she had feelings for Jack and when he came back – *if* he came back – she would be here waiting.

# CHAPTER 6

# 1915 Jim and Jack

Jim Cunningham was 5 years older than Jack but had been working in the shoot since he was a child of 10. He started as a picker and then went onto bird driver. By the time he was 15, Jim was one of the Colonel's best shoot staff, but there was, however, one drawback in that he was left-handed.

He did nearly everything right-handed but couldn't hit a barn door at ten yards if he shot right-handed. It didn't really get in the way but most of the guns on the estate had a right hand bias which made the fact that Jim very rarely missed a shot even more remarkable. Shooting a shotgun was one thing but shooting a right-handed rifle was extremely difficult, not least because the ejected cartridge would bounce out of the breech and thwack him in the face.

As a 21st birthday present the Colonel had a left-handed rifle made to measure for Jim, a sure sign of the high esteem in which he held his shoot manager. Jim was an exceptional shot and didn't miss often, but when he met Jack and saw him shoot he knew he had met a natural and that there was very little to do to improve his results.

Granted, there were things that belonged in the book of the marksman that were missing from Jack's technique, but the facts were that when he took a shot, he didn't miss, ever. Jim had never seen anything like it.

It didn't take them long to become friends. Both had very similar traits and familiarity soon became friendship. Jim knew that Jack was a trustworthy and conscientious colleague and had no worry about leaving him to carry on groundwork and preparation for the upcoming shoots.

His attention to detail was impressive, even to the point of adding hides that Jim had never considered. Jack's natural manner in the field and knack of being able to hide quickly in any cover had cost Jim several shocks as Jack suddenly appeared as if from nowhere.

The Colonel had also noticed Jack's ability and had taken him away to Scotland as a shoot manager when Jim had fallen ill with a heavy cold. The shoot had been hugely successful with the culling of three stags, one an emperor – a seven pointer, whose belligerence and dominance were on the wane. It was a kindness really, to relieve him of his herd before some young usurper beat him.

The shoot also gave the Colonel an opportunity to show Jack's skills to his old Army colleagues and guests. All marvelled at Jack's natural skills, especially during a game of hunt where Jack would hide camouflaged in the undergrowth or woodland in his ghillie suit. Handmade from some old netting and sewn to his overalls, Jack would weave heather and foliage from wherever he was.

He could blend into the background with ease, and with some dirt rubbed into his exposed skin, he would disappear into his surroundings like a ghost only to reappear and touch an unsuspecting guest on the shoulder or foot before the victim ever knew he was there. Grown up hide and seek, the Colonel called it, but the real show was to see Jack shoot. He was deadly.

It was on this trip that Jack was introduced to a military Captain from London with the unusual name of Hex Hesketh-Prichard. He was an extraordinary man who had been born in India to a military family and who had returned to England as a young child, but he had explorer's blood in his veins. He was older than Jack but younger than most of the shooting party.

He had taken a keen interest in Jack's skills and was very interested to hear where Jack had learned his trade and field craft. He was astounded when he found out that it was just a natural talent, albeit honed and encouraged by Jack's mentor Jim, who was at home in bed. Jack didn't really understand all the fuss, but he did notice that the Colonel and his guest talked more than some of the others and that it was about Jack they were speaking.

It made him feel uncomfortable.

# CHAPTER 7

# Jack Joins Up

What the Colonel and Captain Hesketh-Prichard had been discussing would change the course of Jack's life.

On return to the estate at Langwith, Jack was summoned to the Colonel's private office. On arrival he was met by Jim, and as ever, he was greeted by a huge smile and kind eyes from his friend, as well as a warm, firm handshake.

The Colonel's office door was open and Jack could see the heavy curtains moving in the wind; the large sash windows were open and the smell of cigar smoke was blown into the hallway, embracing the two men.

There was the sound of a conversation taking place which stopped as Jim tapped the huge door with his knuckles. The Colonel opened the door and looked straight into Jack's eyes. Kindly eyes framed by heavy lines, Jack could see the grooves at the side of the Colonel's head where the arms of his spectacles fitted a little too snugly, his short hair greying at the sides and slicked flat by hair cream. Jack couldn't ever remember seeing the Colonel without a hat. It struck him he had never seen the Colonel in the large house before either.

Colonel Alcot invited Jim and Jack into the office where Tim Alcot, the Colonel's son, was standing with Hex Hesketh-Prichard by the fireplace. Jack and Jim both smiled and nodded their deference to the young Master and his guest.

The Colonel spoke first. "I believe you remember Captain Hesketh-Prichard, Jack?"

"Jim, let me introduce this fine young officer." Jim and Hex shook hands and instantly liked each other, which was affirmed with a gentle head nod.

"I think what I am about to tell you might suit you both well. The war is taking its toll on our young men, and I know you two have been keen as mustard to join in the fight. Well, I won't let you go, do you hear?"

His voice was loud and firm, and as if being admonished for some misdemeanour, both Jim and Jack looked down to the floor. The Colonel realised instantly that the frustration in his voice had been mistaken for anger, and stepped forward to place a hand on each man's shoulder as would a father.

In a calm, quieter tone he said, "At least I won't let you go as cannon fodder, and that's where young Hex here comes in."

'Hex' Hesketh-Prichard had applied for a commission as soon as war was declared, initially to the Black Watch, but when they refused him, the Guards. Both Regiments refused saying he was too old at 37 and that this damned skirmish with the Germans would be over in no time, so he had applied to the war office.

They saw his past experience as a very useful asset and he was commissioned as a Press Officer, but they had ideas for such men as Hesketh-Prichard and Press Officer didn't really cover the job description accurately.

He was there as an ideas provider, someone who could look at the bigger picture of war on the front. Not to participate as a fighting man, but perhaps to see where there might be an advantage gained over the Germans.

He was sent to the front line in early 1915 as an eyewitness to the carnage that had quickly become a stalemate. The fighting had stagnated into trench warfare and the new weapons introduced by the Germans had been used with great effect.

Within days he had seen enough; the terrors that had been unleashed by his fellow man – such as men gassed like vermin – had left him disgusted and angry. There had also been another detail that had caught his eye: in reports to Headquarters there was an alarming amount of men being shot each day, not by misfortune of position, but targeted and hunted by sharpshooters.

The number of casualties was growing daily as men 'took a peek' over the top to see if they could see the offending sharpshooter. If they did ever see them, no one knew. Very quickly, the men learned that to look over the top was a death sentence. Hesketh-Prichard quickly produced a report on the matter. The problem needed to be countered, and countered rapidly.

He devised a dummy head made from papier mache which puffed smoke like a real Tommy. This was done via a small tube running from the dummy's head and into which a real soldier would puff away at a cigarette hidden safely below the parapet of the trench. It was very realistic. Due to the rigid straight line of the British parapet, the enemy sniper would quickly spot any movement and one shot dispatched the poor unsuspecting target.

In time, the design of the trenches would have to change but for now it served his purpose to maintain these clear lines of fire. Once the dummy had been shot – always in the head, because that was all that was visible – it was a simple matter of triangulation and mathematics to pinpoint the sniper. Then, a rain of artillery fire would fall on the area the shot had been fired from.

On his return from the front, he had been rewarded with some well-earned leave, and had chosen to travel to Scotland to join a shoot his Uncle had received an invite for. Colonel Alcot had kindly invited his uncle and a guest to his Scottish lodge for a week's shooting. It was at this shoot that he first came across Jack and he instantly saw the advantage he had been seeking to combat the German snipers.

On his return to London, Hesketh-Prichard reported back to his seniors with the seeds of an idea that he felt would make all the difference.

They listened to him with nods of approval as he presented his idea that snipers could be trained. Every unit had marksmen, but as snipers, they would also be taught the art of concealment and observation. They would then be taught how to communicate this information back down the line.

He told them of the games played for entertainment by Colonel Alcot's man, Jack Adams. They could scarcely believe him but he was a convincing orator. They gave him the opportunity to train more men like Jack but first they needed to recruit one Private Jack Adams because he might just be the answer to a problem that was costing 100 men a day at the front.

Back in Colonel Alcot's office, there was an air of resignation. The Colonel had known that he would lose staff to the war effort, and indeed he already had. The hunt had been reduced to the bare minimum of staff as man after man joined the ranks.

As a military man, he was both proud and expectant that his men should contribute to the war effort, but as a father he was concerned that his young son was coming of age and was already asking if he should join his father's old Regiment.

The reports coming back from the front about the war were bad. At the colonel's club where he met other old comrades, all the talk was of how dreadful the commanders were and what a waste of good men this war was. Any optimism of an early end to the fighting was dashed once the Germans had created a line of deep defences along the whole front.

It was with a heavy heart that he had agreed to let both Jim Cunningham and Jack Adams join in with Hesketh-Prichard's plans. Duty had called and Colonel Gerald Alcot wouldn't stand in its way. Both men would leave and if it was God's will, both would return safely after this fiasco in France was over.

Both men were delighted to be asked to join rather than be ordered, as truth be told, both had wanted to do their bit but neither wanted to leave home. No one had demanded they enlist, but the general feeling of the village was that anyone who could serve, should.

So the time had come. For Jim, he had no family save his wife and, of course, the Alcots, who he worked for and had committed his service to for most of his adult life. For Jack, it was his parents he had to bid farewell to and, of course, Alice.

Jack sat in the best room of the Barber's little house, the best cups and saucers sitting on the best table cloth and Jack, Harry, Alice and her mother were their best clothes. Sunday clothes, but it wasn't Sunday – it was Tuesday and this little tea had been arranged because Jack had some news for everyone present.

Alice sat quietly in the chair biting her bottom lip as Jack told everyone he was about to leave for the war. Harry stood behind his wife who was sitting at the table, his hand on her shoulder as if to give her strength.

It was a sad time and everyone noticed Alice had the red eyes they had hoped never to see again. Enough tears had fallen because of this war and in Harry's mind, the sooner it was over the better, but for his lovely daughter there was no escape. It had happened once already.

She was obviously keen on Jack and Harry wasn't at all disappointed in that. Jack was a good man, honest and conscientious and with a firm handshake, an honest handshake in Harry's mind. Of course, they understood – expected it even – but it didn't make this evening any easier.

The inevitable goodbyes were tense as Jack said his farewells to Alice and her parents. Firm handshakes would have been the norm but Harry placed his left hand on Jack's shoulder whilst shaking his right hand, a touch of familiarity that showed how much Harry thought of Jack.

"Take care lad, keep your head down and come home safely. You are always welcome here, Jack. You do know that, don't you? I'll keep an eye on your parents and I'll make sure they don't go short."

Jack nodded to Mrs Barber, and holding his cap in his hands, he turned to the door. He looked at Alice, into her moist eyes; her soul bared, the tears running freely down her cheek.

The candlelight reflected her tears like precious diamonds as they ran down her wet cheeks and disappeared, only to be replaced by new ones. He held her hand, the pain in his heart unbearable and he felt sure he would break down and cry along with her.

She pulled him towards her and kissed him on the cheek. He wasn't sure how to respond. He held her and kissed her on her beautiful lips, his first ever kiss, awkward and clumsy, but she kissed him back and they parted.

"Come home to me, Jack. I'll be waiting for you."

His heart missed several beats, his mouth dry unlike his eyes, as he realised he was crying as well.

"I will," he said. "I'm sweet on you, Alice."

He turned and was gone.

Those words would keep coming back to him with painful regularity over the next few weeks. His new love had three stripes on his arm and a striking moustache. Well, that's what his new training Sergeant told him.

# CHAPTER 8

# Training

He felt sad but excited. Initially, the two men would be learning the basics of soldiering during training, but both men had a far more important task ahead.

It took just twelve weeks for Jack and Jim to finish training, and although it wasn't easy, it was tolerable. Marching, shooting, drills and eating all came before sleep. Inspections and shouting day upon day and week upon week made Jack appreciate the quieter moments in his life.

Letters from home made him sad, and as he wasn't very good at letter writing, he only replied at weekends when he got a spare hour. He stored all his letters from his mother and Alice in a leather letter case he had been given and kept them safe in his trunk under his bed.

Jim was a wonderful soldier, who found all the discipline of training easy to cope with as he did with the housekeeping and uniform preparation. He helped others less able than himself at every opportunity but once they got onto the ranges, Jim found it very difficult to shoot his rifle. He could strip it in seconds, clean it like new, reassemble it in the dark with a blindfold on, but shooting the damn thing nearly beat him.

All Lee Enfield rifles were made for right-handed shooters, and there were no exceptions. Jim worked tirelessly to master this new discipline, and although proficient, he wasn't even considered an average shot.

Jack would prove to be an outstanding marksman, and spare rounds collected over the two-week range period were fired surreptitiously into Jim's targets, on one occasion scoring above the maximum allowed. When the range staff counted the successful shots, Jim had scored a remarkable 21 out of a possible 20, and Jack smiled at his friend who had the decency to be embarrassed.

The score was "recounted" and Jim had passed with an outstanding result in marksmanship. It was at this stage that the commanding officer of the training camp summoned the two soldiers to his office.

Privates Jack Adams and Jim Cunningham were marched quick time into the CO's office where they were met by a familiar face. Both their records were lying on the desk in front of Major Hesketh-Prichard. Newly promoted, he had been tasked with setting up a training establishment for snipers. This centre would be based in France away from prying eyes in the French town of Linghem, Pas-de-Calais.

Today Hex had come to collect his first two recruits.

# CHAPTER 9

# France

The camp at Linghem was basic, really basic and small. It didn't need to be big; there were only four people there. There was no welcoming party, just two Officers waiting by an office door. This was the British Army's first Sniper School.

It was shared with another training unit for injured soldiers, who were ready to return to the front but who had been wounded badly enough to be away from the action for more than six months and needed a refresher in all things military, and although it wasn't classified as "secret" it was still "hush, hush" for now, at least.

It was raining, and the tents waiting for their new occupants stood with canvas doors flapping in the wind. The wind wasn't cold but it wasn't like Blighty either, it was just different somehow. Corporals Jack Adams and Jim Cunningham had arrived.

There was mud, a whole sea of mud; everywhere one looked there was mud. For the first two weeks there had been rain, wind and the occasional bright day, and the ground was a quagmire of biblical proportions; nothing was dry or clean.

On the ranges, Jim was disappointed to learn that although he could fire the Lee Enfield rifle through iron sights, once the scope was fitted for snipers he couldn't use it at all. Shooting the rifle wasn't what Major Hesketh-Prichard had planned for him, however; Jim was there to teach field craft and observation skills. It was Jack who would be the leading light on the shooting ranges and he couldn't teach anyone how he shot because he didn't know, he just knew he didn't miss.

All the skills in concealment had been passed down to Jack from his mentor and friend Jim. These skills had been passed down from generations of gamekeepers, poachers and shooting men for a hundred years. Jim Cunningham had perfected most and he was generous in his sharing of these talents with his young apprentice, Jack.

In turn, Jack had added things to established methods and this thirst for new ideas coupled with his shooting skills made Jack a 'natural' as a sniper. The plans to build a sniper school had been formulated in offices in London who needed men on the ground to see what conditions were like, but no one could have prepared any soldier new to the front for what they were about to see.

They travelled the short distance to the nearest trenches. Here was devastation on a scale no one had ever seen before. There was a landscape of, well, nothing; wire, mud and tree stumps were the main things a man could see, but here and there lay a body indistinguishable as to allegiance or creed. The area in front of the trenches stood thick with wire, like no wire anyone had ever seen, row upon row upon row. This truly was hell, and out there hidden in holes and trenches were the men, cold and wet, tired and resigned.

Resignation is a dreadful thing in a man, the realisation that you could end your days here in the mud of France. This feeling of malaise and certainty had been spreading like a plague amongst the men in the trenches. On average, 10 men a day were falling to the enemy snipers and things had to change. Jack could sense the misery, and it made him so angry. The damned Boche shouldn't have it all their way and from today the changes would begin.

Back at the camp, a wooden hut had appeared, apparently liberated from a disused French camp and delivered by a truck. This was going to be the office, the Officer's mess, and for the time being the armoury and store.

Jack liked Major Hesketh-Prichard. He seemed a happy chap with a canny eye for detail and his plan to train snipers had been well received by the high command.

The first part of his plan involved gathering a veritable armoury of hunting rifles, elephant guns and large game rifles, but the thing that fascinated Jack most was the new optical sights.

For Jim, in his role as observation instructor, there were new telescopes. Jack marvelled at Jim's ability to see detail. It was the smallest things, like the freshness of rabbit droppings, newly broken bracken in the hills, footfall of deer and how he could tell the size of the beast just from looking at the imprint left by its hooves. He had tried to pass on this information to Jack but Jack wasn't anything like as able. Everyone agreed that between the two of them, the perfect hunter lived.

To see what they were up against, both men had to go and spend time in the front lines. Different battalions of men were constantly moving up and down the line, but Jack and Jim just stayed and watched. Each battalion had its sharpshooters with rifles and scoped sights but the standard of shooting was at best average, and in Jack's eyes it was very poor.

On one day in late June, Jack had a pop with the rifle of a marksman, just at a sandbag. He aimed at the centre of the bag and squeezed the trigger, the Lee-Enfield kicking back hard into his shoulder.

Jim blew out a long whistle; Jack had missed by a foot. He had never seen Jack miss anything, even in training when the rifles they used were just standard iron sights, not zeroed in for anyone. Jack hit the bull at 200 yards, but this rifle had a telescopic sight, so how could he have missed?

Jack looked almost shocked. The soldier took the rifle back off Jack, telling tales of how he didn't ever miss. Jack asked him to put a round down the line, and this too missed by a foot. When asked, the soldier said it was a kill shot, but Jim said only if the target was two foot wide and Jack laughed. He laughed so hard there were tears rolling down his face, and within seconds all were laughing, some men nearly being sick and coughing painfully from laughing so hard.

It was a harsh reminder as to what these men had endured with the many gas attacks they had been subjected to. The awful truth had struck Jack and Hex and indeed Jim. The soldiers using these rifles were good shots but none of them had any idea about how to use a telescopic sight; the sights were off by a country mile, and on further checking, they were all the same. All these sights had just been handed out as part of trench supplies by over-worked supply Sergeants, who neither knew nor cared what was in the new leather pouches. The sights were given with little or no instruction and fitted any standard rifle. In truth, only one in 10 shots had hit anything, not quite what was intended for these new marksmen.

Once back at camp, Hex had a meeting with various Commanding Officers and agreed that he would second some of his men to help in the trenches and that he would also set up a training school as quickly as possible. It was time to take some shots back at the Germans who – it was felt – had had it their own way for far too long.

Jack was sent along with Jim to the trenches in the Beaumont-Hamel region, about 7 miles from Albert with its once beautiful church and a golden Madonna which, due to the shelling, lay at a somewhat alarming and precarious angle at the top of the steeple.

Armed with two rifles specially set up for Jack and a new telescope for Jim, the two men reported to the trench of the 9 Loyal Lancashire battalion who had been in the area for several weeks and had suffered badly at the hands of various German snipers. It became immediately obvious why there were so many casualties: there were no precautions and no matter what was said, the officers were adamant that there would be no significant changes.

Jack walked along the duckboards, along the length of the trench for about 600 yards whilst Jim did much the same in the opposite direction, each one looking over the top with periscopes. It both surprised and shocked them that there were no steel shields for the men to take cover from the enemy bullets. The sharpshooters had to lie virtually on top of the parapet to even take a shot, exposing their whole head – little wonder no one was keen.

There was one spot marked with a wooden post and on it a wooden board said "beware snipers" with an arrow pointing upwards. Jack raised his periscope to see what was there and could make out several steel shields standing on the top of the German trenches. Each shield had a small loophole big enough for a rifle barrel to be pointed through it whilst completely hiding the man behind, protecting him whilst he aimed and fired. Jack had found his first target.

He waited for Jim to join him and help make an area safe for him to shoot from. They manufactured a safe shield from two thick plates of steel given over to them from the quartermaster, all done in the cover of darkness, and by morning there was a new, safer place for the observer to stand and point his telescope.

The detail was all important and Jim soon saw that most of the enemy loopholes were either false or blocked. Within an hour of daybreak he had narrowed it down to a possible three places where this enemy sniper was taking his daily shots from. It was fairly unsophisticated, really, but no one had thought to look closely at the place where the German marksman could pick his targets.

It didn't help that the officers were so regimented in the procedures of "taking a peek at the Hun" at 10:00 am, and again two hours later. Popping their heads over the top with field binoculars, it took them vital – and sometimes, fatal – seconds to focus the glasses on the other side's trench. Each time there was a shot the officer would fall, dead. This was followed by rapid fire at the enemy lines by angry comrades, with little or no effect.

Jim asked the 10 o'clock 'peeker' if he could try something, and was readily granted his wish. Jim had a dummy head fitted with a steel helmet. The Major had first introduced it last year and from a distance it looked quite realistic. With the aid of a hefty stick he slowly raised it to 'peek' over the top. They didn't even hear the shot, the head just rocked back and fell into Jim's arms with a neat hole just above the right eye and a corresponding hole at the back on the left. With a steel rod, Jim followed the hole in a perfect straight line from back to front.

Jim raised the head again, but this time with a periscope pointing in the direction that the shot had come from. Sure enough, a second shot hit the head and this time Jim knew exactly where it had come from. He looked closely at the area through his telescope from behind his steel shield and could easily see the rifle barrel and even the scope fitted to the rifle. It took no imagination to see the man behind the sight and hatred boiled up within Jim that he hadn't felt for a very long time.

Jack was soon in place in the next shooting position, his rifle pointing in a direct line to the German loophole, and all they had to do now was wait till the lunchtime peek.

At midday, Jim fixed his dummy head onto the thick broom handle ready to raise it above the parapet. Jack checked his rifle. It was a hunting rifle lent to him by the Major, and it was fitted with an expensive scope sight. With this weapon, Jack was deadly. It was agreed that Jack would take a shot as soon as he was ready. He slid a round into the breech with a slick practised movement and settled himself, waiting.

In the trench opposite, Hans Swatch took a last drag of his cigarette and checked his watch: it was time. He knew that within the next five minutes he would consign another "Tommy" to his grave. He stood and loaded his rifle, chatting to his mates and laughing.

"Time for another, Hans?" one called.

He turned and slid the loophole cover open, slowly slipped his rifle through, and then waited.

Jack saw the barrel appear. Closing both eyes, he breathed in deeply and then slowly let his breathing settle. He kicked his foot, signalling to Jim to raise the head. Slowly, Jim raised the dummy just above the top of the trench.

Hans saw the head and thought it looked a bit odd. He blinked and took aim, but before he could fire his rifle, he was dead.

The bullet had come through the loophole and struck him just above the right eyebrow, the back of his head crumpling and then exploding outwards. If Hans had been alive long enough to feel the fatal shot, he would have applauded the skill of the fellow sniper. As it was, he lay dead in the foot of the trench, overlooked by his shocked colleagues.

Jack saw the end of the rifle fly skywards and knew instantly that his shot had hit its target. Indeed, just for a second he was sure he had seen the bullet find its mark. There was a short silence then a loud cheer from a small crowd of soldiers who had gathered to watch with curious eyes the simple culling of an enemy who had avoided his fate for several weeks.

Jim clapped Jack on the back and said, "Hit, good shot Jack!" He had watched via his telescope and he had seen the bullet hit. He knew it would, but it still felt like a job well done.

Then the reality hit them both: they had killed a man, for the first time and without any emotion, only the satisfaction that a job which needed doing had been done.

This was only the start. Both men knew that the tide had to turn, and like King Canute, they were going to turn it.

Over the next few weeks both men worked closely together. All along the line, new observation posts were being built and the officers were being tasked with a new role, as sniper and intelligence officers. They helped the new arrivals build shooting points with iron shields and new loopholes that had a movable cover over the hole so that it wasn't always open. But, more clever than that was a second plate behind the first to make it virtually impossible for the enemy to shoot through the holes and kill the soldier hidden behind.

In turn, more German snipers were slain, either at the hands of Jack or by artillery shells brought onto an unsuspecting enemy from the new observers, who were being taught new skills and observation tactics by Jim.

Under the tutelage of Jim Cunningham, the new men learned how to see things that had been previously hidden, such as newly disturbed soil indicating activity and digging, and even the number and size of the rats were noted. For each week the pair spent in the trench system, one day was spent training with the new sharpshooters back at the camp.

It was turning colder and the nights were drawing in fast. It would soon be the start of a new year and Jack was due some leave, maybe even enough time to go home and see Alice, whose letters were a constant reminder of the happier times before this dreadful mess had started.

When the leave pass arrived it caught Jack by surprise. Major Hesketh-Prichard handed over the paper which said he had two weeks. Hex told Jack that there was a truck about to leave; if he got a move on he might just be able to get away tonight. Jack saluted, turned on his heels and was gone.

He ran into Jim and showed him his precious leave pass. Jim already knew and gave Jack a bottle of Cognac to take home for the boys in the shooting lodge. It took them a couple of minutes to say goodbye; this was the first time they had been parted for over six months and both men knew it would be strange to be without the other.

Jack climbed into the truck and headed home, home to Alice and his parent. He had been bad at writing letters home but he would explain when he saw them.

# CHAPTER 10

# Home On Leave

It took three days for Jack to arrive home, and he got off the train and started walking along the street. He had long ago decided that if he ever got this far home it was to Alice he would walk.

The butchers shop was just as he remembered it, bustling with customers, all chitter chattering about nothing in particular. Jack waited in the queue until he got to the counter. He never spoke; he just waited for Alice to look up. She hadn't seen him in the line and he had removed his hat from his uniform which he thought smelled a bit ripe but was better since he had dry scrubbed it on the train, removing most of the mud carried from France.

Alice looked up right into his eyes, first with shock, then horror, and then with wild delight. She shrieked and Harry nearly lopped off his fingers with a meat cleaver as he jumped.

"Good God, it's you!" she cried.

Jack was confused and didn't know if she was happy or sad; the tears ran down her soft face as she wiped her hands on her pinny and fell around the counter to hold him.

The shop went quiet. No one spoke, some smiled and some cried, but no one spoke in case they broke a magic spell.

Harry called to mother to come see and took Jack's hand in a firm, warm handshake. "Hello lad, how long before you have to go back?"

It broke the silence and there was a huge intake of breath, followed by an outpouring of affection for one of their own. For the first time, perhaps in his entire life, Jack knew what home meant.

Alice had calmed down a bit but was ready to cry at any moment.

"I have ten days, sir."

"Sir, sir, hark at him," said Harry. "Sir indeed! It's just Harry to you lad, and proud to know you I am. Have you seen your mum and dad yet?"

Jack looked down to the floor feeling a little deflated; he really should have gone home first.

"Good lord you haven't, have you? Get on that there cart and let me run you home, quick smart now. Our Alice can wait a while and go and clean herself up. Let's see what we can find in the way of some grub to take with us. Your mum doesn't know you're here; she was in this morning and didn't say you were coming, so I would have to guess she won't have dinner for you."

He wrapped some sausages in a paper parcel along with a fresh rabbit and then wiped his hands. Replacing his straw boater with his outside hat, he took Jack by the arm and led him to the cart outside to take him onward to meet his parents.

Alice would follow later on her bicycle, but for now it was a tale for Harry to hear and one for Jack to tell.

# CHAPTER 11

# France Again

Things had been quiet since Jack had gone two days before. There had been the start of the training course and Jim was busy teaching the new students. He had been introduced to a new group of students called the "Lovat Scouts," a great bunch all from Scotland. Jim had problems understanding what was said when they were together, and especially when they got animated, which was often.

These Scouts had fantastic skills as observers, being mostly employed as highland ghillies before the war. They were used to the equipment now available, such as the new telescopes that gave up such detail in the right hands, and these fellows had the right hands. Jim fitted in well with these men; he was one of them in many ways, having learned most of his skills in the highlands of Scotland.

It was after a day with his new chums that he was called into the Major's office.

It was here that Jim learned of a serious problem that was resulting in a very high casualty rate further up the line: a German sniper the men had named Wolfgang was causing a major concern to everyone from the high command to Tommy Atkins in the trench. This sniper was exceptional and it was felt that he should be dealt with as a matter of urgency.

Up to now, his score was known to be at least 50 men over the past two weeks. No one had any idea where he was lying, or indeed if he was even mobile, but his reputation was causing as much trouble as his exceptional marksmanship and he had to be eliminated.

Jim was to go to this area and look to find Wolfgang, and he was to work with Private Blackie who would be the sniper. It was a job that Jack would have copped without a doubt, but he was skiving at home on leave.

The two men were to leave immediately and report to the SOS officer at the reference given on his map. Jim left to collect his things and met Blackie. Blackie was a good shot – better than that, a great shot – but it would have been so much better if Jack was there.

However, both men knew there was a job to do and they were to get on with it. They left in a truck to meet up with more men moving up to the front. The last part of the trip would be on foot and there was a long march to get to the right spot on the map.

# CHAPTER 12

# Delville Wood

As part of a marching column, Jim arrived at a spot he had heard of but never seen before: Delville Wood. To call it a wood seemed a bit generous, however, as there were only tree stumps to be seen and the highest of these was only about 8 feet.

The problem was that there were literally hundreds of areas where Wolfgang's lair could be positioned. Blackie dropped into the start of the trench system and made his way along towards the front line, encouraged to see that shooting shields were all along the line. This, in turn, caused him more worry that Wolfgang must be a very steady shot; to score such a high hit rate in these conditions was impressive.

Jim talked to the sniping officer and heard what they knew about their prey. At the back of the trench system there was an elevated shell hole, it wasn't much of an advantage but any gain in this war was worth having. Both the sniping officer and Jim crawled slowly towards the shell hole, as the sun started its slow descent into dusk. It would be in their eyes when they looked at the panorama before them.

Once in the hole, Jim carefully scraped a rut for his looking glass to rest in, whilst the officer looked through his binoculars along the line of trees that formed the enemy positions. There was nothing to see that was obvious, but with the skilled eyes of a scout Jim picked out five areas that he would place Jack. If this Wolfgang were as good as the rumours said, he would be in one of these five areas.

There was an old turnip patch, a fallen tree that had a huge root system, a hollow that had a wispy grass thicket, the remains of an old building, and a clump of tree stumps that formed a mass of cover from this side but that he could see was hollow on the back side. All were within a ten minute crawl from the German trenches and all were near perfect for sniping. All that remained was to see where he was.

The sniping officer went back to the trench system at nightfall and left Jim to his work. It was night time and dark but it was the dark arts that Jim specialised in. The night held no fears for him.

For three days and nights Jim looked on from his hiding place. He had donned the ghillie suit to afford him even more cover and he knew without a doubt that he was invisible to anyone who didn't know he was there. Indeed, he had startled a family of rats who were looking for a new home. He just remained motionless apart from his eyes and toes, which he wriggled to help any blood move in his lower body.

Toileting had been done where he lay, even to the point of urinating into the towel he had placed under his body. He hadn't moved more than two inches for the whole time he had lain there. He had heard three snipers shooting and knew all their locations. He even knew which regiment they were serving with as he could see the flashes on their caps to indicate whom they belonged to. But he also knew that these three weren't his prey: they were average and the guy he wanted wasn't. He was exceptional, but he hadn't fired a single shot for three days. Of course, he could be out of the line, resting in some bathhouse with a clean uniform waiting and wine to drink, or perhaps 'schnapps'.

Jim let his mind wander. He was tired beyond tired. His eyes were red, his stomach ached for lack of food, he had water but only took small sips to reduce the need to toilet, it was getting dark, and he knew he needed sleep. Tomorrow he would be rested and Wolfgang would once again be the hunted and Jim the hunter. But for tonight he would sleep out here, in the hole; it would save the long crawl down and back again tomorrow.

Jim eased himself back below the lip of the shell hole, scattering the rat family who all ran out over the top of the lip. He cursed his stupidity; this was just the sort of careless mistake he was waiting for Wolfgang to make, not himself.

It was still dusk and the last of the day's sun gave its dying warmth. There was cloud tonight but it was high so no rain, just a gentle breeze. Jim pulled his ghillie suit together to help retain his body heat and within seconds he was sound asleep, the sleep of the dead.

Tonight was going to push that particular phrase to its very limit.

# CHAPTER 13

# Gas, Gas, Gas

Jim could see the horses pulling the plough, great big powerful animals, with plaits tied into their long manes and bobbed tails. Behind them walked Jack, following on slowly in a perfect line. The sun was beating down and Jack was sweating. He wore a bright red neckerchief and a clean white vest.

Behind Jack, Jim could see the haystacks, neat and orderly. Edith, Jim's wife, was sitting there with freshly made lemonade and a lunch made of fresh bread, cheese and pickled onions. Jim could hear the crump, crump, crump and although it made him stir, it didn't disturb his sleep. He could smell the mown hay in the fields. He felt restless and could hear distant shouts and a rattle, a football rattle.

It all felt so wrong. This was his sleep, why were there men shouting and creating such a din? He coughed, cleared his throat, and blinked himself awake.

The rattle was constant and he coughed again, this time taking a deep breath to clear his throat. It burned and now he wasn't sure whether he was asleep or awake. He heard someone shout gas, he knew it was gas, he heard it clearly: gas, gas, gas.

He opened his eyes but couldn't see anything because he was in a cloud, a pale white, repugnant, deadly cloud. Jim coughed, his eyes running and the tears burning his face. He coughed more and knew he was doomed. The gas shells had landed behind him whilst he slept, but being heavier than air, the gas had clung to the ground and rolled down the slight hill to settle in the lowest hollows, dips and gullies.

Jim had been asleep in the lowest hollow of them all and a quilt of death enveloped him, caressing him and wrapping her arms around him as would a new lover, determined never to release him from her impassioned embrace.

Jim had fallen face first, and as he fought for his final breaths he saw the light, and felt his swollen face take its final resting place on the very towel he had pissed in for three days.

Then it was over and all became dark; his struggle had ended as had his war.

# CHAPTER 14

# Medic

It was several hours later that Jim heard a voice talking to him, quietly and calmly. The voice was a gentleman's voice.

"Lie still, Corporal. You have been gassed and are in the hospital. There is a bandage over your eyes, try not to touch it. It would appear you have been very lucky. It seems that you fell unconscious with your face in your makeshift gas mask. That was extremely clever and probably saved you."

Jim didn't understand what he meant, makeshift gas mask? Then he realised the towel he had laid on, covered in his own urine, was just like the early designs of gas masks, and because he had his ghillie hood on, the gas didn't really have any way in.

He had taken in a huge dose of gas, but when he fell he saved himself by falling on his face. Who would have thought it? He tried to smile, but as he did he was racked with a coughing fit so severe he vomited. The medic helped him sit up and held Jim's hands away from his face, which burned as he sweated.

He coughed again and the medic told him it was a good sign. "Cough it up, lad."

The shell hole he thought might be his place of safety was very nearly his grave, and if it hadn't been for the sniping officer and a couple of men risking all to collect him, there was no doubt he would have died.

It was a blessing he couldn't remember anything about the journey back to the first aid post, but once there, his face was washed with water. In fact, it had been tea that had gone cold in the big urn but it was perfect for getting the remains of the phosgene from his skin.

His eyes, though, were a terrible mess, swollen to twice their normal size, red and watering constantly. The itching was unbearable so they were covered with a dressing and Jim Cunningham was sent down the line to a base hospital. It hadn't actually taken long for him to get here.

He had vague memories of being in the back of a motor ambulance with another chap whom he could hear groaning with a strange cat-like meow noise, he just wasn't really sure what it was all about. By the time they had arrived, the crying from the stretcher above had stopped. The medics didn't seem in a hurry to remove the now quiet man and Jim later discovered that the poor chap hadn't made it.

Once at the hospital, he became aware of more things going on. He couldn't see because of his bandages, but he could hear the wounded crying for help and thanking those who offered it. Every now and again he would hear a lady's voice. She sounded like an angel and it struck Jim that he hadn't heard a lady's voice in an age. In time, another man came along, calling "Corporal Cunningham, is there a Corporal Cunningham in here?" He sounded vaguely familiar.

"Here," said Jim. "I'm here, I'm Cunningham."

"Jim, it's me," said Bob McKenzie. "From the school. The Major heard you were wounded and had arrived here, I've been looking for you for hours. How you feeling?"

"Bob, Oh thank Christ, what happened to me? I understand I've been gassed but where am I? My eyes aren't good, mate. Will I be able to see? Am I blind?" Jim could hear himself babbling, question after question, and he apologised to his visitor.

"It's early, Jim, but fingers crossed. We're at a General Hospital near Calais, and you can smell the sea from here, Jim. There are pretty nurses here as well, but you were quite badly gassed and no one really knows how long it will take for you to get better. You're going home to Blighty; they're sorting out your ship passage right now. We don't know where you're going but don't worry, the Major is writing to Edith to tell her you're alive. No doubt she will hear from him before you get back."

"How's Blackie?"

"I'm afraid he didn't make it, Jim. He was hit by Wolfgang the day after the gas attack. I'm sorry; I know you two were pals."

Jim sat back on his cot bed, feeling his emotions building up: anger, grief and even a bit of self-pity welled inside him. His eyes started stinging with new tears. He wasn't sure if it was the news or the gas, but either way he wished it would stop. His guts ached and he needed a toilet.

"Mac, where are the toilets? Can you guide me there?"

"Hang on, Jim. I'll get the orderly, he'll help you. I have to get back, but I'll find a nurse to help you."

This was no way for a man to be: helpless, needing to sit on a toilet, not being able to do anything himself. His heart hurt and so did his stomach. What would become of him now? A blind gamekeeper. He pondered his future and his mood was as dark as his view. He sat on his bed, blind, lost and needing to shit.

It would take a couple of days for the swelling to go down

they had said, and once he was back in England the medics would be able to assess his recovery a little better, but for now it was eye washes and showers.

His uniform had been thrown away and he was in some clean clothes; the gas had stayed in the cloth of his field uniform and so had to be disposed of. He had been sent a clean uniform from the School and Mac had fetched some spare vests and long johns. Along with all the showers and clean clothes his hair had been washed and cut short, right down to the bone. He was waiting for the boat back to England and hopefully he would be able to see his lovely wife.

Jim wasn't alone in his wait; there were many men just like him, blind. Each one held their own frustrations and each one had learned to laugh at each other's misfortunes. One man fell over another's outstretched legs and tumbled through the door. This brought about hysterical laughter between the men, and even the poor unfortunate victim had made some quick remark and joined in. It amazed the nurses where these men found the courage to make light of their condition. But in reality all the wounded had been blessed, both with a ticket home to Blighty and – despite some of the most horrific injuries – life.

Within the week they were ready for evacuation back to England. All the casualties were sorted into priority and loaded onto the hospital ship *HMHS Glenart Castle* which set sail back to Southampton.

It wasn't a particularly long trip but they had to wait for the tide. Jim heard that they left at night, but to Jim, all was night. His bandages had been replaced with new ones and his eyes felt more comfortable, but the continuous weeping from his eyes left them sore and raw, and although he could just about cope with his eyes, it was the coughing that made him so sick.

He wasn't able to keep food down at all and although he was made to drink, it was a challenge not to cough at each swallow. If he could have seen the sputum he was producing, he would have been sick even more; even now, days after he had been gassed, his secretions smelled of gas, but worse, he swore he could taste it.

The thing that made him retch most of all, though, was the others coughing and heaving up their lung contents. This invariably caused a wave of nausea and then more coughing from the others. In time it would ease and everyone would rest, safe in the knowledge that it was only a temporary reprieve. He could smell the smoke from the single large funnel; strangely, it made him think of home. It had been a long time since he had smelled coal smoke and for the first time really since his injury, he realised he was going home.

The docks in Southampton were busy and bustling, and the noise was deafening to Jim. His hearing had become very acute in the last weeks and as men were offloaded from the ship and into the waiting ambulances and train carriages, Jim was reminded of the chaos he had left behind on the fields of France and started to shake. He felt a hand placed on his shoulder and he instinctively put his hand onto it. It was a woman's hand and as she whispered in his ear, he felt reassured and safe like he had never felt before. Just a few simple words had changed fear into courage and Jim knew from that moment on that he would survive.

From Southampton they went by train to a nearby hospital in Netley. The hospital had been built after the

Crimean war, but had the advantage of seaward facing wards. Outside, there were tented wards with canvas walls that could be rolled up during the day so that the healthy sea breeze could blow up the ward. It was an ideal way for the men to get plenty of fresh air.

The wounded men just sat and talked, whilst the gassed men were encouraged to take walks around their new temporary home in long lines with a hand on the man in front's shoulder. Along the line a nurse or orderly would offer guidance, and despite all the worries in the world, each man felt safe and for most part, happy with his lot. These walks gave men time to think without the incessant noise of the battlefield and because of their blindness, their hearing had adapted to become for most, very acute.

Good food, rest, and oh the quietness of Blighty. Corporal Jim Cunningham had come home.

## CHAPTER 15

# Back To The Front

Jack was restless. He had no desire to go back to war but he knew he was needed at the front. Everyone had been so friendly when he came home but Jack knew his time here was nearly done. Tomorrow he would leave for London but for tonight he wanted to be here with his Alice. That alone had been a difficult decision; he needed to see his parents but Jack's heart wasn't at home any longer.

Alice was in love, of that she had no doubt; this man made her so happy she never wanted him to leave, but she knew he must, and she had to stay strong. On the walk back to his parents' house he was dreading saying goodbye and decided that he would just hug them and try not to show how much he didn't want to leave again.

He was a grown man and not known for his gentle touch, but as Jack hugged his father he saw he had tears in his eyes. It wasn't the first time Jack had seen his father cry, but it was rare enough that Jack felt thoroughly awful about leaving.

No one really talked about what Jack did in the war – no one really knew – and he wasn't going to tell them; they were just grateful every time they saw him. The post boy made all too regular deliveries to the townsfolk of Langwith and the vicar was kept busy making visits to the newly bereaved.

Jack kissed his mother and held her tight, hugging her and closing his eyes. The tears wouldn't stay inside and he felt one run down his cheek, soaking into his mother's hair. She offered him her handkerchief and he dabbed her eyes with it, wiping his own eyes with the back of his hand, which was clean for the first time he could remember, the dirt of war washed away.

With a final squeeze, his mother pulled away. "Go on lad, that lass won't want to see her brave soldier with teary eyes. Tell Alice to come by and see us when you're gone, and thank Harry for the meat he gets for your dad and I. Tell him we are very grateful."

With that, Jack was gone; he left his home knowing that the future, whatever it held, wouldn't see him return here to his parents' home.

He walked down the lane to the junction with the road, where Alice was waiting. The evening sun was on her face and she looked so beautiful to Jack. He wasn't an educated man but he had heard of the fantastic paintings done by renaissance artists and he felt sure that Alice was beautiful enough to be in any one of them.

She knew how sad Jack was; she could see the sadness in his face. She knew he had been crying and she knew that soon, she would be as well. Her Jack was bound to go in the morning and she wished every minute would slow to an hour, but they were ticking by far too quickly and she knew that tomorrow's dawn would see her heartbroken once more.

# CHAPTER 16

# Back To France

Jack was in a sombre mood; the trip back to France carried with it a foreboding. There was a love deep within him, and although he was tired from walking with Alice the previous night, he found sleep elusive. When he did sleep it was fitful. He hadn't really got used to the quiet of a rural England. It struck him that the noise of the battlefield was a strange thing to miss but he had and now he was hearing it again. Even at the coast of France he could hear the distant thunder of artillery barrages carrying all manner of evil to an unsuspecting and fearful recipient.

Jack had seen the effects of the gas shells and the sheer carnage that shrapnel could cause, but for him there was an air of safety, an imponderable belief that 'it won't happen to me'. Each soldier Jack had met shared that feeling but Jack had seen the effects wear off once these soldiers had been exposed to the vileness that was the trenches.

Superstition was a strange bedfellow but just about everyone Jack knew, and he included himself in that, had a superstitious habit. It appeared that fate alone wouldn't offer safety and Jack knew that other chaps found great delight in seeing what the others did to secure a safe return. Jack had a new one; it started only last week when Alice gave him a small crucifix to wear around his neck. He knew this was his keepsake, and from now on he would never take it off. He held it in his fingers and kissed it before letting it fall back down the front of his shirt. He closed his eyes and could feel Alice in his arms. In his mind he could smell her hair.

In one week at home he had given his heart up, found a new reason to survive this carnage. He opened his eyes. He was looking forward to seeing Jim; the lads left behind had wonderfully received the bottle of cognac Jim had passed to him. All had wanted to hear of the exploits the two of them had been up to and even the Colonel had asked Jack to stop by.

Colonel Alcot had told Jack that Tim had taken his commission with the Derbyshire regiment; he had a reputation to uphold because it was the same regiment with which the Colonel had served with such distinction. Lieutenant Alcot had gone to Sandhurst just weeks after Jack and Jim had left for France, and the Colonel said how keenly he missed his boys. It made Jack feel very proud to be considered in the company of the Colonel's closest.

By the time Jack had boarded the train to Linghem, he was feeling his tension returning, although he didn't overly mind. In his job, tension could keep you alive. Being alert was the major requirement for any sniper and just as he had felt all the muscles in his body relax when he returned home, he could feel them all tightening again now.

At the station platform there was a lorry about to leave and Jack managed to cadge a lift. He had no weapon with him and there were curious, even suspicious looks cast his way; a soldier in France without his rifle might well be a soldier going the wrong way.

A military policeman stepped into Jack's path and challenged him. "What's your name corporal, where are you going to, what regiment do you belong to and where is your weapon?"

Jack looked at the Sergeant; he could see the coldness in his eyes. "I'm Corporal Jack Adams, I'm from the school of sniping and my bloody weapon had better be in the armoury or there will be hell to pay. I'm just back off leave."

The Sergeant just tutted and said something about "fucking poachers". Jack ignored him and jumped on the back of the lorry. He had very little kit to carry but he did have a parcel tied with string which was full of clean underwear and socks, some spares for Jim, as well as a large tin of rub for Jim's pipe.

It took nearly an hour to get back to camp; he reported back to the guard hut and was surprised to see that the Major was sitting there. He knew instantly that something grave had happened.

"Gas," the major said. "Damaged lungs, eyes damaged, blind, a Blighty one for sure, probably the end of Jim's war, but he was alive."

Jack knew there were many words in-between but had heard none of them. Dear God, this war had caused so much pain and heartache but this was like a punch to his stomach.

The Major told Jack what he knew to have happened, how 'Wolfgang' was still at large despite several crack shots looking for him. The best observers had been attached to the front line regiments to try to locate him, and even the Major had been on the line but there was no sign.

Jack said instantly, "He is either on leave or wounded, sir. No one has seen him because he isn't here, but he'll be back soon and then I'll find him. Wolfgang old son, your clock is ticking."

It made perfect sense, how could he have not thought of that himself? Hesketh-Prichard acknowledged with a nod. In the meantime, Jack was being attached to the new boys in the line; the Derbyshire's had just moved up into the trenches, in a place called 'Beaumont-Hamel' and there was a big push coming. The date was June the 10$^{th}$ and in just fifteen days, it would be the start of the biggest push so far. The battle of the Somme was planned.

It took Jack and two others six hours to travel the fifty miles or so to the trenches at Beamont-Hamel. Jack had two weapons, his short magazine Lee-Enfield rifle and his very special gift from the major, a Nitro-express rifle fitted with superb optical sights. At the conclusion of their journey the three men, each with orders for their new attachments, split up.

Jack soon found the Derbyshire's and was astonished to walk straight into Lieutenant Timothy Alcot. The two men made their way into a small dugout that Tim called his home. Jack was amazed at how much Tim had grown up – not just grown up but aged; he looked haggard.

The dugout was furnished with homemade chairs and a table of sorts with bits of lighting lamps hanging on the walls along with some candles for the night. There were two beds in the room, one for Tim and a bed in the corner for someone else, certainly not Tim; he looked like he hadn't slept for weeks.

"It's a dreadful place, Jack. Up to our left going up a way are the lads from Newfoundland, great bears of men. God help Jerry if he ever gets into a scrap with them. We get shelled every day but we haven't lost many, just a couple of men and a pack mule, but the men are all jittery and we have only been here a month, and up in the line for less than a week."

Jack took an offered cigarette and smiled as Tim coughed, not yet used to the smoke. It felt good to Jack; he took the smoke deep into his lungs and let it out slowly. He felt much calmer when he had a smoke.

"Do you have everything you need, Jack? I have orders here for you, and by tonight you will have met Captain Taylor the Sniping officer, he's a good sort, from Bolsover."

Jack said he was about to get settled, but had been told to go back down the communication trench for his billet. It was only a quarter of a mile back to his bunk and he had dumped his stuff but wanted to get back here to have a quick look around. "That's when I came across you, sir." Now it was Tim's turn to smile, glad of a familiar face.

"You know you have quite a reputation, Jack; my lads have been following your success like a football player. How many is it now, Jack?"

Jack didn't like to say, but he knew it was over fifty. In fact, it was fifty six, and he remembered each and every one of them. He never talked about how many, just how the shot went; striving for the perfect shot was typical of Jack. Others were just glad to have had a hit but to Jack it mattered that each shot was deadly and efficient, and as far as he knew, every one had been.

"Oh I don't know, sir, never keep count, it's the next one that matters not the last."

In time Captain Taylor came in to the dugout and Jack saluted him. It was expected down here but never up top; it was a sure way to get an officer shot by saluting in full sight of the enemy.

"Corporal Adams, reporting sir."

Captain Taylor was a tall, slim man who looked drawn but had a huge smile and the kindest eyes that wrinkled in the corners when he smiled, which was often.

"Ah Adams, good, you're here. Did you have a good leave? Well overdue I'm sure. I hope you don't mind but I asked for you personally. I was away up at the School when I met Hesketh-Prichard, he said you were just the chap I needed to help me out with a few issues we have here in this sector. We seem to be troubled with damned machine gun nests in just about every direction, and they are well dug in. We know where they are but the damned things seem impervious to artillery so I thought maybe a rapier instead of a mallet."

Captain Taylor produced a map of the area for Jack to look at. On it were marked all the areas that housed a known machine gun post, of which there were eight in total. The furthest from the front trench was four hundred yards, and deciding that this one would be the hardest, Jack marked it number one. He then went along and marked each one in turn, one to eight.

Number eight was a mere hundred and fifty yards. Jack's job was to make sure these posts were wiped out. He picked out a spot where he would have a clear line of sight for as many as he could and marked on the map a point where he could easily see six of the eight. The simple fact was that from one point on the map he could sweep round in a large semicircle and have a shot at each, making his life both easier and yet, in an ironic quirk of fate, more dangerous, because if he could see them, they would have a line on him.

He would only have his skills as a chameleon to ensure

they couldn't see him. He would be able to take one shot at each before they knew he was onto them but then he would have to move to a new location.

It was agreed then: Jack would position himself for the following dawn. He knew it would take him at least an hour to crawl into position and he would add another hour to ensure he was well settled before the sun came up behind him. He then had to wait for the morning to warm a little so as not to give away his hard earned advantage of concealment with the first shot; he had noticed that some snipers had given their position away shooting at first light because the smoke from the end of the barrel hung in the cold air like a balloon, and it had inevitably ended badly for the careless sniper.

Captain Taylor had arranged that at the morning 'stand to' some of the chaps would "bang off a few shots to irritate the Hun." They all knew that it would start a fight and that the Germans would think an attack was on its way. All hell would break loose with trigger happy and tired German soldiers all getting involved. Lieutenant Alcot was to ensure that no patrols were out and about either in no man's land or indeed near the enemy trenches until it was all over. Jack knew he had at least six shots to get away in pretty sharp order so that he could duck back and avoid any stray bullets heading his way.

It was starting to get light by about 03:30 so Jack had to be on his way by 02:00, meaning that he had about six hours sleep before he left. Everyone agreed the plan and watches were synchronised. Stand to was planned for 06:30.

Jack had seen exactly where he was going to set up his temporary sniper's den the day before. There was an old well that had collapsed with all the shelling of the farmhouse that had stood on that piece of ground for a hundred and fifty years. The roof of the well had collapsed and jammed itself tight against the walls of the shaft of the well. Under the roof there was twenty feet of rubble that had been either thrown in or blown in by the shells, or by soldiers who had visited this site in the recent past.

Jack knew that both the Germans and the French had held the farm for periods and both groups had poisoned it with dead animals, or worse: the dead bodies of fallen enemies. So to ensure no one drank from the well, it had been collapsed and filled in nearly to the top, but with a little bit of excavation work it would make a perfect hide. It had a solid floor and quite a few of the bricks that formed the wellhead had been left in a state of ill repair. There was no skyline to silhouette the laid down marksman and with a minimum of effort he was invisible to the human eye.

He had on his sniper's hood and had deliberately got his uniform muddy on the back by crawling and rolling in the mud. He was filthy and it all helped him become as one with the muddy tumbledown that was his new home. He undid his rifle from its case and took out his spyglass, with which he could clearly see what was going on around his area. It was getting close to first light and Jack looked down his sights and was astounded at what he could see: nothing.

The early morning mist was heavy and thick; he could barely see the back of his own trenches let alone the 150-yard target. He hoped that the sun would burn off the mist double-quick but thought it unlikely. In the event of a heavy mist would Lieutenant Alcot hold back on the wake-up call for Jerry? If he didn't, then Jack still wouldn't be able to see his targets, and he would have to wait.

He needn't have worried. Alcot was a bright young officer and he had seen the problem even before Jack had. He fired a very pistol into the air and Jack saw the flare emerge out of the mist and fly skyward. It was an iridescent green and cast a strange, haunting shadow on the mist. He now knew that the planned shoot out would be delayed. There were a few shots fired from the enemy trench, more in anticipation of an attack rather than at an actual attack, but it confirmed to everyone that nothing could be seen.

It would be at least another hour before the mist lifted but it was all in Jack's favour because the sun would be right in the German's eyes when he did start shooting. Jack settled himself with an eyeglass to keep a close watch on the areas he had made note of. From those areas death was delivered by the German machine guns, but death had turned his sharpened scythe and today Jack would be wearing the cloak of the reaper.

The early morning sun was quickly warming the land. There was a peaceful tranquillity around, precious because of the rarity of the quiet; even the morning birdsong seemed loud today. The fog was lifting and was now no more than a slight haze over the fields. The ghostly silhouette made the French countryside look as if she was wearing a grieving veil for her lost countrymen, many of whom were lying out there in the mud, marked with a makeshift cross or marker of broken trees.

The buildings now started to poke skywards through the thinning mist. Now Jack could see the enemy lines clearly, and as he looked he gently slid home the first bullet into the breech of his well-oiled rifle.

Lieutenant Alcot heard Captain Taylor shout for his men to take ten shots each to wake Jerry in his dugouts. "Ten rounds rapid fire, fire!" There was a crackle of gunshots, and within seconds of the command there were eight hundred aimed shots heading towards the enemy positions. The British Army were well known for their rapid fire skills and eighty men could move more ammunition in a very short time than any other group of men.

Each 'Tommy' was more than able to fire 15 aimed shots in one minute and the initial response from the German trenches was slow, but within minutes there was a cacophony of noise with rifle fire and, for Jack, the all-important MG08 machine guns pouring four hundred rounds a minute back towards the British trench.

Jack could see the twinkling muzzle flash from all six of his initial targets, and with a silent prayer he looked through his telescopic sight for his first shot. He never considered a target, just a shot, and with majestic calmness he squeezed the trigger of his rifle. There was barely a bang and the first German was dispatched. Inside the bunker, the German slumped forwards onto his gun, his dead finger releasing the trigger as he slid sideways. The gun toppled over off its feet, no one wanting to right it; they knew it was suicide to start firing. There was a sniper shooting at them, and they were safe as long as they stayed away from the back of the MG08 – no one wanted to be there.

Jack slipped another bullet into the chamber and loosed another deadly shot; this was the second target, slightly further away but still relatively easy. Within two minutes, all six German machine gunners lay dead. Jack slid his feet to the side and changed his position so he could line up on the final two shots. These were more challenging but Jack liked a challenge.

He could see from the smoke that the wind was coming virtually from behind his left shoulder so he allowed for a fraction of an inch further left for every hundred yards he had to the target. Once more his rifle cracked, and this time the German was lucky; Jack had overcompensated and the bullet glanced off the side of his helmet smacking into the man standing behind him and killing him instantly.

The gunner looked surprised and turned his head to see what had happened, and in doing so exposed his left temple. It wasn't something he had time to regret. The 303 round hit him next to his ear, and as if hit by a shell, his head just erupted into a mass of blood and bone. It had taken Jack just two seconds to reload his rifle, make the mental adjustment, aim and fire. There was no conscious thought, it just happened.

The result was two dead Germans within the count of five; indeed the last man hadn't stopped twitching before Jack had moved on to the next and final target. Six hundred yards isn't very far for a bullet. Jack had aimed one inch above the muzzle flash of the MG08, the bullet had left one barrel and within the blink of an eye was travelling up the barrel of another. Just as a round from the German gun was about to explode outwards, it was struck by the point of Jack's and the whole gun exploded, bits of shattered gun metal showering all the men in the small bunker where they were meant to be safe. But today death was hungry, and two more Germans died right there and then.

Jack stopped. His breathing had become too fast and he was angry with himself for rushing the last couple of shots.

He wasn't to know the carnage he had caused; with the last three bullets he had killed four Germans and in total he had fired nine shots in just over three minutes.

He took deep breaths and laid his head down. No one could see him, and he was invisible once more. He knew that the German snipers would be looking for him, as would every other German with an optic scope. He needed to lie low for at least the next two hours and then he could move; he could make his way back to the trench for breakfast.

He stayed laid down for the next half an hour; he couldn't see anything but he could hear that the shooting had stopped. He knew this was a dangerous time for him. Everyone would be looking as to where he could be but he also knew he was never going to be seen. He had dropped below the cover of his newly-made hide and felt it was ok for him to roll over onto his back and take in the fresh air.

Whist he laid there, looking up to a clear blue sky, he could hear an aeroplane above. It was shooting but Jack couldn't see any other aeroplanes. The German aeroplane was behind Jack and as it came round a copse of trees, somehow spared from the shelling, Jack could see what he was shooting at. It was a group of stretcher-bearers.

There were six of them in total, each two with a stretcher carrying a wounded man. The men struggled to move without dropping their precious cargo, the German swooped round to fly directly towards them and Jack once again heard the chatter of the guns from the aeroplane. This time two of the bearers fell, the poor fellow on the stretcher bouncing as the bullets struck home. This wasn't war; this was murder, and Jack felt the bile rise within him.

The four other bearers stopped and lay over their

casualty, covering his body with their own, each hoping that the German air machine would pass over them and that they could then run for cover and safety. The bullets struck the earth all around them but missed the targets they were aimed at.

Jack loaded his rifle and bent up his knees to offer some support for the barrel. He could see the German aircraft coming from his left at about six hundred yards. Jack shuffled his shoulders back so he was resting his back on the wall. At this stage, he was dreadfully exposed to anyone looking for him, and more than that, he was moving and nothing caught the eye of a watcher more than movement. But, whether it was good fortune or just good timing, no one saw him and he was now in a position to try to shoot the murdering scum flying the aeroplane.

Jack eased himself into position. With the barrel of his rifle laying along his knees, he brought the scope to his eye. He could clearly see the pilot but he was moving faster than Jack had thought and the first shot hit the tail of the plane.

The second didn't hit the pilot either but it tore into the petrol tank behind and within seconds there was a fire. The third shot hit the pilot in the neck. He didn't die straight away, but he did have time for the blood to fill his throat, chest and cockpit. Still, he didn't die; the fire would do that but he had lost control of his flying machine, and with smoke bellowing out from his fiery coffin, the plane rose skywards, the engine screaming as it tried to grab the air. Ultimately, it failed, and the plane rolled over onto its back and hurtled into the ground.

Jack realised instantly what he had done and ducked his head into his shoulders. He had committed a great crime: he had given his position away to the enemy. He knew he had to move and pretty damn quick; the shells would be in the air within seconds.

He was right; he heard the first scream of a falling shell followed by the more incessant screaming of several others. Shrapnel and high explosive shells rained all around but today was Jack's day; the huge crack he heard wasn't a shell landing, it was the wooden floor he had been lying on breaking and giving way beneath him. He felt himself fall.

He only fell about ten feet. He realised that the old well roof had been his bunker's floor and it had held him well whilst he was still, but when he moved it had first creaked, then snapped and like a rifle shot he was down, down in the mud and rubble of the inside of a collapsed well. He wasn't hurt, and he started to laugh. The smell was awful, but the shells would be lucky to find him in here.

It had been an interesting hour but Jack had a new problem now: how was he going to escape from here? No one knew where he was, and no one was expecting him back for at least another three hours. He didn't have any cigarettes and his water bottle was up top. He was safe but stuck.

"Hello, hello down there, is anyone there?"

Jack could see the face of a man looking down the well. "Hello," said Jack

"Are you hurt?" the man said.

"No, I don't think so. Can you help me get out?"

"I'll get some help," said the stranger, and then he was gone.

It took another two hours before Jack was rescued from his safe but damp hole. It was the stretcher-bearers who had come to the rescue, and with the aid of a rope they had pulled him out. His rifle was lying right there without a scratch on it.

Jack just shook his head. It had been a close shave today. He had broken the rules of a sniper and it had nearly cost him but he wasn't hurt, not a scratch. There was backslapping and handshakes. Both parties thanked the other for what they had done. Everyone was quite happy but Jack could see the new bodies wrapped in a tarpaulin ready for burial and he realised that because of his own stupidity he would, but for a huge slice of luck, have been lying there next to them.

Jack bade them farewell and slowly made his way back to his trench. It was two o'clock in the afternoon and Jack felt that he'd been gone for days, not hours. He made his way back to Lieutenant Alcot's dugout, aware that he smelled worse than the men who clapped him on the back as he walked along the trench.

A huge Sergeant stopped him. He had a kindly face, dirty like an urchin, a young man with an old man's eyes. He offered Jack his hand. "Thanks lad, I saw what you did and I saw the murdering Hun fall out of the sky. That was really some shooting, you'll get a medal for that if I have my way, but I can offer you a drink. Here, have some rum. You'll have missed your daily ration so have it now and then you can have mine."

Jack took the offered cup, and as he drank he felt the warm rum slide down his parched throat. He thanked the Sergeant and walked back to the dugout.

# CHAPTER 17

# Back Home

Jim was doing better. The hospital Chaplin had written to Edith and explained that Corporal Cunningham was fit enough to be moved and that he would be travelling within the week to Aldershot. If she wanted, she could visit before he left but there was no accommodation or anywhere she might stay at Netley and it might be better if she could wait until he had settled into his new accommodation.

Colonel Alcot had been magnificent; he had offered all the support and help Edith could have wanted. He even offered her his car and driver and so today she was leaving to see her wounded husband, but she wasn't going alone. Alice had heard the news of Jim's wounds, and much worse than just being wounded, everyone was saying he was blind. There was talk of him going to a specialist unit in London for treatment, but before that happened, Edith had asked Alice if she would travel to Aldershot to see Jim in his new hospital.

Like the hospital at Netley, the Cambridge Military hospital had been built following the war in the Crimea. Jim had been transferred there a week ago and a fellow patient had written to Edith at Jim's request. In it he said he was doing splendidly and that his breathing had become much easier. He still had a few problems with his eyes but the bandages were being changed daily.

The nurses were very kind and gentle with him. He was on a ward with men, many of whom had received dreadful head wound injuries and suffered from gaping facial wounds. A young army doctor called Captain Gillies was treating these men, and he was using a new surgical procedure called plastic surgery. It conjured images of hideous features but Jim still had his eyes bandaged and so consequently couldn't see how badly mauled these poor lads were.

Alice and Edith travelled like Royals in the Colonel's car. There had been a hotel booked, again by the Colonel for the two ladies, but Edith was too scared and excited to settle for the evening, knowing her husband was only a few miles away. She hadn't seen Jim for months, but just knowing he was alive and healing made her heart ache with joy.

So many men had died in this dreadful conflict. Edith was mindful that while Alice's new found love was still there fighting, hers wasn't, and although her man had paid a high price, at least he'd got a ticket back home. It caused her such mixed emotions; she was happy and then sad with every changing second.

The main entrance to the hospital could be seen for miles: the clock tower, lit at night, was like a beacon. Huge, massive double doors, flanked by wounded men in blue hospital uniform, waited to greet them. Inside there was a table with a sergeant who directed them to the ward where Jim sat waiting. They walked along the lengthy corridor, which was bustling and busy with wounded men and nurses, until they found the right ward. The chest injuries ward was directly opposite the eye ward, and Jim could have been a patient on either, but they knew it was the eye ward they sought.

The long wards were cool, with the windows opened fully to let the fresh air flow along the length of the Nightingale wards. These ones carried the name of Florence Nightingale, the nurse who had designed them some forty years earlier. There were more beds than planned and each one held a man who, despite his wounds, thanked the Lord he was there, as opposed to the thick clawing mud from where they had been wounded.

Jim was seated on the balcony at the back of the ward, along with other men who were sitting around smoking and chatting, swapping news and stories from the front. They all shared a similar history of being wounded weeks ago, prior to being moved either directly here to Aldershot or via other hospitals such as Netley or Portsmouth. Some had been visited by family already but most waited to see their loved ones. Many were in the first stages of recovery and awaited another transfer to a hospital nearer to where they lived or where they had family in the area.

Jim was worried that the sights that abounded here might scare Edith; he had heard wives cry in anguish when they saw their husbands. It was a heart-breaking cry, knowing that the man they were now looking at bore little or no resemblance to the handsome men they had waved goodbye to however long ago.

The two ladies were met by the sister of the ward, and she showed them to the dayroom where a silence quickly descended. The men who could move moved away, and those who couldn't move were helped. It was all done with a delicate choreography that only comes naturally to men who understand the emotions about to be visited on one of their own.

Alice felt slightly awkward but the nursing sister took her arm and suggested that a cup of tea might be helpful if she would care to help. Alice felt relieved to be able to help and the nurses, who were all used to the situation, were all so helpful.

Today was an important day in the life of Corporal Jim Cunningham; two events were occurring, that up to this point he hadn't allowed himself to think about. Today his wife would come to see him, and if God was merciful – and he prayed that he was – the bandages would finally be removed from his eyes. The darkness that had become his daily life would be lifted. He felt the fear well inside him once more. "Please dear Lord, let me see."

He felt her standing at his side, heard her breathing, and reaching out with a trembling hand, he felt her touch his fingers.

"Hello love," she said.

At that moment in time he felt a surge of relief gush through him. The fear left him and he stood to face her. "Edith, sweetheart!"

She put her arms around him and he held her tightly,

"I'm alright, lass. I'm alive; it could have been so much worse. But I'm home."

She held him, unable to speak as the tears ran down her face and dripped onto his shoulder. Jim wasn't sure if she was happy or sad to see him, as he couldn't see the warm smile that accompanied the tears.

In the beat of a heart she told him that she loved him and then sat him back in his chair. He could hear her sniffles and tried to reassure her, but she told him that she was happy, not sad, and inside her the dreadful knot of fear unravelled and she knew that all would be well.

Her tears had stopped and been replaced instead with warmth and pride and relief: these were the overriding emotions now. Edith told Jim that Alice was with her and he was delighted that they were both there. He felt he owed the Colonel a great debt for looking after the girls and he was determined that he would repay it any way he could.

Alice joined them with tea. Jim held her like a daughter and kissed her on her forehead.

"It looks worse than it is, Alice. I cough a bit with the gas but it's easier than it was a couple of weeks ago, and I won't be going back. Have you heard from Jack?"

She said she had a letter but that Jack was hopeless at writing and they all sat and laughed. For the first time any of them could remember, the laughter was heartfelt and it felt good.

Within a couple of hours, the nurses said visiting was over but that they could come back tomorrow. Kisses and hugs were exchanged. The girls hadn't been gone five minutes when the doctors came to remove Jim's bandage.

The bandages were slowly removed. Jim's eyes were shut tight and he closed them even tighter as the bandages got lighter with each layer being unwound. Through closed eyes, Jim could sense rather than see the light: it was yellow and warm.

"Open your eyes slowly now; it will take a bit of getting used to," said the doctor.

Slowly, Jim opened his eyes. It was painful at first but then he blinked and blinked again. His eyes were watering and the nurse dabbed his eyes with a gauze swab. His vision was blurred but he could see shapes, and as time went by he could see more clearly. He focused on a pretty nurse standing behind the doctor's shoulder. He could see her smiling.

"Hello," she said, and with a huge smile that lit up the room he said hello to the world again. He could see.

CHAPTER 18

# 24<sup>th</sup> June 1916

The bombardment started. History would show that the battle about to commence was amongst the bloodiest battles in the history of the British army. What history couldn't communicate was the noise. Over a thousand artillery guns all firing at the same time again and again, time after time; the noise was deafening.

Jack was stunned by the cacophony of noise; he had never heard anything so loud or constant in his life. He could only compare it to the sound of rolling thunder in the highlands with the boom echoing from the hillsides, but that was just the occasional boom – here there was no silence, there was no rest, no peace.

There had been thunder the day before but it was from nature's armoury and accompanied by rain. The rain was heavy and the trenches quickly turned muddy and waterlogged. Beaumont Hamel was away to Jack's left, a small village that had been occupied by the Germans for months now.

The stalemate of trench warfare had become the norm. From where Jack was lying, he could see the village down a slight hill and he could imagine even now what wonderful farmland it must have been before the war. Away to his right in the distance was the area of Thiepval. Nearer to him was the area where the Newfoundland Regiment were in the trenches and to his left were the Lancashire fusiliers – and a rum bunch they were as well.

The sheer number of men and the activity around him astounded Jack. Each day there was more and each day his job was to go and try to make the enemy keep their heads down. Down the valley, he could see a cloud of gas that had been drifting towards the German lines. He hated gas. It had cost him his best mate and Jack wondered how Jim was now, back in England.

Jack felt sorry for the Germans; it wasn't the first time he had felt pity for the enemy but gas was by far the worst thing he could imagine. The rumour was that there would be an attack within the week and Jack knew that this bombardment was the beginning.

Today he wasn't shooting, he was observing, and from what he could see the Germans were copping it. All along the miles of line he could see huge explosions lifting dirt into the air like a water drip, but one made of dirt, soil and no doubt men – men wounded and maimed by shrapnel. At least when he took his shot he knew that the target wouldn't suffer and wouldn't know what had hit them; it was a clean, swift death.

What did surprise Jack was the lack of shells coming back; maybe this would be the end and maybe there wasn't anything left of the German artillery. Jack hoped but doubted that was the case. He was right to doubt it: the next day there were plenty of enemy shells coming back. The day was warmer and indeed brighter with a gentle breeze that dried him and his wet clothes. Today was a better day for sniping but he had only taken a few shots. Each one was a hit but the Germans were now gone as far as he could see.

The news was that Wolfgang was back and Jack was being kept there to find him and kill him as quickly as possible, but as yet Jack hadn't seen anyone with the reported skill of Wolfgang so he didn't really think he was here.

German snipers were still there, though, and every day Jack had to ensure he found them and knocked them out. He knew they were looking for him as well: a prisoner had said there was a bounty on the head of the English sniper known as 'Jack'. It was a made up name, a generic name used by the Germans because not all Englishmen could be called 'Tommy' just as all Germans couldn't be called 'Fritz', but the fact that they were using his real name shook him when he'd heard.

It was the 26th June and the shellfire continued. It hadn't really stopped or even slowed down, and the constant crump, crump, crump of the exploding shells were making all the lads feel jumpy. Captain Taylor had joked that if they thought it was bad, how did 'Jerry' feel – he was right under it.

It was obvious that Lieutenant Alcot was nervous and Jack had taken a brew to him, asking him to come and look. Jack had an observation post from which he could see quite a panorama of the front lines, both German and his own. From here, and with the aid of his eyeglass, he could see everything that was going on.

He thought that Tim might feel better if he could see the constant bombardment the Germans were under. Jack had also learned that the attack was planned for the 28th June and, noticing that the intensity of the shelling had increased, he believed it. Lieutenant Alcot couldn't say of course, because he didn't know, but Jack could see Tim was wobbly. He wasn't yet more than a boy but within a few days he would be a man, a man with the memories that haunted other men for the rest of their lives.

Jack looked out at the scene of destruction; all he could see was shell holes and wire, vicious barbed rusty wire, rows upon rows of it. The plan was to destroy the wire but it was obvious that it hadn't worked.

Jack knew that within a couple of days there would be an attack. It was clear for anyone to see, and if the Germans needed any warning signs they would have had them by now with the incessant artillery barrage. Jack thought there must have been millions of shells landed as the bombardment had been going on for days and surely no one would still be alive in the German trenches.

Men were going mad in the British trenches just listening to the constant racket. In fact, the shelling had been going on for a week, and for Jack not much sleep was taken apart from the odd nap. He was amazed to see in the line that some men were fast asleep. At first he feared they were dead, the victims of a sneak gas attack that he had missed and been spared from, but then he heard the oddest noise he could imagine: snoring. Despite all the chaos of war flying overhead, delivering such destruction, men were actually sleeping like babies.

The 28th June came and went, still with no attack. Jack had been stood down, he hadn't seen a German for three days and he was sure they must all be dead.

Captain Taylor called him into his dugout and told him that the plan was for the attack to go in on the 1st July, but before that Jack had to take a spot to ensure he could overview the area in case the Germans had reinforcements back in their communication trenches. Jack said something about there not being any Germans left but Captain Taylor said there were reports that there were plenty of Germans left, more than enough to spoil the party on the first attack.

In the meantime, Jack and Captain Taylor were to go and have a 'look see' to establish what wire might be left to impede any attack. They made their way to the top of the ridge and were amazed at the landscape. The wire had mainly gone but there were Germans to be seen over the fields moving around and smoking, as if nothing was happening.

Jack thought it odd that these men could just be wandering around but his blood ran cold when he saw that they were walking away from a machine gun emplacement that no one had noticed. It was well hidden in a copse of bushes that was marked 'Hawthorne ridge', and as Jack followed a line down to his left he could see clearly why it was there.

Along that line the Lancashire Fusiliers would move forward and Jack understood that there would be a sister gun further to the left to give a cross fire, but try as he might he couldn't see it and neither could the Captain. But they both knew it would be there and that they needed to warn the men of the Lancashire's of what they had seen.

From his vantage point, Jack could easily deal with the threat but not knowing where the other was could prove to be disastrous. He would have to wait for it to start firing before he could engage it and shoot the operator manning the gun, and by the time he had taken care of it many men would have paid the ultimate price for his slowness. He shivered again. Today was the 30th June and the attack was planned for tomorrow morning. He had to warn the lads below, so the two of them made their way back to the trench.

They were able to cadge a lift on the mini railway that ran down to the sunken road area where men were safe from enemy shellfire because it was behind a ridge and out of sight of the German observers.

Jack and the Captain were shown to the operations officer who looked about twelve years old to Jack. He was a young Lieutenant from Farnworth in Lancashire, a place full of mills and soot, apparently. The men in the trench were jolly; they seemed quite happy to be there and were looking forward to the job at hand.

Jack met with the snipers from the battalion and showed them what he had seen on a map. Hawthorne Ridge was marked as a fortification and indeed there appeared to be very little damage to it from the shelling, but Jack knew that the blasts from hundreds if not thousands of shells would have disabled anyone in the area. He had seen for himself the many explosions, due to the gas released for the past week on the area. There was hardly any wire left. He felt confident that he could manage the machine gun post but was worried by a nagging feeling that he had missed something. It was at this point a happy Captain Taylor called him away from the maps.

"There's a bloody great mine under it," said Captain Taylor.

Jack stood and shook his head: a mine. Right under where they stood there was a tunnel that lead to the mine under the Hawthorne Ridge redoubt. It had been laid by the Royal Engineers tunnelling company and by all accounts was indeed a 'bloody great mine'. About eighteen tons of explosive made this a huge mine. It was planned to go off tomorrow morning, just before the attack went in along with nine other mines along the line. All the mines were going to be set off at 07:30, apart from this one – this one was going off ten minutes beforehand because there was a chance that the advancing troops might be a bit close by 07:30, and there couldn't be that many Germans left.

It was at this point that Jack recognised what the nagging feeling was: it was dread. He knew there were a lot of Germans in their trenches; he had seen them only this morning. All the talk of no one being left alive or fit enough to put up any kind of fight was untrue and Jack knew it. The plan was that the soldiers would advance onto a huge hole in the ground and make it secure with Lewis guns, digging in ready for any counter attack by the Germans.

The commanders were so sure that the attack would be a walk in the park that they had a camera to film the whole thing. On the way back to the train, Jack could see the camera with some chap who apparently was a famous moviemaker.

Jack remembered the times he had been to see films with Alice at the picture house in Derby. Thinking of home just hurt so much he rarely allowed himself to do it but today, quite unexpectedly, a wave of homesickness overcame him.

# CHAPTER 19

# 1<sup>st</sup> July 1916

At 05:00 Jack was dressed in his ghillie suit. He had a brew in his hands and a woodbine between his lips. He had about an hour and a half to get into position. He knew he would be witness to something awesome today but had no idea what it would be like.

He had a meeting with both Lieutenant Alcot and Captain Taylor, who were both moving up and down the trench, chatting to those men making themselves ready for the upcoming battle.

One man started to laugh when he saw Jack walking towards him in the trench. "Ey up, we've got a tree in the trench, don't let the Sergeant see you lad, he'll have us polish you." The rest of the men joined in the laughter, nervous at first and then hearty. Even the two officers joined in the laughter and Jack could see the tension in all the men's faces. He made a comment about how he was disappointed he could be seen and the lads all laughed again.

Captain Taylor had a map for Jack to look at. The other three snipers had already been briefed and had left to join the rest of the lads for the push. Today, Jack would be working alone again as Captain Taylor and Lieutenant Alcot would be leading the advance at 07:30.

"Jack, you have to take out that damn machine gun, before we get to the whistle." He placed the map for Jack to see.

There weren't any changes to the map he had looked at before but there was now a cross at the point where the mine was. Jack's position for the day would be up a slight bank where he could overlook and, more importantly, overshoot the main advance. There was to be several waves of infantry advancing here today but if all went to plan it would be a walkover. Jack prayed it would.

There were handshakes all round and Jack told Tim to take care and keep himself safe. He didn't add 'sir' at the end of his sentence; this wasn't an Army thing, this was a personal thing. Jack knew just how much the lad meant to the Colonel, his father, back home.

With a nod, Jack was gone. It took him an hour to move back towards the communication trench where he could make his way to his position; it was nearly impossible to move against the huge surge of men all pushing their way towards the front trenches.

Jack climbed the ridge slowly. The shelling was heavy and every now and again there was a ping as a stray bullet from the Germans ricocheted overhead. Within the hour, Jack was positioned perfectly; he had set up his rifle and wiped the glass clean on both his riflescope and on his looking glass. He was in complete control of his own destiny now, invisible to anyone who didn't know exactly where he was positioned. There was nothing to see.

He was no more than five hundred yards from the German front line and he looked towards the machine gun post positioned carefully at the right hand side of the copse of bushes known as the 'Hawthorn Ridge redoubt'. He moved slowly and looked down towards the Lancashire Fusiliers in the collection point. He could see them having a tot of rum, Dutch courage he thought and they would need it today, God help them.

He couldn't have one; it might make his arm shake and affect his aim. He never had a drink of rum before he was going to shoot, although he didn't mind a slug when he had finished, as oddly, it helped him calm down. In his mind he toasted the men he had killed that day, a silent toast to eternal sleep, a job well done.

He looked at his watch: it was 07:15. The sun was already warm but the day was overcast. Jack liked to have a sighted round at a target but today there wasn't anyone to sight it for him so he looked for a target at the same distance he needed to shoot at.

Jack scanned the area and found what he was looking for; a discarded German helmet was sitting on the surface just to the side of the machine gun post at about five hundred yards. Jack wondered what had happened to the man who owned the helmet, but he didn't have to wonder long; when he looked through his eyeglass he could see the owner lying dead just about ten feet away from the helmet.

Jack took his rifle and worked the bolt a couple of times, although he didn't need to; it was oiled perfectly and the round slipped into the breech effortlessly. He took some deep breaths, long and slow, breathing in and out. The air was fresh and cool and Jack looked through his riflescope to find the helmet.

Jack always blinked once before he fired, both eyes closed just for a second, then he was ready. He looked and picked out the target, and with one last breath, he slipped off the safety catch from his rifle. The shot was lost in the cacophony of noise from the artillery, the helmet jumped, did a somersault in the air and landed virtually in the same place it had left just a second before.

Jack clicked his sight up one degree. The round had landed short by about two inches, hitting the metal peak at the front of the helmet and flipping it over. He knew that it would take one more shot to make sure it was perfect, so he slipped another round into the breech. This time the bullet hit the helmet exactly in the middle of the forehead. Either side of the new bullet hole there was a ventilation lug and Jack was a bit disappointed because it was at one of these lugs he had aimed. He was about two inches wide of his target but to the untrained eye it would have been an amazing shot. Jack altered his sight again by one click to the left. He didn't need to take any more shots, he was confident that he was spot on.

It was 07:19. Once more, he looked down to the sunken road where he could see the camera set up by a man he had heard called Malins. He was pointing the camera at Hawthorn Ridge.

Jack felt the earth quiver, and he looked at the ridge as it convulsed like a huge mushroom, growing by the second as more and more earth lifted towards the heavens. The roar was deafening and smoke swirled like a dragon erupting from the bowels of hell.

Jack inhaled hard in order to try and catch his breath, stunned by the vision he had just witnessed. He looked down his eyeglass to find his target but it was gone. The helmet had gone, the copse of trees had gone. There was nothing left as it had been just one minute before.

Within seconds of the last piece of earth falling to the ground and the smoke clearing, there were the first signs of a huge crater left where there had, just minutes before, been humanity. Now there was just smoke and devastation, crowned with the clawing smell of cordite that hung heavy in the morning air. Vegetation and all things living in that true hellhole had now ceased to exist.

Jack could hear the cheers from the men below and the ominous clatter of a machine gun away to his left in the distance. Then there was silence, a very odd event given that the biggest attack of the war to date was about to take place.

Jack listened, but there was nothing. No shells exploding, no machine gun fire, no rifles going crack. He thought he might be deaf but a cough soon showed that he wasn't. He looked at his watch: 07:30. Within a second of him looking at his timepiece, there were a series of loud rumbles that became even louder, gradually building to a crescendo. These were the other mines all timed to go off at precisely 07:30. Then there were the ear-piercing high-pitched whistles of the troop commanders calling the men to arms.

Then, there they were atop the trenches; Jack looked as thousands of men raised themselves from their underground world of the trench systems. Up wooden ladders, or through cut outs that had been covered to hide them, men poured like wine onto the French countryside, and within a heartbeat the wine was turning red.

On the far bank of the ridge, Germans poured out from their dugouts, safe and deep underground. The shelling stopping had been the signal they'd been waiting for. Now, with most of their number mad with rage, they clambered to their firing points along the trench.

Worse still, within the same time, another group had run into the still smoking crater and were setting up a new machine gun. They set about their work with the sadistic passion of revenge; they started a deal with the grim reaper and cut down the advancing allied troops.

Jack could hear the carnage below, the rat-a-tat of machine guns was constant and he looked on in horror as men fell like skittles before they were even away from the trenches properly. He had to get some shots off, but where to start?

With all the vengeance of a jilted lover, he was searching for his first target: a machine gun on the ridge was dealing out real problems for the Lancashire lads and Jack put a bullet through the head of the first gunner he saw. But within a second, the gun was firing again so Jack shot the second gunner as well. It fell silent.

Jack moved his rifle round to the right, looking for the second gun. He couldn't distinguish where the noise was coming from but then he saw the muzzle flair and knew he had found his second target. Behind this gun, the gunner was pulling the trigger wildly, just fanning the gun from left to right. From this distance he wouldn't miss; there were bullets finding their mark literally left, right and centre.

Jack's bullet hit him just below the nose. The second round hit the new gunner in the chest as he stood to look over the gun. The shot had been aimed at his head but by standing, he exposed his chest. He screamed before he died, scared. The other men on the gun wouldn't get hold of the weapon but by now the damage had been done.

Hundreds of dead and dying men lay out in no man's land, the screams dulled by the noise of battle. Medics ran with stretchers, dropping to their knees when they came across a fallen comrade. Time and again they stood back up and moved on to the next man, leaving the dead for later.

Now there was new shelling and it fell on the advancing troops. Shrapnel blasted down from the German guns firing from away in the distance behind Beaucourt sur Ancre, a small village some 2000 yards behind the German lines.

From his vantage point, Jack could still see where his friends had left the trench system. He fired and fired again but his barrel was getting too hot and the rounds were flying erratically. Nearly every one hit its intended target but not all were killing shots and Jack could feel a mix of delight and despondence as the darkest side of mankind found its way to the surface.

He could hear the voices of compassion crying to the roar of depravity. Wounding was preferable to killing; hurt them as they were hurting ours, he heard the voices in his head say.

He stopped shooting to consider what to do next, as his efforts had been futile. He could feel the tears of anger running down his face, rage and fury allied with wretchedness and desolation. He felt helpless, empty but for the dark melancholy of a lost soul.

In time, Jack could do no more. He had fired all his ammunition and had to leave the battle to the poor tortured men on the field. He had a dreadful thirst, and with his water all gone, he made his way back to the trench.

When he got there it was chaos, men pushing up to the front, getting in the way of the wounded, and exhausted men returning after a failed advance. There were no faces he recognised, no one familiar to ask how it had gone for the Derbyshire's. Jack saw quite a few Lancashire fusiliers and a sorry state they looked, no longer the defiant face of determination but the haunted look of beaten men.

Jack made his way to the operations post to refill his drinks bottle and ammo pouch. He was going to go back to his spot and continue covering the lads as best he could, but when he went in the dugout, it was empty.

"Where is everyone?" he asked.

"Out there," said a shattered young soldier. He was from the Derbyshire's but Jack didn't recognise him.

Jack refilled his bottle from the urn, and then saw a corporal with ammunition who was handing it out to the lads who needed it. Jack *did* recognise this chap; he was from the quartermaster's supplies department and had returned wounded a few weeks ago from a patrol out into no man's land. For the time being, he would be working as a stores man, handing out supplies.

He saw Jack and called him over. "Need more ammo, Jack? It's a fucking disaster out there."

Jack asked him if he knew anything and the store man just said there were hundreds missing, including Captain Taylor and Lieutenant Alcot. That was just from this section; all the officers had copped it and most of the NCOs as well.

There were wounded men lying on stretchers and the walking wounded were helping as best they could. Medics were running around giving morphine to the most badly injured and the regimental aid post was quickly overrun. Men lay groaning, holding bloodied bandages against bleeding wounds. The padre was walking up and down, administering to the faithful and none-faithful alike.

The thing that struck Jack most of all was the constant

cry for lad's mothers. It made him think of his own mum at home. The heat of the July sun was warming, and despite the early hour, the heat in the trench was stifling. A man grabbed Jack's bedraggled suit and pleaded for a drink. Jack looked at the stretcher bearer who looked drained himself, the yoke of the carrying strap cutting into his burdened shoulders as the man on the stretcher moved.

"Not yet lad, let the MO see you first." It was as if he had said it a thousand times but still with the compassion of a new father.

Jack once more felt useless. He quickly filled his pouches with bullets and turned to make his way back to his lair. As he turned, he looked straight into the eyes of Lieutenant Tim Alcot. He had a bandage on his thigh and another one on his shoulder, blood had seeped through the scruffy bandage, and mingled with the blood was sweat and quite a few tears.

Jack offered a hand, helping Tim into the dugout and sitting him down. Once sat, Lieutenant Alcot broke; he lowered his head into his shaking hands and sobbed. Jack felt humbled and awkward, not sure what to say or do, so he put his hand on Tim's head and then, like a father, hugged him and held him close.

"It had been a cock up from start to finish; the mine had gone off too early and the Germans knew we were coming. The shelling stopped instead of creeping ahead and the shells that did fall were falling short onto our own men. The machine gun posts were everywhere and hadn't been disabled or knocked out; if it hadn't been for Corporal Adams, the butcher's bill would have been much higher. Captain Taylor fell dead within the first ten yards, taken by a sniper." Lieutenant Alcot was in full flow.

The Intelligence officer, a Major from some regiment or other, was collating notes from those men who had survived, and it was heart-breaking work. The Lancashire Fusiliers had lost most of their battalion within the first hundred yards, and further up the line the Newfoundland Regiment had been decimated. In fact, all along the front the results had at best been disappointing and at worst catastrophic. The 'Pals' battalions had suffered grievously and all along the front adjutants were compiling lists of the casualties. There were hundreds still missing in no-man's land, wounded and dead all mixed together, but the medics had done a sterling job and but for them, hundreds and maybe thousands more would be dead.

The attack was to continue again tomorrow, but for now, everyone had to do their best with what they had left.

The Intelligence officer ordered Lieutenant Alcot to see the doctors. He only had a slight wound – a bullet graze to his leg – but he had fallen in the mud and a discarded bayonet had pierced his shoulder; it had gone right through and was remarkably clean but it needed medical attention before it became infected.

As he went to leave, the Major with the notepad turned and said, "I have a directive here for Corporal Adams; it appears he has been awarded a medal for his work shooting down an enemy aeroplane. Not any medal, either: you have been awarded the Distinguished Conduct Medal, Adams. Good man and congratulations. Well done today." With that, he was gone as indeed was Lieutenant Alcot, as the medics helped him with his rapidly stiffening leg and increasingly painful shoulder.

Jack was alone. The noise of the battle had quietened a little but he knew it was still a desperate struggle out there and that he must go back and lend a hand.

# CHAPTER 20

## *Albert Hagerman*

The events of the day had been devastating in so many ways and lives changed forever or indeed were snuffed out like a spent match. It would have been easy to be victorious and celebratory but for the fact that Albert's very humanity had been pushed to its very limit.

At forty years old, Albert was very much older than most of his peers and would have had no part in this stupid war apart from his astonishing skills as a huntsman. He was nationally famous for his marksmanship having been the winner of several national titles for shooting over the last twenty years, too old to join the army of the Kaiser.

His father had served his time as a soldier in the last stupid war, again against the French, but this was before he was born. He had grown weary of the tales of war and killing at an early age. The truth be told, his father had changed after the war. Albert didn't know, of course, but his mother told him when he was but a boy about the brave man that left and the broken man that was his father when he returned. War had a way of doing that to men, he thought.

In his den he was alone, safe for the time being; there was no more shelling and the rages of the advancing British had calmed, for tonight at least, but he knew they would be back tomorrow.

Albert was a Swabian. He lived in Tuttlingen near the Black forest; it was a beautiful town, near the mountains and relatively new since the huge fire that destroyed most of the old town over 60 years before he was born. Even now, people still referred to the old town and the new. There at home waited his wife Monica and sixteen-year-old son, Hans. This war had to be over soon, before Hans had the chance to join the Army. Albert had seen so many young men give their lives away so cheaply and he didn't want Hans to be another life wasted. He prayed to God he would be home before long.

Albert had been brought into this war by the town Mayor. He was really too old and had no appetite for fighting, so he wouldn't fight if it could be avoided, and so far he had managed to avoid much of it. He had been sent to the army as a marksman and his job was to shoot the enemy officers. Prisoners who had been captured during the pathetic little raids that both sides insisted on, sending raiding parties out every night, had told his superiors that there was a monster amongst them, cold, ruthless and deadly. A sniper, and they called him 'Wolfgang'. There was a price on his head: a week's leave to anyone who shot or killed him with the bayonet. Wolfgang? What a stupid name.

Albert wasn't German, he was Swabian, and yes technically it was Germany but he didn't really feel German. He certainly wasn't proud of being German and this pointless, stupid war was proving the pig-headedness of his superiors on a daily basis. The only thing that was more stupid and pig-headed than the officers on his side were the arrogant upper class idiots on the British side.

His job had been to dispatch as many of these fools as possible and up to now, even though he said so himself, he was doing a pretty good job. Recently, however, things had changed for Albert on a number of levels. Someone was trying to kill him and it wasn't only the enemy sniper known as 'Jack', it was someone on his own side. Someone he knew and had spoken to once too often. It wasn't that Albert was generally disrespectful, he just had no respect for this particular bunch of officers. Prussians: the same, all of them. He spat his disgust into the dirt.

No, this was one of the officers and Albert thought he knew which one and, indeed, why. He had told one of the Prussian officers – a certain Hauptman Berger – that he wouldn't shoot a wounded British soldier who was lying out in no man's land and who was groaning continuously. He was grievously wounded but needed medical assistance, not a shot from Albert's rifle.

The Hauptman had decided this soldier must die because he was disturbing the rest of the men and he sent out a party of men to silence him. Albert had said at the time that the medical bearers would pick him up and the Hauptman declared this was the plan, then the machine gunners would mow them down like the swine they were.

Albert was incensed at the cold callousness of this upstart officer. He looked him directly in the eye and said, quietly and in private, that if any such thing happened to the British rescuers, then he himself would shoot Hauptman Berger and he wouldn't miss. In due course, the German stretcher-bearers picked up the lad but he died anyway.

But the dye had been cast and now Hauptman Berger wanted Albert dead before he could either tell anyone of the atrocious behaviour of this Prussian officer or make good his promise and kill him. Albert's missions were becoming more and more like suicide missions and the Hauptman ensured that Albert needed all his wily skills to avoid a fatal ending. Albert noticed that the other men were helping him; Berger was an animal they said, not fit to wear the uniform they said, but Albert was worried. He became more independent and even more careful each time he went out.

Today had been too much. The two huge mines in their sector had shaken men to the core and the constant shelling had unhinged many men, but Berger was in his element. He himself had shot ten or twenty men, and his bravery wasn't in question, right up until he shot the five prisoners who had been captured. He shot them like animals, in the back of the head with his Luger pistol. Quite clearly, he had cracked.

One young Oberleutnant had tried to intervene and had been shot on the spot like a traitor. Most men just shook their heads and walked away but Albert knew, and Berger knew he knew.

He waited until the Hauptman was looking straight at him then he loaded his rifle and nodded towards the officer. "This one will be yours, Hauptman, it's got your name on it."

Both men turned and walked away.

Tomorrow would see more fierce fighting and every man had to survive. That's all that mattered now: to survive. Berger would get his comeuppance and justice would be done, Albert had already saved a round to ensure it was so.

Most people thought Albert had been affected by the war but Albert knew the truth: he had become disaffected.

Albert's mission in this war was to shoot people one at a time. He was too old to be a trench soldier, and so he had his job to do. Armed with his rifle and a pouch full of ammunition, a gas mask, water bottles and his camouflaged uniform covered in mud and lice, Albert looked every bit the killer he was, but something had gone out in his soul. The hatred he had for the war and the British had been replaced by a new loathing and more than a little bit of fear because he knew that he wasn't going to survive this war; Hauptman Berger was going to see to that. But before he could rid the world of Albert, Albert was going to rid the world of him.

Albert had to set off to make sure he was in position to take the British officers out of action tomorrow morning, because tomorrow again they would come.

The Germans liked the way they had a 'Wolfgang' to match the Tommy's 'Jack'. Each of the two men had a destiny but neither could have imagined in what direction it would lead them.

# CHAPTER 21

# London Gazette 22<sup>nd</sup> July 1916

**Distinguished Conduct Medal**

*"For conspicuous gallantry and devotion to duty under heavy machine gun fire from an enemy aeroplane 8961, Corporal Jack Adams remained calm and engaged and destroyed the aeroplane with his rifle, saving the lives of medical staff who were tending to the wounded."*

Colonel Alcot reread the citation again, but this time out loud, and then he shouted to no one in particular, "I'll be damned, he's a hero!"

Sitting on the desk, next to the London Gazette, was a postcard. It was a simple brown field card from his son and on it, it said he was wounded but fine. The Colonel wouldn't have even seen Jack's Commendation but for the fact that his only son, Tim, had been promoted from Lieutenant to Captain, and for the blessing that he had been wounded – but not seriously – and spared by God on that dreadful first day of the Somme.

He was quite certain that Tim would have died on the subsequent attacks if he had been in a position to lead the men. Of the 28 officers in the front line that week, two had survived, both wounded, one severely enough that he would never return to action. So it was that Tim, now Captain

Alcot, would continue to uphold the honour of the family name.

Colonel Bradley, the commanding officer of the Derbyshire Regiment, had written to the retired Colonel to say how impressed he was with young Alcot. He had done sterling work on the initial attack, and the regiment had shown great courage and determination in the face of difficult conditions. He was sorry to have to inform him that Lieutenant Alcot had been wounded, albeit not too seriously and indeed he was expected to make a full recovery at the base hospital in Calais. He was also delighted to report that his man Adams had been awarded the DCM for downing a Hun aeroplane.

Colonel Alcot reached for the brandy, a celebration. Later, after afternoon tea, he would take a drive down to both Jim Cunningham's place and Mr and Mrs Adams. This medal was for all of them and by God they all deserved it. He would invite them to dinner as his guests.

There was no denying that Colonel Gerald Alcot was a caring man. He was also exceptionally thankful that two of the three men he had committed to the war were doing well and that the one who had come home had come home covered in glory. Yes Alcot, he thought, they've done you proud old man, and now you should show them how proud of them you really are.

So, with a sip of fine brandy and a fresh cigar, he called the housekeeper Mrs Millward to plan dinner. He wanted it to be a 'special night' so he told her to make sure there was plenty to drink as well. He was renowned for his fantastic parties but he wanted this to be a bit more personal. Still, that didn't mean he couldn't roll the carpet out a bit.

Things here on the home front had been a little tense, but after today's good news maybe things were looking up. Cunningham had settled well back home. Yes, his chest was buggered, but that seemed to be about the sum of it. His eyes were getting better by the day and he seemed in good spirits, glad to be home with his family, he said, but the Colonel knew he worried about his chum, Adams.

Truth be known, the Colonel worried about him as well; he had this damnable talent with a rifle, and although it wasn't the type of war the Colonel might have wanted or indeed accepted in his day, he was a great credit to the uniform. Still, it was a rum do and in such circumstances you had to fight fire with fire. He cursed the Germans for using Gas. For God's sake, gassing men like rats... it was despicable behaviour, even in a war. Just despicable.

The Colonel reflected on the year as he looked out of the window over the garden. The spring had been dry here, but not in France. The summer sun had ensured a decent crop in the rural countryside; the farmers would be happy.

There would be no shoot this year save a couple of days' rough shooting, and if Jim could manage it, he would take him to Scotland for some shooting. But in his heart he was doing it more for Jim than himself; the fresh air would do him the power of good, it would do *both* of them good.

He realised just how much he missed his lad, Tim, hardly the boy anymore but he would always be a lad to him. The fact was he was a grown man now, a Captain in the Derbyshire's. He remembered his time as a Captain, too many years ago to want to count. It was a different world then, a simpler world where a soldier did as he was bid and the officers had breeding.

He finished his brandy and stubbed out his cigar; it didn't taste as good as it should have and he was aware that missing his son was nearly as painful as missing his wife. She had died twenty years ago, giving birth to a sister for Tim and a daughter for him. Both mother and child had perished, there was nothing anyone could do. He had kept those feelings buried as deeply as any man could but now, with a heavy heart, he wept.

He sat down in his study chair and ran his ageing hand through his thinning hair. At that moment in time, he shared the same emotions that millions of families were feeling, a national grief for a generation they were losing. On a daily basis, men were dying and more still wounded and maimed. Breeding was no guarantee for safety, not for anyone. And when this war was over, nothing and no one would ever be the same.

# CHAPTER 22

# The Set Up

Jack had been tasked with a simple job today: harass the enemy. That was all he had to do, but it was a tense time for everyone. Things seemed totally different since the July attacks; nothing had come of them, just thousands dead for very little gain, and for the first time in a long time Jack felt the fickle fingers of melancholy take hold of his spirit.

He could see no point in this war now, but worse than that was that he could see no end to it. He had shot a lot of men, and in his mind he could relive every shot apart from the ones on the 1st July. Of those he had very little memory, other than they were shot in haste and in anger, two things that were certain to get you killed out there as a sniper.

He had been lucky. Major Hesketh-Prichard had been to see him in the trenches to congratulate him on his award. Jack felt no great pride in receiving it; for his money, the poor blokes that were being shot at with the stretchers deserved it far more than he did. It was a nice little break from the front to go back to Headquarters and to be presented with it though.

There were some very brave soldiers that day, each with a story to tell, and Jack listened eagerly to as many as he could, but no matter how hard he tried he couldn't place himself in the company of those brave men. That night, they had been allowed to have drinks and it didn't take long for the effects of those drinks to take their toll; within a few hours of getting the medals the drink and quiet made most of the lads fall asleep. It was a restless, fitful sleep, but sleep nonetheless.

Within days of getting those medals of bravery, some of the recipients were lying out in the mud, dead. This war was such a waste.

All this was going on in Jack's mind. He was in a routine now, and not always concentrating on what the job in hand was. His greatest enemy now wasn't the Germans but complacency. Jack had a price on his head and still had Wolfgang to find and stop. No one could seem to pinpoint Wolfgang but as the Major pointed out, no one had found Jack either, and they were looking. Every day they looked for him and every day he avoided detection, but for how long could he last? It was a question he had hoped he would never ask himself, but now that he had, he hoped it might help him last a bit longer.

Jack was attached to a different bunch now; The Derbyshire's had taken quite a beating and had been pulled back to rest and for new reinforcements to join. Now Jack was with the York and Lancaster's or the 'Young and Lovelies' as they were sometimes called, but Jack was never sure if it was a term of endearment or a bit of army Mickey taking.

It wasn't going to be for very long; Hesketh-Prichard wanted Jack to go back to the snipers school for a while to pass on his newly acquired information and skills. It was an agreement between the Major and the commanding officers that he had first dibs on Jack.

Jack thought the change might suit him well so was quite keen to go. It would be a few weeks away yet, but in the meantime he would stay on here and look for Wolfgang.

At the last count he had shot eight 'Wolfgang's', each one a sniper, but Jack wasn't convinced any of them were the true target. Five of them had made silly mistakes and it had cost them dear – it had cost them their lives.

Three had taken skill, first to find them and then to get a shot away at them. Jack had reported that the camouflage of the German snipers was superb and was in fact only bettered by their cunning in the field. The last one Jack had shot had been hidden in a model of a dead horse; the horse had been killed a few weeks before and had lain where it fell. Troops were using it as a reference point. It overlooked the British lines and was so obvious that no one in the British lines ever paid it any attention.

The Germans did. They spirited it away and replaced it overnight with a model in which a man could hide. This was all done under the cover of darkness. Jack and the Intelligence officers marvelled at how well the model had replicated the dead horse. Mostly used for observation, occasionally it had been used by German snipers, and on the day Jack was there he had been staggered when he saw the set up.

A sniper had crawled into the belly of the beast in darkness, set up his shot and rifle and then waited. He had waited for the whole day and no one had a clue he was there. He'd shot and killed five men before Jack saw him. Jack took one shot and the German shot no more. The discussion and thought was that it had been Wolfgang but Jack wasn't convinced. He admired the gall of the man but this was sloppy. Not only sloppy but greedy too.

To shoot one man or even two from the same spot was the normal practice, but never three. Five was amateurish and for all the things Jack had learned about Wolfgang, amateurish wasn't one of them.

This wasn't Wolfgang, but it was no doubt Wolfgang's idea, and at one time no doubt his lair. It suited the powers that be to make out it was the German sniper, though, as it was good for morale.

There was no end to the ingenuity of the opposing snipers; just to find them when you knew where they were laid was truly difficult. To try to find them out there when you were being shot at was nearly impossible. In the past, just knowing they were in a particular spot was enough to call in an artillery strike and decimate the area, but now – as up in the sky in the air war, with the opposing pilots – things had become personal.

The battle between Wolfgang and Jack was more intimate than that. There was a respect, as would a hunter respect his prey or a stalker and a stag. Yes, that was more accurate: Jack thought of himself as a stalker and Wolfgang an emperor stag. It added a bit of normality to a frankly abnormal situation. A duel between the top shots, but for those who thought this was just about the shot, well, they were the dead ones, lying out there in their hides and lairs. These were the ones who didn't get to see the sniper who killed them because they thought that sniping was only about marksmanship. Both Albert and Jack knew that the shot was only part of the process and that was why the two of them were the cream of the crop.

With his head back in focus, Jack thought about and planned a way to draw Wolfgang out of his hide. Much as Jack respected his opponent, it was his job to kill him and Jack had a plan.

He was going to go out into no man's land and set up his lair, and he was going to stay there for maybe a week. He had food enough stored in the reconstructed shell hole as well as water, and over the past few nights he had built his hide. He even called in a small barrage to disguise the new ground works that left the tell-tale signs of new digging and disturbed earth.

He had learned about digging from the tunnelers who had helped him with his chore of getting rid of the new spoil, but to make extra sure there was no sign he had been working there, he had asked for a few shells to be sent over to cover his tracks. The shells that landed around had made sure the new site was invisible, even from the air. It was a masterstroke.

Jack was nearly ready to make his way to the new hide but he needed a diversion, and that was going to happen tonight with a fake attack, lots of noise, flares and chaos. It was his time to go.

The attack started at 11:00 p.m. There was a green flare set off in the west of the line and within minutes patrols were out and trying to take prisoners. In reality it was an everyday occurrence, trench raids happened all the time, and the raiding parties were hard men, used to fighting hand to hand.

Jack tagged on with a raid until he reached his spot. He dropped into his hide and within seconds was gone from sight. He would have to wait until first light to get his stuff together but all was nearly done and so he curled up into a ball and tried to sleep. It was about an hour later that he heard the patrol coming back, completely oblivious as to his presence.

He smiled, just for a second, and then he heard them talk, a whisper only, in German. Jack slid his hand down to his revolver, the Webley mark 4 was sitting at his side and he felt comforted by the fact that at close range it was deadly. Its 11.9 mm bullet had a lot of stopping power but if he had to use it, all the hard work of the past week would have been for nothing. He could feel his heart pounding in his chest as he held his breath.

The German patrol was right outside his hide. He thought about shooting them, after all they didn't even know he was there, but something stopped him. Suddenly, a German stood in his shell hole. The soldier stumbled and stood on Jack's leg, and Jack had to bite his lip so as not to cry out. The German fell onto Jack and grunted his disgust; he was certain he had fallen onto a dead body.

The soldier jumped up then ducked down. Making that much noise was a clear way to draw machine gun fire onto his group and Jack was aware that the men standing around him were crouched at the lip of his shell hole.

Sure enough, there was the familiar rattle of a British machine gun. The bullets landed wide of the mark and the parachute flair that was sent skywards cast an eerie iridescence over the lunar landscape. Within a couple of minutes, the temporary daylight scene had returned to the dark and the Germans crouched down low and moved on.

It proved to Jack that his hide was invisible. He checked that there was no damage. That had been a close call, and for now, sleep was out of the question. The German patrol would have to return later and Jack was careful to control his noise and his breathing. It was time for him to disappear again, but this time he would be mindful that he wasn't safe from the dealer of bad luck. It was the only way he would be found – of that he was confident – but lady luck could be fickle, so he said a silent prayer and hoped that tonight's God was English.

The rain started again, a steady drizzle, and Jack was pleased he had covered his hidey-hole and that he wasn't exposed to the elements. It was, after all, still summer and the day was just as likely to be bright and sunny as well as hot, so having cover was important.

He unclipped his spyglass and unwrapped his rifle from its waterproof bag. He then wiped and cleaned the working parts, preparing to start his work at first light. The night had started as per plan but had quickly gone south with the German patrol. It was now back on plan so maybe some sleep was a good idea; he needed to be awake and alert for tomorrow.

He finished his cleaning, checked his revolver, pulled his hood over his head and let himself drift away into a restless but much needed slumber. The rain eased and the night became clear and still. In the distance there was an artillery barrage that played like an overture with the shrill rat-a-tat of the occasional machine gun; it sounded like an orchestra and Jack realised he was dreaming.

On the edge of sleep, he was awake enough to be aware but in a place where the war was hidden: the recess of his mind.

# CHAPTER 23

# Set Up Part Two

Albert lay, watching. It had been quite a show. He was impressed that the British sniper had taken so much time and paid so much attention to the finer details of his hideout. In truth, Albert had seen Jack on the first night, but he didn't have a clear shot and as he watched, he became more fascinated by the thoroughness of this 'Tommy'. He was meticulous in his detail and it hadn't taken very long for Albert to make up his mind that this was the infamous 'Jack'.

He could have shot him a number of times if he had felt so inclined, but here was a man of a similar skill to his own. It suited his plan for Jack to live. There were many parts to Albert's plan but uppermost in his mind was getting home alive and not left out here to rot like so many of his countrymen, and indeed the countrymen of the British sniper not forty yards away.

Albert decided that he was too close and that for the best results, he should move back. He slowly crawled out of his hide, invisible in this light. He moved with the stealth of a predator, hunting, looking for his quarry. In the whole time it took him to move twenty yards further back, his eyes never left his prey. It had taken Albert two hours to move that short distance but it was imperative that, come daylight, there must be no sign that he had been there. If the roles had been reversed, he knew he would see the line he had taken. So he made sure he left none, no sign or lines that would or indeed could be seen; it was as if he had never been there.

It had come as no surprise to Albert that Hauptman Berger had been asking where he was heading to. As Albert had predicted, Berger was taking a very close interest in where he was and what he was planning to do next.

Albert had given Berger the wrong coordinates; it was a risk because normally you gave this information to ensure there were no attacks in your location. But this night, depending on who you were, things weren't going to turn out quite the way they should.

Albert had made sure he had been out by about fifty metres. Whilst he was out, dug in, he heard the click then pop of a trench mortar being loaded; he knew the sound too well. The mortar rounds were in the air, loaded with the smallest launch charge and aimed virtually vertically. The three large cylinder shaped bombs rose into the night air. So slow that Albert could see them, black against the night sky in the air, they reached the very top of their flight then tumbled back to earth. Each one landed within ten metres of where he had told the Hauptman he would be.

Death was a certainty if he had been there. The murdering scum who was supposed to be his officer had indeed set his own weapons upon him. It was no more than Albert had anticipated but it still made him sick to the guts with hatred for the man. He now had a choice to make: go back and alert Berger that he was still alive or stay out here.

Here was safe, no one knew he was there. To Hauptman Berger and his comrades, he was dead; this was his chance to finish this crazy war for himself. Unfortunately becoming a prisoner of war just wasn't that easy. If the British found him out here they might just kill him; he was a sniper and snipers were treated like vermin.

He was well hidden and had supplies. It had been a nice distraction when he had spotted Jack. It had helped him make his decision.

## CHAPTER 24

# 20th August

Albert watched as Jack slithered on his belly. He was on the edge of his shell hole and then he was gone. Albert smiled. He liked the Britisher; he did the same things Albert would do and he was supposedly the best. By spotting Jack, he had confirmed it.

Unfortunately for Jack, Albert wasn't the only one who had seen him that morning. Another German from the Bavarian regiment in the trenches opposite was watching a fight. Not humans – that was commonplace and he had seen it a thousand times before – but two rats. The two rats were fighting over a grizzly prize: the remains of a young soldier. Dead for less than a week, he was bloated and had the skin colour of a bluebottle. Within the next couple of days, the corpse would have burst and, depending on the wind direction, he would have either returned home or been responsible for the awful sweet smell of death.

The answer was well known by both sides: just shoot the dead body, the bullets would release the pressure and gas build up and the body would lay quiet. It was called killing the dead. No one liked doing it. It felt wrong, bizarre, given the madness that was daily, living here in the front line. Nevertheless, it was a shot that no one liked.

Whilst he was watching the fighting rats, something else caught his eye, a movement. He could have dismissed it as insignificant but the thing that made it stand out was there was nothing there to move. He couldn't see anything that might move. No rats, no wounded, no patrols. There was nothing there but he knew he had seen something.

He called for his corporal. "There, just past the shell hole, near the broken wire, look closely. There was something moving there and I don't know what it was. It shouldn't be there, that's why I noticed it."

The corporal called for one of the many snipers in the line to see if he could see anything. The trained eye of the sniper looked for the obvious and dismissed it instantly; his eye was trained to see the less obvious, the new spoil, nothing, water pooling where it shouldn't, nothing.

Then he saw it: the perfect round aperture of a rifle muzzle. A near impossible sight, it was perfect but it shouldn't be perfect, nothing in nature is perfectly round like that. It didn't move but he was intrigued, and he asked if he could take a look from a little closer. He felt sure he had spotted a sniper and who knows, it could be the infamous 'Jack'.

The thought of two weeks away from the front as his reward for killing the most-wanted sniper in the British lines appealed to him very much. He was ordered to go and see what he could find, and he collected his things. It would only take an hour for him to work his way around the side.

He was delighted the corporal had called him. He was the senior sniper now Albert was dead. Shooting 'Jack' would give him bragging rights over all the other sharpshooters and hunters back in the line. He would be as famous as Baron Von Richthofen, the Knight of the air war. He left the trench system with high hopes of leave, fame and honour. What more could a Prussian want?

Karl Mattes was a good shot. Not the best, not by a long way, but at the moment he was the best there was in the German trenches and he was on to a target. Slowly, he manoeuvred his way out of his trench and made a wide arc around to his left. He dropped into the first shell hole some two hundred yards from Jack's position.

He had been very clever and moved between huge night-lighting flares, sent up to see what was going on in no man's land. He knew the British would respond with the same. It was like a choreographed fireworks display. On the odd occasions that anything was seen, there would be a furious display of firepower aimed in the general direction of the shadows and into the wire. Rarely was there anything there, but tonight, he was, and he knew that the most wanted man on the front was sitting in a hole not more than two hundred yards to his right.

There would be the first signs of daylight in about two hours so Karl had to keep moving, otherwise he wouldn't get the shot he wanted. He needed to be in front of the target and to do that he tracked around to the right using the shell holes as cover; he crawled through the mud and slime, he even crawled through some of his old friends and foes. Most of the dead were still here, British and German alike, enemies in life and comrades in death. It felt right to think like that because no one had come to collect them. If you fell out here, here was where you would stay.

He made his way very slowly, moving no more than ten yards within thirty minutes. He could feel the cold but he was soaked in sweat. His heart was pounding and his hands were sore from being in the wet mud. His rifle was held on his back by two shoulder straps and the optic sight he had was safe in a leather case, protected.

Mattes made his way and in time found the right hole to take cover in. He had removed his helmet because the chinstrap rubbed, making his chin raw and sore. He looked at the breaking dawn. It was beautiful. There was a songbird singing and the air was fresh. He unclipped his shoulder straps and attached his sights to the pristine rifle. He had already slipped a round into the breech, and with one final, silent click, the rifle was ready. He was glad of the precision German engineering; it was perfect.

Whilst he still had some darkness left, he moved the soil from the top of the crater, just a small 'V' cut into the bank top. He made sure his face was dirty and spread some mud onto his sweating hair. It quickly matted and then he slid his rifle into the premade groove. He took his first peek at his pray. It wasn't easy to see him – in fact, it was nearly impossible – but there it was again, the perfect round hole at the end of the barrel.

Karl marvelled at the disguise; the chances of seeing this were ten thousand to one, but there he was looking, literally down the barrel of a rifle. He knew that the sights would be to the left of the hole and the head of the shooter would be just one inch to the left of that. He couldn't see any distinguishable features to show there was a head there at all, but the rifle would fire at some stage and when it did he knew exactly where the sniper's head would be. This sniper had one shot left. It would be his last and Karl felt sad that one of his countrymen had to die for him to be able to kill the British sniper. But he couldn't think of that now; the dawn was upon him.

Exactly 350 yards to the right of Karl Mattes lay Albert Hagerman, who had watched Mattes make his way into a position. He was full of contempt for the Prussian. Albert thought Mattes was clumsy and careless. He had spotted him two hours ago in the near darkness. He knew what Mattes was doing but was disappointed that he was there at all.

Jack hadn't seen anything. He had been busy waiting, with his head down in his crooked arms, not sleeping but resting his eyes. He had heard the birds singing and the distant howl of a dog. It sent shivers down his spine; it was such a mournful howl. He had a routine when he was out in the mud: he would open his eyes and roll them, and then he would smile and wiggle his ears. Next came his feet. He would wiggle his toes and tighten his leg muscles, then tense his buttocks and relax. Then his hands, one at a time and always down by his side, slowly. He would then take a look down his scope to see what was right out there in front of him. He would only take one shot then, and as soon as the kill had fallen, he would lower his head and wait for another hour.

The first ten minutes after his shot were the worst, waiting to see if anyone had seen where it had come from. They never had of course, otherwise he would be dead, but it didn't make him feel a lot better for knowing that. He was fairly sure he wouldn't attract any attention because when all was said and done, he was bloody good at this sniping and hiding. A deadly game of hide-and-seek, he had never been found yet.

Karl Mattes looked down his sights. There was nothing new to see but from now on this was the danger time. It was first light and he knew the sniper would be looking for his target, maybe even as he was looking at his. What he had absolutely no idea about was that he in turn was being watched, through a scope attached to a rifle. But unlike Mattes, Albert wasn't going to wait.

Jack looked and saw what he was after, a bloody great big German with a fancy hat, obviously an officer, and in a second or two he was going to be meeting his maker. Jack wished him a safe journey and took a deep breath, ready to breathe out and shoot.

It was then that he saw a movement just off to his right. It was a huge rat coming without any fear, right towards him.

At the same time as Jack took a deep breath, he moved his rifle less than an inch. Karl Mattes saw the movement and clicked off the safety catch on his rifle, also taking the first pressure on the trigger. He wasn't alive when he pulled the trigger.

Albert's shot hit him just behind his right ear, his head rocking sideways. If he had had an ear it would have hit him on the shoulder, but his left ear – along with the rest of the side of his head – was mixing with the mud, as was most of the brain he had been so proud of when he was alive.

Jack never got the shot away. There was a splash of sand and he ducked instinctively. What the hell was that? He needn't have asked himself; he already knew the answer.

He had been spotted and someone was shooting at him, but they had made a fatal mistake; they had missed. He looked through his sights. Right there in front of him, not more than two hundred yards away, there lay a body. It hadn't been there a minute ago, he was certain. He looked again, this time through his spyglass. That body and soul had only just parted company, Jack could see the fresh blood. He lowered his glass. What the hell had just happened?

Albert slid down once more. That had given him more pleasure than he thought it should. He had just shot one of his own men.

He now knew he could shoot that pig Berger and feel nothing, which left him feeling elated. He wasn't sure if the British sniper had been hit, but when he looked, it was all still in the sniper's lair. He would have done the same thing: go back to ground and wait. Don't move, not a muscle. For the next two hours, lay still and breathe. The breaths you are now taking, Jack, are mine. You owe them to me, he thought, and then he himself put his head down.

This duel was over. Karl Mattes lay dead. A tear ran along his already chilling nose as if in recognition of his failings, but the tear wasn't water, it was blood.

Jack didn't move for the next three hours, as cramp burned his legs and disbelief burned his mind. He was always careful, meticulous in every detail. It had served him well because it had kept him alive. This was a huge setback, and as he slowly moved his legs, he knew it was time for him to move, to withdraw and go back to his trench. Time for him to reflect on how anyone could have seen him and if he was getting careless.

He had been hugely lucky today. The sun was high and the warm summer's day helped his sullen mood. He checked the dead German once more with his spyglass; the flies were already starting its natural disposal, feeding off his fresh blood. Jack knew that the rats would be next. The rats, he thought. Maybe the same ones that had saved him today, had made him look.

He had questions aplenty but the one he daren't ask himself was who had shot the German. In the hours that had passed, Jack had looked for some sign of who had saved his life. He had already worked out that someone must have shot him; there had been no shelling, so it couldn't have been shrapnel. It must have either been a very lucky shot, a misfire or a sniper.

Jack didn't really believe in much luck, and misfires were unheard of really, so it must have been a sniper. He hadn't heard of any British snipers working in the area but clearly there was one. When he got back he would ask; he owed the man huge thanks. With that decision made, he started to pack his gear. It was going to be a long day, as he couldn't move in daylight and he mustn't risk taking any shots. He wasn't even sure if the shaking in his hands would let him squeeze the trigger. He took a sip from his water bottle and promptly vomited. For the first time, Jack Adams knew he was mortal.

By dusk, Jack had pulled himself together. He had packed all his kit and started his slow crawl back to the front line. He would try to eat once he got back, then he would ask around as to the name of the sniper who had saved him. One day he might be able to return the favour.

It took Jack over an hour to get back, and once back he made his way to the rear lines and the billet he had been allotted. He made his way over to the company headquarters of the returned Derbyshire regiment and Captain Alcot.

Freshly returned to duty, the Captain had physically come back as before but Jack could see there was a change inside the man. His eyes told a different story than the bravado he blustered. These were dangerous times for the Captain and Jack felt he had to keep an eye out for him.

There were many new men sent to replace the old guard who had fallen on the first day back in July. There was a big Sergeant, who he had since found out went by the name of Bill Savage, still there but like most of the men who had survived the first attack on July 1st he was different now. Bellicose and quarrelsome, he would argue black was white but with Jack, he was calm and quiet. A shared understanding of what had happened helped the survivors adjust to the new replacements. Today Jack had survived again, so maybe he was blessed after all.

Jack couldn't find anyone to thank. In fact, there had been no other snipers out for the last week. Jack had been out when the orders came in for another attack, scheduled for the beginning of the week coming, so all the snipers were firing from the trench. Jack was very confused but accepted that there may well have been a sniper from another battalion further up the line.

It was all highly irregular. Jack and, indeed, all the other snipers had daily briefings as to who was where, and no one owned up to having taken a German sniper.

Jack remained in the dark.

# CHAPTER 25

# Going Back

Having spoken to Captain Alcot and the new sniping officer who had replaced Captain Taylor, Jack was keen to get back into the saddle. He felt the need to go back to the hide hole because it offered him a superb overview of some of the German trenches. Everyone agreed that Jack had had a lucky escape, and the only explanation was a misfire of the enemy sniper's rifle or a lucky shot. Jack felt he needed to know but couldn't tell anyone that he planned to go and collect the dead German's rifle to see if it had indeed misfired, just to make sure.

There was an attack planned for two days' time, not a huge attack but a moderate advance to try to occupy a new stretch of trench that the Bavarians had just moved into. No one liked the Bavarians, but they were better than the Prussians who had reportedly just moved out of the line.

Jack went with the blessing of his troop commanders with the idea that he might be able to collect valuable information about how many and, if possible, which regiment was sitting in front of the British line. To the left of the British were the Canadians and they were scheduled to advance at the same time.

Jack knew it was more of an opportunity to blood the new boys, so many regiments had been decimated by the attacks in July, and now they had replaced the dead and injured, it was time to get the new troops into action. The opposition was going to be tough, though. The Bavarians were known for being tough buggers so any information Jack could collect would be invaluable really. It was agreed and Jack collected his gear and made ready to move.

Within the hour, he was under the wire and on his way. He had fresh supplies to last him for two days but the truth was he didn't like to eat when he was out because it made him need the toilet more and he didn't want to do anything more than a pee in his hide. Anything more had to be collected and buried, unless you wanted to share your home with it; Jack didn't ever do number two's whilst out.

It took him about four hours to crawl to his hide, but he stopped short of going in and rested in a shell hole about forty yards from the hole he had so nearly died in. He thought that before he went in to set up he would go to look at the dead German.

He was again focused and alert, a good combination for a man who is only two hundred yards from the enemy trenches. He made his way slowly past his hide and onto the shell hole that was the final resting place for Karl Mattes.

Jack could see the rats had had their feed for the last two or three days; Mattes lay face down in the mud but there was precious little left of his face now. The rats had eaten all the soft parts such as his eyes, and around the huge hole that was all that was left of his head, flies had laid their eggs just about everywhere there was any old blood.

There, to the right of the body, laid the rifle Jack wanted to collect. The sights alone warranted great interest and within a few minutes Jack had relieved the dead man of his gun. It took less than a second to realise that this gun hadn't misfired. The last bullet to leave this rifle was aimed at Jack but, for whatever reason, it had missed.

The bullet with his name on it had gone astray but someone had shot this poor fellow in the head, and looking at the wound, it didn't take a genius to realise the shot had been fired from this side of the trenches – an own goal. A German sniper had shot this poor soul, one of his own. It must have been a mistake. A sharpshooter thinking this dead German was in fact a British sniper. The poor lad, thought Jack. He felt sad for his family, what a waste, but he nearly nailed me and I didn't see him coming so he must have been a good one.

Jack looked back at his hide. From this angle, there was nothing to see apart from a tiny aperture where his rifle should have been, and he knew it was there so that was cheating. He realised that was what this dead German had seen but when he had looked at it, there had been a rifle, and Jack knew he had been a very lucky so and so.

He wanted to spend a little time with Karl, just to pay a fellow sniper a last respect. It was an uneasy hour for Jack, but an hour it had to be just to ensure that no one was watching him. He said his goodbyes to Karl and a silent prayer, it was the same one he used for 'Fritz' in the trench but he felt sure neither would mind if he shared the same.

There was an artillery battery venting some mournful anger for the men it had lost but it was quite a few miles away. Jack was sure he could hear the sound of an accordion coming from the German trench. There was certainly singing, but Jack didn't know the tune. He looked down at the mud and for the next half an hour he crawled with his face no more than two inches above the stinking French landscape.

In time, he fell back into his initial stopover, looking again at the hide to make sure it hadn't been disturbed, which it was clear it hadn't. There were no signs of movement at all so he started his short journey to his personal observation point, safe in the knowledge that he had built it and that it was invisible to the rest of the world. He felt safest when he was 'dug in' although in this particular hide there was very little digging to be done. Once he was inside, it would be only a couple of minutes before he was once again totally invisible and unseen.

When Jack got into his hole, there had indeed been a change; shellfire had disturbed the far wall and a long piece of corrugated iron sheeting had been blown into the wall. Jack thought it was a good thing to have as he would be able to put his things under the tin to keep them dry and safe. He decided he would get settled in first then he would make the alterations to his precious, safe hideout. It took Jack a few minutes to settle his stuff then he lifted the sheet of tin, dropping it instantly when he saw the barrel of a pistol pointing right at his head.

# CHAPTER 26

## *Albert Meets Jack*

Albert had moved into Jack's shell hole the day after Jack had departed. He was impressed and satisfied when he saw the detail in which Jack had set out his stall. There was even a 'pissen gruben' or pee pit. It was very well made and totally invisible from more than ten yards.

He had dragged in a sheet of tin cladding to protect himself from the weather. He didn't want to disturb any of Jack's fine work. He knew Jack would come back; he had to. Just as curiosity had killed the cat, it would eat away at Jack's mind to find out why that shot had missed him.

Albert was very pleased it had, because Albert had plans for Jack and when Jack did finally return to this superb lair, Albert would be waiting to greet him. In the meantime, Albert had to do some extra work within the shell hole to ensure Jack didn't see him and when he was finished, he hoped that Jack in turn would be as impressed with what he had done as he was with Jack's work.

If Jack was invisible from ten yards then Albert had to be invisible from three feet, and in order to achieve this, he had to dig a grave. It had to be into the side wall of the den because on the floor was too obvious and the spoil from the hole had to be dispersed away and out of the hide so that Jack couldn't see there had been any changes to his home;

there must be nothing different apart from the tin. If it were, then Jack would fly away like a bird on the wind or worse, shoot him, in which case the hole he had called his grave would truly be just that.

# CHAPTER 27

# Hello Jack

Jack looked into the eyes of a killer. Blue and cold, a hard stare, but there was no malice in those eyes.

Albert looked into the eyes of a truly worried man.

What now? he thought. He had been planning this meeting for the past few days but now that he was here, and it had all gone exactly as planned, he was a bit confused as to what to do next.

Albert spoke only two words of English ("thank you") and Jack spoke absolutely no German, so thank you was all they had. It seemed as good as any words but when push came to shove "thank you" wasn't going to get them far.

What was needed now was an action, and Albert was the first to react. He looked Jack straight in the eyes, holding his glare and slowly raising his hands as in surrender.

Jack was stunned; he couldn't move.

He was held in those eyes like a rabbit in a headlamp and all that Albert could say was "Shhhh, thank you." It was calming and the atmosphere was easing but it would all go badly wrong if there were any bangs or sudden movement. "Shhhh, thank you," he said again as he lowered his pistol, "Sie sind Jack?" and he pointed his finger at Jack. Turning his finger on himself, he said, "Ich bin Albert oder Wolfgang."

Jack's heart froze. He had no idea what this man was saying but it was clearly not a threat; it was calm and easy.

How did he know Jack's name? Then when he pointed to himself he said "Albert", was that who he was? Or was he from the place 'Albert'? Then he had said "Wolfgang". Was he Wolfgang? And if so, why was he not shooting Jack?

That was a lot of questions for Jack, and he didn't really know the answer.

"Kamerad" said Albert, and offered Jack his Luger pistol.

Jack sat down. He was totally confused. Where just two minutes ago he thought he was captured and perhaps to be shot, now, he found he was in fact being asked to take this German prisoner.

He couldn't deny Albert was far better at concealment than he himself had ever been. Jack believed this man was, in fact, Wolfgang, but he also thought Wolfgang was a made up name so maybe he was Albert.

Albert reached slowly into his tunic and produced a small flask, offering it to Jack. He then realised that the poor man in front of him was still quite stunned and in a state of shock, so he undid the cap and took a much needed sip of Kirsch.

He was still as frightened as Jack, but he had the advantage of age on his side. He offered Jack the flask again and Jack took it, taking a sip. The warming nectar was strong and sweet. Jack closed his eyes.

Here were two men, neither of whom wanted to be here, both experts at what they did and both with a bounty on their heads, sitting in a shell hole in the middle of a war-torn field that would no doubt have been good farming land before this damn war, and now they were drinking cherry brandy.

He shook his head. "Hello Wolfgang, my name is Jack."

"Mein name ist Albert Hagerman, nicht Wolfgang."

The two men looked at each other. They had been committed to killing each other just a week ago but now it seemed that was no longer the case.

Jack passed the flask back and reached into his ghillie suit pocket for some refreshment of his own, some good old fashioned rum. It tasted foul after the sweet kirsch and it was an offence that Jack had any at all. It was strictly against the rules to take any away from the nip given daily as a rum ration but Jack had been allowed to have some for his hip flask and it did indeed keep the cold away when he was lying overnight in the mud of no man's land.

Albert took a swig and coughed.

Jack laughed and said, "Sorry, it's a bit rough."

Albert smiled.

"Kamerad," said Jack, offering his hand.

"Kamerad," replied Albert as he took it. "Now what?"

Albert reached back and very slowly pulled his precious rifle out from under the tin, offering it to Jack. Jack looked at it and Albert pulled back the cocking handle to eject the bullet sitting in the chamber. He again offered it to Jack, who looked at the one he had just picked up from the dead sniper out front and Albert nodded. He mimed out a gunshot wound to the head, just behind the right ear and pointed to the dead Karl Mattes.

Jack's eyes opened wide. "You shot him, didn't you?" He pointed at himself, then at Albert and then at the dead man.

Albert nodded.

"Why? He was one of yours." But it was no good. Neither man understood the other and for now a smile and a drink was all they could share.

They had to get back to the trench, but Jack needed to

understand why this man had shot his own. How on earth was he going to communicate that to Albert, who was clearly not in the slightest bit worried that Jack had no idea what to do next?

Jack indicated with a head nod that he had to go and Albert nodded back. He pointed between Jack and himself and then back to the British lines, putting his wrists together as if in handcuffs. Jack understood that he wanted to become a prisoner; he was giving himself up. It was time to go back to the trench; there was an attack planned for tomorrow and Jack wasn't meant to be here. They left together.

# CHAPTER 28

# Interpreter Needed

When the two men got within thirty yards of the top of the trench, Jack called out a password. No one shot at him so he assumed he was ok to advance into the trench. There was one man awake at the sentry point. This was the only way into the trench from no man's land; any other way would have been met by a soldier with a bayonet so it was understood by all to come in the 'front door' as the slipway was fondly known.

It was all excitement when Jack led Albert into the trench.

"Who's the Hun, Jack?" asked one.

"Not like you to bring someone home," said another.

Albert felt entirely uneasy. He had planned for all this but it still made him very nervous and he worried that he might be shot at any moment, so he kept his hands in the air where they could be seen.

One corporal went to kick Albert up the arse but Jack grabbed him and pushed him into the trench wall. "Don't touch him, he is my prisoner." Jack looked hard at the corporal who looked resentfully back.

Jack looked at the other men who were all staring at Albert with sharp, untrusting eyes, filled with hatred and loathing. "Anyone tries to hurt this man and I'll shoot them right where they stand." Jack meant it as well. Out there over the top there were no rules, but in here, under his protection, there were his rules and his rule said no harm comes to Albert.

They made their way to the Captain's dugout, and by this time there was quite a stir. Things needed to be ready for the morning and Jack's early return wasn't expected.

Captain Alcot looked stunned at Albert's presence. "Who the hell is this, Corporal? And, more to the point, what is he doing here?"

"Well sir, I thought you wanted to talk to one of them? This chap is a better sniper than me, he could and should have shot me out there, but he didn't. This man is the man I owe my life to. This, sir, is Wolfgang. His real name is Albert Hagerman. We need to ask him some questions, sir. *I* need to ask him some questions. You speak German, don't you?"

Captain Alcot did indeed speak German; he had spent time studying in Berlin as part of a life tour. It wasn't something he made public, otherwise the damned General Staff would have him in the headquarters doing translating rubbish, which was the last thing he wanted and interestingly the first thing his father had wanted once he had returned from the hospital.

"Corporal, keep your voice down." It was no good; everyone had heard, and it was only a matter of time now until someone in authority learned about his ability.

Captain Alcot moved next to Jack, hushing everyone back outside into the trench. There was just Jack, Albert and himself for now, but he knew it wouldn't last long. "Jack, you know he has to go back for interrogation, don't you?"

"Yes sir, but I need some answers. Can you ask him for me, why he was in my dugout and why he didn't shoot me, and more importantly, why he shot one of his own men to stop him from shooting me? And, is he Wolfgang, or who the hell is he?"

Alcot quickly introduced himself to Albert and asked him the questions, adding why he had surrendered. The answers stunned him.

"OK, Jack. Here you go. Yes, he is Wolfgang but he hates the name so please call him either Albert or Hagerman. He was in your dugout because he wanted to meet you and he wants to meet you because he has a mission. He shot the other German, well he called him a Prussian prick, but he shot him because he had spotted you and was going to shoot you. He is dead to his own, they tried to kill him, well one man has: a Hauptman Berger. He is the officer who has shot several of our men after they'd been taken prisoner and Albert here protested too loudly. He wants to point this Berger out to you, because he wants you to kill him. He is quite happy to help us, but he needs to go back down the line. You can go with him if you like; you look shattered and I'm sure it's been quite a week for you. Take him back with a letter I'm going to write. He needs to let his wife know he isn't dead as well. Now get me some tea, will you? There's a good man, and I'll sort out you going back to brigade headquarters with our guest. He has already been very helpful, it's the 6th Royal Bavarian Division that are opposite us, and our chaps think they are one of the best enemy units. Jack, these chaps are not the sort of men to cut your teeth on, and we need to get a message to command pretty damned quick. In light of what he has told me I think it's important that I come back with you. Is he really better than you, Jack?"

"Well sir, I would have to say at this snooping around the

place he is; I never saw him at all and he was nearer to me than you are now. He could have shot me anytime so I feel like maybe I owe him one, sir."

And so they left for the brigade headquarters, Albert, Jack and Tim Alcot. The clock was ticking; no one wanted a repeat of the July fiasco.

# CHAPTER 29

# *Over The Top*

Albert's revelation that it was in fact a crack Bavarian force that faced the inexperienced British troops was indeed alarming, but in the big scheme it made no difference to the high command. The attack was set and Captain Alcot had an attack to prepare for and, indeed, lead. There was a look of resignation in his eyes, more casualties for a pointless gain.

The men were all ready. There was again a wave of jingoistic enthusiasm mixed with fear hanging in the air. The old sweats remembered the same feeling just two months earlier before the killing started. They didn't share the same this time and left the new men to it.

There were reasons to feel optimistic. If the cost in men of the July attacks had been severe, then lessons had indeed been learned. The simple facts were this war wasn't just going to end, and if they were to force the Germans to surrender then attacks like the one planned had to continue, whatever the price, but today's attack was to see the first real advancing barrage, not only with artillery but with machine gun fire as well.

The plan was simple: artillery would start shelling the middle of no man's land and enemy trenches, whilst at the same time Vickers machine guns would fire over the heads of the advancing troops, landing their bullets onto the

German trenches. In effect, the rolling barrage would make the Germans stay in cover deep in their dugouts, and when the barrage finished or went over the top of the trench, the British troops could just drop into the trench and do their grizzly work with the bayonet and bombs. Maybe, just maybe, this time they would get it right.

At 04:00 hours the shelling started on the German trenches. It was only a short barrage in comparison to the days of shelling the Germans had to endure for the July offensive, but the lessons learned continued and the shells this time were high explosive and not shrapnel.

The aim was to blast away the deadly and omnipresent barbed wire. The German wire was designed and made to stop men, as opposed to the allied wire designed primarily to stop cattle. Like so many things in this war, the Germans had prepared better. The wire had long rigid spikes or barbs. Thick and ugly, it was a deadly menace. It had been a significant factor in the failings of so many attacks previously, but high explosive shells did destroy large areas of it and this, in turn, gave the advancing soldiers a chance to move forward. The second reason for the short shelling was to avoid warning the enemy that an attack was imminent. The shelling was to be accurate and short lived.

Jack was back on machine gun cover for the next attack. The lads going 'over the top' where always thankful that the best static shots were in a position to do good work, killing the enemy before they got a chance to kill them with their deadly machine guns.

At six o'clock, the shrill whistles sounded like a siren of the damned. Over the top went brave and foolish alike, but this time the British had learned that walking in a neat line was certain death, so they had adapted and now broke up into smaller groups, advancing under the cover of the rolling artillery barrage.

Jack found his targets easily and, as ever, he was deadly. He had moved along the line to the far right flank, past the entrance he had used just yesterday when he returned with Albert, who was now in the headquarters awaiting the return of Captain Alcot to continue his 'interrogation'. It wasn't so much an interrogation as a friendly chat; it was very strange and extremely civilised.

Jack was in a good position; he could see all along the front. The Germans were very quiet and Jack wasn't sure if this was a good sign or not. He had only fired four shots, all of which had found their mark and the enemy machine guns had fallen silent. As part of his shooting, he had taken to actually hitting the gun if he couldn't get a clear shot at the gunner. This had the same effect, as the gun would be useless because of the cooling water covers that were punctured, and then the barrel of the machine gun would quickly overheat and misfire. Jack had learned this from another sniper, following his tragic efforts in July. Everyone, it seemed, had learned something, but the question now was would they all remember what they had been taught?

The chatter of the machine guns from behind slightly unnerved him, but looking out ahead, it was clear that the new tactics were indeed working. The advancing troops were only just short of the German lines and indeed some were dropping into the trench.

Within minutes, hundreds of men were in and the shelling moved its way into the distance to discourage an immediate counter attack. To Jack, it looked like there were very few casualties; there were cheers coming from over the German lines and Jack watched as lines of prisoners walked back towards the British lines, escorted by jubilant troops who had tasted the blood of their first battle and now felt invincible.

In the German trench, things were frenzied. The fighting had been hand to hand and savage. Bombs were thrown into doorways, and deep in the dugouts, the toll of the dead and wounded was high.

Captain Alcot had been right at the front. As if he had a point to prove, he led the men courageously and with a determination that was unshakable. He had emptied his Webley three times like he was a wild man, kicking and punching as he advanced along the German trench.

At one stage, a German appeared from the entrance to a dugout to find himself behind the marauding officer. He raised his rifle to shoot Alcot in the back, then screamed as a bayonet emerged from his stomach; Sergeant Savage had stuck the huge blade into his left kidney and just kept pushing. The German dropped his rifle and fell to his knees, a look of fear and resignation on his face. He knew he was going to die and Savage stabbed him again and this time, mercifully, it pierced his pounding heart and ended his misery.

Alcot looked the Sergeant in the eye; both men had the 'rage'. Killing was easy when you had it and all vestiges of civility had left. It was very much a case of kill or be killed.

Then it was over, and there was much work to do now. The trench system had to be reinforced and the parapet needed to be prepared for the impending counter attack. Sandbags needed to be placed on the back of the trench lip to give the cover needed to repel the expected German attack.

The Germans were very good at the counter attack and, more often than not, soon gained the ground they had lost in the initial advance by the British. It was much easier, of course, as there was hardly any wire to contend with. The back of the trench was much more difficult to defend than the front, and so whilst the artillery continued to drop its shells behind the now newly-taken trench, it was only a matter of time before the Germans wanted their trench back.

In the German support trenches it was pandemonium. The supporting troops were the Prussians who had handed the trench over to the Bavarians only last week. Hauptman Berger was screaming to his men to get ready, his mood ugly and dark; he had only killing on his mind and he felt nothing but contempt for both the British and the Bavarians.

The communication trenches were full of soldiers all pushing and getting ready. There were shells landing and exploding above and all around him, but he was incensed. There had to be an attack and it would be driven by revenge. Berger looked above the trench and could see in the distance the prisoners being led back to the British lines.

Disgust welled in his already heaving gut as he screamed, "Cowards! Fight back, why don't you?" He checked his men were ready and jumped over the ledge to start the advance to regain his trench.

"Hold, Hold!" yelled Sergeant Savage. "Don't let the bastards back in; this is ours now."

The battle was in a very small area. Along the trench were large junctions where the communication and support trenches fed the front line, and this was now packed with angry Germans who were determined to gain the trench they had lost.

There were explosions as grenades fell amongst the heaving throng and bayonets thrust into the faces of the defending troops. Again, the fighting was hand-to-hand and any weapon was a good weapon: shovels, spades, clubs and daggers. All were used, and along with the grenades and rifle fire, the casualties mounted on both sides. Dead and dying mounted up and the wounded were dragged unceremoniously back.

The situation was getting hopeless and Captain Alcot was trapped; he couldn't get to the front of the fighting because the sheer number of men in such a confined space made movement impossible. What he needed, of course, was for fewer men but he had all but lost control, and now there was a mob facing each other.

It was a desperate struggle at the front of the heaving morass and Alcot realised he would have to retreat; the number of Germans was too great. He put his whistle between his trembling lips and blew hard three times. All the men heard it above the clamour and quickly regained their senses. The Sergeant pulled men back and told them to go, and that he would hold this space until they could give him cover.

One by one, the men stumbled over the top and headed back towards their own line. Captain Alcot pulled and pushed the men back onto the top to help them retire. He was weary, all the strength he had was drained; now it was only character and stubbornness that kept him going.

One by one, the line thinned until there were only half a dozen men left, and it was much easier to defend with that many men, as each man had room to move and manoeuvre. Then, the next two men to go were shot down and within seconds, the trench was overrun. The Germans had broken through along the trench and now converged on the one area still being fought for.

But now they had the problem of too many men in such a small space; instead, rage and anger, revenge and bloodlust all conspired to get in the way. Conversely, fear and determination to escape helped Captain Alcot and Sergeant Savage. In a bound they were over the top and running, running like all the hounds of hell were after them.

Giant heaving mushrooms erupted all around as the German artillery joined the already finished party. Their chests heaved and lungs burned with the tainted air of cordite; each breath was trying to get out as another tried to get in. They ran crouched and zig-zagged, each stride taking them further away from the danger and a stride closer to safety. Bullets pinged and ricocheted all around them but miraculously neither was hit.

They were about a hundred yards from the German lines and two hundred from their own when a shell exploded right next to them, lifting them in a blinding light and tossing them like flotsam on a summer breeze. Savage was dead; cut in half by the blast, oblivious to any pain. He never even heard it coming. Captain Alcot tumbled in the blast; Sergeant Savage had done him one last favour and saved him from the worst. He landed in the wire and rolled suspended in the air, tangled in an agonising dance between being free and being held firm on the wire. Unfortunately for Alcot, the wire won.

He was hung on the wire, a nightmare for anyone. He was only slightly wounded – nothing but a few splinters – but he was covered in blood; it was the blood of his Sergeant who had, unbeknown to him, saved Captain Alcot's life, again. Twice in one day.

Alcot was in trouble, he knew he was. There were stretcher-bearers out there but he was in an awkward position; both his legs were trapped as were both arms. His right arm was pinned across his chest, and with a bit of effort he could reach his whistle, but if he blew it he would draw attention to himself. Not only the British would hear his distress call but so too would the Germans and although he was facing the British lines, he was in clear sight of the Germans. His shoulder burned but he could feel his fingers wiggle so he assumed all was OK. Just a graze, another wound to tell the folks about back home.

In time, all the men had returned from the initial attack, all the wounded were accounted for, and the butcher's bill for the day had been reckoned up. Dead were numbered at forty five, wounded ninety, and missing sixty. Amongst these were Captain Alcot and Sergeant Savage. There were many reports of the men's brave attempt to cover the lads as they retreated back into no man's land, but no one had seen them fall. There was hope.

Captain Alcot was thirsty, hellish thirsty. There was no water and his mouth was as dry as the desert. He was very much aware that the evening was closing in; it was cooling quickly now the sun had started its slow descent to night time and the safety of darkness. He thought it might be better to wait until night-time to blow his whistle. The bearers would be out looking for the wounded and if he could attract their attention, he would be released.

Darkness came with an eerie silence. In the daylight there was noise, but at night, out here there was nothing. His ears had stopped ringing from the previous day's battle and mayhem and now there were no sounds or indeed anything to see. At least whilst there was daylight he had had the hope that someone would come back and see him, but in the dark there was nothing moving.

At odd times he would hear a chatter of a faraway machine gun and occasionally he would be lit up by a night flare, but no one came. For the first time that he could remember, he was scared. As a child he was scared of the dark, and nanny or Misses Millward would have a night candle lit in his room. Now there was darkness, his shoulder ached and the sharp barbs of the wire cut into his flesh when he tried to move. All he could do was wait, the bearers would come, he knew they would.

He was surprised that it was so cold; the warm autumn sun made the days quite pleasant but at night he had needed an overcoat, and that was before he had led the attack. Now, in his battle dress, he was shivering. If he had known what was about to happen he would have been shaking, not from the chill of the night air, but from fear.

# CHAPTER 30

# *War Crime*

Hauptman Manfred Berger was an evil, sadistic and damaged individual. Anyone who had ever met him would have had no qualms telling you. Albert Hagerman knew it. He had witnessed things done that shouldn't have ever been done, not even in a barbaric war like this one.

Albert had made two mistakes since joining up and he considered that the first. The second was telling Berger he had his number. He should have just shot him, quietly and from a distance; it was what he was supreme at. It was a regret now but still a mistake, because from the moment Berger knew he had been challenged, and indeed caught, he was going to make sure Albert died.

This was Berger's mistake: he had assumed that the trench mortar had killed Albert. He was so sure he didn't even send anyone to look, although if he had it wouldn't have made much difference; they would have found a dead German sniper lying in a shell hole and would have reported that back to Hauptman Berger, but he didn't send anyone anyway.

As the morning sun ended the short night, Berger was awake and on the prowl. They had to be ready for another attack; the one yesterday had been costly, and there were hundreds dead or wounded. The British attack had been very successful initially, and the Prussian was appalled by the weak capitulation of the Bavarians.

He never gave any credit to the now more experienced British or the fact that the Bavarians couldn't come out of their bunkers. The air was thick with lead, raining machine gun bullets, and for the Bavarians to emerge from the safety of their bunkers would have been both futile and fatal. The attack was better than good; it had been perfect, and if Berger could have seen past his arrogant self-righteousness, he would have realised he would have done the exact same thing his Bavarian counterpart had done: died.

The Germans had tried to repel the attack but it was far too late; the British were already in the trench system before even a single soldier had made it out of their trench dugouts. The Bavarian Officer had been one of the first to emerge and indeed one of the first to die. Berger was indeed a pig-headed sadistic disgrace to his uniform that many had thought but none would dare say.

As he walked along the duckboards of the trench, he saw the remnants of the soldiers who had so destructively visited yesterday. Odd bits and pieces: a bayonet lay there and a striking match for the hand bombs lay over there. The detritus of war was everywhere. He looked over the parapet towards the British lines to see that the sun was getting higher, bringing the safety of light. It was then that Berger saw the entangled body that was Captain Tim Alcot.

At first he was sure it was dead, but now he wasn't so sure. Had it just moved? He looked again, this time through a pair of field glasses, of which he was very proud. Made by Ziess, they were as good as any in the world, and Berger had acquired this pair in a wager with a young Oberleutnant in a game of chance.

The Oberleutnant had lost more than his field glasses; it had cost him a posting to the east to fight the Russians and now he lay dead along with thousands more of his unfortunate countrymen, killed not by the enemy but by the weather and cold. Russia wasn't a place to be in the winter.

Berger looked and saw a definite movement, better still with the power of the glasses he could see the man was an officer. Typical, he spat, not even the courage to stay and fight, now caught like a rat in a trap. He called his orderly, who was at his side within a second. "Get me a rifle with a scope on it, now." The rifle was demanded and fetched within ten minutes.

Berger stood on the footstep and rested his rifle on the parapet. He had always prided himself on being a good shot, but that wasn't a requirement for him as a Hauptman. He had plenty of excellent shots within the battalion, so this was purely for entertainment. He smiled to himself as he pulled the trigger. The first bullet missed but whistled past Alcot with a familiar and fearful 'zing', and Berger reloaded.

Alcot wasn't sure if it had been a bullet because there was no reason for anyone to be shooting at him, but he had recognised the sound of a bullet whipping past and thudding into the mud just in front of him. He tried to get the whistle into his dry lips as a slight panic rose within him.

The second bullet didn't miss. It struck him just below his right knee, through his leather boot and into his calf. It felt like he had kicked by a horse and his leg snapped straight in an involuntary jerk. He blew his whistle hard; the loud shrill could be heard above any other noise, partly because it was so urgent. It sounded like the cry of a wounded animal.

Berger thought about firing a third shot but decided that he might have a coffee first. He handed the rifle back to his orderly and told him to wait.

The bullet had hit Captain Alcot in the right calf but had been deflected by his boot. Instead of entering from the back and leaving an ugly exit wound in the front, it had veered to the right and exited out of the side of his leg. Not a huge wound, but very painful once the initial shock had worn off. Alcot jerked in an attempt to free himself from the wire but to no avail; the more he wriggled the more he became held tighter. He couldn't understand why anyone was shooting at him from the German lines, but they had stopped, so with a bit of luck they might think he was dead.

Coffee finished, Berger came back to continue his depraved game. Sliding a fresh round into the breech, he aimed at the trapped man's other leg, higher this time. The bullet hit Alcot in the left thigh. It smashed into his leg just below his left buttock and shattered his thighbone as the bullet exited just above his left knee. The whistle screamed like a demented steam train and fell from his lips, followed by an agonising and pitiful cry.

Berger and his men heard the agonised cry and he told his men that this was what the brave British officers were like: "they cry like baby girls," he mocked.

Tim wasn't crying, he was wailing in agony. For now, the game was over. Berger's idea was to induce as much pain to the poor unfortunate man, but not kill him. He wanted the screams to pervade the British trenches and drive the British to try to rescue their man. He had a machine gun trained on the area and he would massacre the rescuers en masse. He would leave the man to scream for now. He wasn't going anywhere and Berger knew it.

Back in the British trench, each man knew what the game was. It was depraved and sadistic and the officer in charge called for the telephone to the headquarters. He needed the observation officer to isolate where the shots were coming from. His intention was to call for an artillery barrage to land on the trench; after all, they had the distance from yesterday. It was an exact science but even if they got it wrong, it would stop the dreadful torture of one of their officers.

He was disappointed to hear that the lines had been cut so he called for a runner. Never had a runner run so fast. Captain Alcot was a popular officer and his suffering was keenly felt by each and every man able to hear the mournful cry of pain.

The sun was high in the midday sky and Captain Alcot was nearing an unconscious sleep. Fearful that it might be an eternal sleep, he fought to stay awake.

The runner returned but it was not the message they wanted to hear. There would be no artillery barrage. The high command didn't want to destroy the trenches opposite, they wanted to occupy them and a barrage would leave them too badly damaged. A rescue party was to be assembled with all haste and volunteers were called for. There were plenty of hands raised. One chap asked if anyone thought it was a trap and the tragic, devious plot was realised. The wire was in an open space, there was no cover, and Captain Alcot may already be dead; there were no cries anymore and the Germans had stopped shooting at him.

Then he called for Jack. Jack ran back to the company HQ as quickly as he could. He had been up the line with Albert waiting for the Captain to return so he could communicate between them. There was no one available to guard the prisoner so Jack had to take him back with him. He did feel a certain kinship with his new prisoner, perhaps because they shared the same occupation. Albert was very keen to stay with Jack; he was all he knew. There was a sense of panic in the air, not an emotion that either Albert or Jack were used to.

Jack thought he had a chance to crawl out into no man's land and affect a rescue. Failing that, if he couldn't rescue him then he was to administer the coup de grace, if indeed he wasn't already dead.

Jack grabbed his gear and was dressed and camouflaged within ten minutes. It was hot today and he could feel the sweat running down the small of his back. He dragged his fingers in the mud of a puddle and smeared it onto his face. There was a mental change as well. Coldness came over him, the calm of a killer. He had killing on his mind: not his Captain and friend, but the heinous murdering bastards that were responsible for the shooting. Albert looked around and felt a feeling of apprehension, the men looking at him in an angry and menacing way.

He had no idea why until a young private soldier said in fluent German, "Someone is shooting lumps out of our officer."

Everyone stopped. Stunned, all the men looked at Private Finch. "You speak their lingo, lad?" asked the warrant officer.

"Yes sir, my mother is German, I've spoken it all of my life, sir."

"Why the hell didn't you say something, you gormless bugger?"

"I didn't want anyone to take the Mick, sir. I ain't proud to be half Hun, sir."

"Ask this 'ere prisoner if he knows what's going on. Why are they doing that to the Captain?" said the Warrant Officer.

Young Finch spoke to Albert. He told him not to worry; there was a flap on because someone was being bloody evil on the other side. Albert said he didn't think it was the Bavarians then. He was confused; it just wasn't the Bavarian way. It was not a gentleman's way and the Bavarians were, in general, better than the others.

"Could he look through Jack's eyeglass?" They thought maybe he would be able to help identify who was opposite.

He looked and his blood boiled. There, past the poor man hanging on the wire, there was a machine gun. He knew it was there; it's where he would have put it if he were going to gun down any rescue attempt. He was also able to see a gunner and on his helmet was a number. It was the number 7 and he knew instantly it was his old regiment, the Prussians.

# CHAPTER 31

# The Rescue

At first everyone just stood and looked at Finch and Albert; they were jabbering away like two old washerwomen.

The Warrant officer coughed, then said, "Finch, wait a minute. Stop talking in that nonsense, what's he saying?"

"Sir, he is telling me that the Germans over there are Prussians, that he knows who they are, and that they had been withdrawn from the line. He thinks they have replaced the Bavarians that we kicked out of the trench yesterday. He's telling me they are nasty bastards, er, sorry, sir. It's a bit difficult to understand him, sir. It's a strong dialect, a bit like one of us talking to a cockney, and I'm not used to talking in German anymore. He seems like a right nice fella though, sir."

"Never mind him being a nice fella, Finch, it's his lot that are shooting our Captain and for me I'd shoot the bastard here and now, tell him that."

Finch relayed the message and Albert nodded his understanding. He said he would feel the same but perhaps he could help. Finch told the gathering audience what was being said.

Jack picked up on something. Maybe he wanted to like this German, but whether he wanted to or not he found that he did. Jack spoke quietly, and it was more just speaking out loud rather than the formation of a plan, but when the WO heard him, he told him to speak up. There was no doubt that Jack had a lot of respect from these lads; all of them, including the Warrant, had seen and heard of what Jack had achieved and what he had been through.

"Sir, I will take him with me, he knows those buggers over there and he might prove useful. I know it seems unlikely but Finch here has done a great job by talking to him. Let me take him and see if we can't get Captain Alcot back. I will need some stretcher-bearers to be ready, I can't carry the Captain and shoot, sir, but I know this German can shoot, and I also know he isn't a lover of that lot. Finchy, ask him if he will help me rescue the Captain?"

It took a couple of minutes to get the message through. Albert looked very confused and then quite happy. He said he would be very pleased to help; this wasn't how honourable men fought and the actions of his supposed countrymen left him feeling sick. He quickly explained to Finch what had happened to him and how, as far as the Prussians opposite were concerned, he was dead, killed by one of his countrymen under orders from Hauptman Berger.

Albert understood the war was over for him and he had no desire to die for any so-called Fatherland and certainly not Germany. He was a proud and indeed honourable Swabian and he wouldn't be able to explain everything, but he was more than happy to help save that brave man out there on the wire.

Finch explained as best he could, and Jack was pleased. He had a familiar feeling with Albert, and it reminded him of how he felt when Jim used to be with him.

It was agreed, but the proviso was that if the German tried any funny business, Jack would shoot him and leave him to rot.

Finch didn't explain it, not quite like that.

# CHAPTER 32

# No Man's land

There was no plan for this rescue to take a long time, no supplies other than a flask of water and a morphine syrette, some wire cutters, rifles and ammo. There was little need to wear camouflage.

It felt a little odd to Albert, feeling his rifle back in his own hands. He didn't have much ammunition but Jack had some left from the magazine of the rifle he had lifted from Karl Mattes. All in all, Albert had about 50 rounds and that was more than enough to do what he had planned.

Jack asked Finch if he fancied the trip, and he was more than ready to help. Three men would make this work: one to hold the Captain still, one to cut the wire and one to shoot any bastard that got in the way or tried to stop them. Everyone agreed on the plan. It wasn't much of a plan, really, but no one else had any ideas, so Jack's plan it was.

The three men crawled out. Jack in front, then Albert, followed by Private Finch. Jack had asked if there was any chance of some covering fire from the machine guns back behind the British front line. It had worked a treat yesterday and no one could see any reason why it wouldn't work again today, but the timing had to be right. Too soon and the enemy would think it was another attack, too late and they would be in the open, standing up and exposed, cutting wire and trying to get the Captain back.

So now it was against the clock: the three men only had two hundred yards to cover but already the Germans had seen them and were taking pot shots at them. Fortunately, there were deep shell holes right across no man's land, but no one wanted to go into them; they held all sorts of gruesome reminders of the war passing this way and then back again.

The dead were in these shell holes, and despite the weather being fairly dry for the past few weeks, there was a clawing, stinking, foul mud in the bottom, hanging onto its lifeless occupants. The shell holes held no side as special, they had a life of their own, and within them, both British and German fallen were comfortable bedfellows. All were welcome. Being in the bottom of a shell hole was no place for the living.

The three men skirted along the sides of the various holes. Just below the rim, there lay relative safety, but even there lay discarded wire, cast aside by high explosive shells in various bombardments, waiting, always there to catch the unwary.

Progress was slow and Jack checked his watch to make sure they weren't behind schedule; rather to be in the right spot early than late. When the machine guns opened up they would only have at best five minutes to cut their comrade out of the wire and get him into some cover. Ideally, they would get him far enough back for the stretcher-bearers to collect him. Then they could give covering fire to keep the Hun heads down. It was about timing.

Jack stopped on the upslope of a shell hole. Albert joined him and Finch, like the good soldier he was, squeezed between them so he could translate. They were in position, just thirty feet away from the start of the wire corridor. There on the left, tangled and limp, was Captain Alcot. Jack checked his watch: they had five minutes before the machine guns opened up.

He passed on his orders to Finch who in turn told Albert. Albert was scanning the horizon for movement, of which there was plenty. He slid his rifle into his shoulder so he could look through the sights, and it didn't take him long to find what he was looking for. Berger.

He could have just shot him like an animal but that was a suicidal thing to do. It would start a barrage of fire and the poor chap left hanging on the wire would surely be caught in the hail of bullets that would come their way.

Albert told Finch who he was looking at, and what he had done to the British prisoners. When Jack heard, he slid his rifle out along a line of fire. He didn't need optical sights, not from a hundred yards. He had used open sights before at a lot further than this, but the problem was seeing the targets. He didn't have his spyglass, either, so he asked to look down Albert's scope.

It made him look up; Jack couldn't believe how clear these Zeiss sights were. He was able to see so much more than with his own optic sights. When this was over, he had to get some of the German sights for himself; he hadn't any idea they were so good. He also knew that in his hands Albert's rifle would be useless, and for once he thought he had made a serious mistake. He was just providing covering fire now, he was the bludgeon and Albert was the rapier. He hoped he wouldn't regret his decision to bring Wolfgang out to play.

Hauptman Berger was in playful mood. However, his sadistic games were an acquired taste, and none of the men around him had acquired it. No one had much to say about it, though, as they lived in fear. Deep down, each man wanted to believe he would go home one day, but each and every one of them had long ago given up any hope of doing so. No one ever spoke about it, but one thing they all knew for certain was that this man Berger was the devil.

Berger called for his rifle: it was time for some sport, and he was certain that the emotional Tommy's would try a valiant but ultimately pointless attempt to save the officer on the wire. They would fail and be cut down like the vermin they were. When this war was over, he would return a hero; his name would be known by all as the victorious Hauptman, or better yet, if he was exceptional – and how could anyone doubt he was? – Oberstleutnant. The name had a ring to it, he thought: Oberstleutnant Berger.

He had his rifle ready, cocked and aimed, and this time he thought he would shoot the officer in the right shoulder. If no one came to help him, he would shoot him in the head tonight but there was no point in fishing without bait, and as every good fisherman knew, if you want to catch big fish you needed live bait.

The first thing anyone was aware of was the chatter of machine guns away in the distance. No one thought anything of it, then out on the flank about thirty yards away there was a cry and a soldier fell, then another, and then it was raining but it wasn't water, it was lead. Little puffs of dust and dirt erupted like tiny volcanoes, men were falling and running for the safety of the dugouts and as Berger looked on, he had no idea what was happening.

The man next to him fell dead. A bullet had hit him just above the rim of his steel helmet, and it had hardly slowed the descent of the deadly projectile. As the British had done in Agincourt some five hundred years before, so they were doing again, and death rained from the French sky.

# CHAPTER 33

# Lift Him Gently

Jack and Finch sprinted over to where Captain Alcot was trapped. There was a low groan from his parched lips and Jack felt a huge lump rise in his throat. It was held in place by the sheer rage and disgust that a fellow man could do this. He started to cut the wire that had entombed his friend.

Alcot was barely conscious, more dead than alive, his left leg shattered. Even without any medical training, Jack knew that was coming off. The right leg looked better but there was a clean hole in the boot, both at the back and side, and Alcot's foot was at an alarming angle. Jack could tell this leg was also broken but the officer's boots were holding the leg in somewhere near the right position.

The wire was thick and tough, and it needed all of Finch's strength to cut it. In the process he cut his hands badly, but nothing would stop him. There were tears running down Finch's face, both in rage and effort.

His love of this man was both shocking and prohibited. His love was only ever expressed in German when the two men were alone. It had been that way for nearly a year now and he had nearly lost his lover once already, back in July. To lose him now would be too much for his already fragile heart. He hacked away, cutting wire after wire. Jack had to stop him; they needed to make rational cuts to release him, not remove all the wire here and now, there was no time.

Jack took the weight of his friend over his shoulder, as would a coalman with a bag of nutty slack. He had considered carrying him over his shoulder in a fireman's rescue lift but he was worried that the wounds to his left leg would bleed further and that it might prove fatal. It meant that the Captain's head was by Jack's ear, and he could hear the laboured breathing of the wounded man.

Jack set off to the nearest safe hole; the machine gun barrage had nearly finished and he knew they had to be in cover before that happened, otherwise they would be sitting ducks. The Germans on the left and right of the Prussians could see what was happening and not one shot was fired. They applauded the bravery of the British soldiers. Hanging men on the wire was barbaric, and no one would condone such a thing.

Berger was back out from under his cover as the last few bullets fell to earth. He was furious that his sport had been spoiled and was determined now to make sure that his next shots caused exquisite agony to the beleaguered man. As the last few bullets landed, he took up his rifle and looked for his target, screaming in anger when he realised his target had gone.

In the shell hole Jack, Finch and Albert started to put a splint on the Captain's legs. He had been offered a sip of water and as the sweet nectar of life had touched his lips, he had opened his eyes. His lips were cracked, his eyes were swollen, and tears had left a track of clean skin on his unshaven face.

At first, he sipped, then he tried to drink and coughed. This caused him to scream in agony; the shattered bone grated and he convulsed with such force at the intense pain that he instantly passed out. It was a blessing all four men could have only prayed for. Jack injected the morphine syrette into the Captain's arm, hopeful that it might help him with the painful journey back to the British line. Piece by piece, they removed the vicious barbs of the wire until he was clean and it had all been removed.

Jack wet his handkerchief and wiped the Captain's face clean, and there, whilst unconscious, he could see the young man he had known for so many years.

He held him close as would a father to a son and whispered in his ear, "Nearly there, Tim. Hang on, old love."

He handed the Captain to Private Finch; Jack was surprised how affected Finch had been by the Captain's plight. "Hold him upright, Finchy, it'll help his breathing."

Finch held the Captain close, but not as would a father but as would a wife to her wounded husband. There was a hidden tenderness in his grasp.

Jack joined Albert at the lip of the shell hole. The Machine gun barrage had finished and it had been replaced by returned fire from the Prussian's side, sweeping along the area. They were safe but exposed to any artillery that might be brought down on them. A knowing nod was all the communication they needed, and both men looked back at the German lines in expectation of the incoming shells, but they never came.

Albert looked along his scope and froze. There, right in the middle of the sight, was Berger. If Albert had been looking for him for a week he wouldn't have got a better view than the one he had right now.

He only said one word, "Berger".

Jack looked but could only see a man; he was standing on top of the parapet, shouting like a lunatic towards them.

Albert breathed out, aimed, and squeezed the trigger at the same time as Jack, and in a heartbeat two bullets had smashed into Hauptman Berger.

One bullet had taken him squarely between the eyes, as if placed there. Exactly equidistant between his eyebrows and one inch above his nose, a tiny rose of red blossomed bright, its puckered petals white and blanched. This was Albert's shot, the other shot – Jack's – hit Berger in the throat. Right in the middle and just above the Adam's apple, it stopped him from making any sound, and like a tumbler in a circus, he performed a perfect reverse somersault back into the trench he had so precariously climbed out of.

As if delivered by the hand of the devil, he lay on the floor of the trench in a perfect cruciform. The man next to him looked on in amazement, and then he gathered all the phlegm, bile and hatred he could muster and spat on the dead man in utter and complete disgust.

There would be no mourning for this dead man. He could barely bring himself to say soldier. There was a collective cheer and all along the line the news of Hauptman Berger's demise had spread faster than any telegram could hope to go.

Jack and Albert ducked back down, hidden, nowhere to be seen. Finch asked who they had shot and Jack said in all honestly, "Nobody."

Albert looked on and said to Finch, "He was the devil, and now he has been sent to hell."

The three men had to plan what was next. It was going to be tough to get the Captain away from here now, but as if in understanding, there was a call from the German lines.

Albert smiled and Finch laughed. Jack was now confused.

Finch said, in between laughs, "They are shouting at you, Corporal. They want you to know you have killed the devil and you can take a free and safe walk back to our own lines. They give their word they won't shoot."

Albert assured them it was true. Jack looked directly into Albert's eyes. Albert had a choice and a huge decision to make. He could go back with Jack or he could go back to his own side.

The three men lifted the wounded and semiconscious Captain. It was only maybe a hundred yards to the waiting stretcher-bearers but each of the rescue party knew that each step was an excruciating experience for their saved leader. His pitiful groans were a constant reminder to the horrors they had thought behind them. This war would perhaps see all of them in the ground, but today they had done something that both sides had approved of. They had shown compassion.

# CHAPTER 34

# The Aftermath

In the following days since their return to the British lines, Albert and Jack had spent quite a bit of time in the rear headquarters. Finch had been allowed to 'guard' the prisoner but in truth, although Albert was held as a prisoner, he wasn't treated as a prisoner in any way. He had made it perfectly clear that he had no desire to fight in the war. He knew he couldn't go home, back to Tuttlingen, at least not until the war was over.

The powers that be in the British high command had sent the appropriate letter to the German Red Cross to inform Ehefrau Hagerman that Albert was alive and well and a prisoner of war. As a special favour they had allowed Albert to write a short note to be attached, under the belief that it would ease any worry she had. Albert was a bit of a celebrity within the German Army as a well-recognised name and indeed a world famous shot from before the war. It was arranged that Albert would be transported back to England to a prisoner of war camp that allowed certain privileges for prisoners in the good faith that they would behave and not encumber the authorities. Young Finch explained all this to Albert. Everybody had mixed emotions about the events planned.

Captain Alcot had been evacuated back to the main hospital and had undergone lifesaving surgery, but unfortunately he had indeed lost his left leg. It had been amputated above the shattered bone and he was now back in Blighty.

In time, he would be invalided out of the army and return home. He had been treated as a hero and the Commanding officer had been to thank Jack personally for his rescue efforts. Jack hadn't seen the Captain since handing him over to the first aiders of the Medical Corps, but news had filtered down and reports that he was alive and well had been a great boost for the morale of all the men, Albert included.

Finch had been promoted to Lance Corporal and Jack was told that he was to be promoted to Sergeant. However, he thought it a bitter pill because the previous incumbent had been Sergeant Savage. They had recovered the top half of him from his muddy grave and he had been buried in an area marked out for just such sad events.

The plans for Albert had been finalised and Finch had translated for the two men. Albert was sad to be leaving his newfound friend and old foe. There was a real respect between them. It seemed at odds that these two men could forgive the things each had done. It provided hope that, in time, when this war was over, the two countries would recover and perhaps old friendships renewed. If Jack and Albert could get on, there was hope for everyone, after all their war was a personal war and very discriminating unlike the machine guns and artillery who didn't seek a target but just found them.

The two men shook hands; it was time for them to say goodbye. Wolfgang was dead to everyone and, in his place, Albert Hagerman had been born again. There was of course a bounty on Wolfgang's head and leave was the reward. Jack ensured that Finch took the credit for handing over Karl Mattes' identification tags and Jack was very convincing that it was indeed Lance Corporal Finch who had dispatched Mattes.

Albert also chipped in and Finch was awarded a break from Hell and allowed a 10-day leave pass. Jack thought he might be able to get a message of goodwill to Captain Alcot back in Blighty. Finch knew what was going on and thanked Jack. It was a touching moment of humanity, again in a world of hurt and pain, and Jack knew there was more of the latter to come in the future.

With a firm handshake and a smile from both men, Albert was led away. He would leave today but if it were at all possible, he would try to keep in touch with his new mate Jack. With no more than a nod, he was gone. Jack felt quite alone.

# CHAPTER 35

# *Sniper School Instructor*

In the following weeks, the front line was quieter than it had been for some time. Jack had been asked if he would return to the sniper school and take up a place as the chief sniping instructor. It seemed like a great opportunity to sleep in a bed and stay out of harm's way. No one could have accused Jack of avoiding a scrap, but he was tired and the fact that he had been found not by one but by two German snipers had shaken his self-belief.

Without Jim to keep an eye on him, there was little doubt he wasn't as good as he had been with the help and support of his old friend. It was a well-kept secret which he hadn't shared with anyone, but he needed the rest.

On his arrival back at the school, Hesketh-Prichard looked at the man he had recruited those long years ago and saw a huge change in the demeanour of his protégé. With a knowing eye, Hex could see a man who was as near broken as was possible. The shelling and constant shock and awe of this man's daily life had literally sucked the lifeblood out of him. Both men knew that if there hadn't been a change in Jack's life, he would have died. As sure as the men he aimed his own rifle at.

Jack was now in the Sergeant's mess with a comfy cot bed and warm blankets, but he found it difficult to adjust to both and often found himself sleeping on the floor with just a pillow and blanket to keep the cold away. The medical officer had been informed about Jack's health, but it was all 'unofficial' of course. It wouldn't do for the new hero to be ill, but he was, and very soon it would prove to be more dangerous than any sniper he had ever encountered.

Jack had flu, and the virus was attacking a very unprotected side of Jack: the inside.

It was whilst in the classroom, giving a lecture, that the first signs of Jack's illness presented themselves. He had felt unwell, and had been suffering shivers for a couple of days, but had carried on. In his words, "There were men who were feeling the effects of this war far more than I am." What he needed was some fresh air, but no matter how much he thought he was winning, this battle was already won and he had lost.

It was in the classroom that he collapsed. The medics took him straight to the medical centre and by the time Jack awakened, he was in the ward for communicable diseases. Burning up with a fever and barely lucid, he drifted in and out of a fitful sleep. The faces of men long since dead came back to haunt him, each with a single wound surgically inflicted with the skill of a surgeon but with the results of an assassin. For Jack, over the next few days the dead wouldn't stay dead; the Pandora's Box of his mind had been opened, and it would be a battle like he had never faced before to close it.

Hesketh-Prichard had seen men like Jack before. None of them had been left without mental scars. Jack was exceptional in everything he had done, and Hex felt there was a debt to pay to this extraordinary man. Jack needed rest, and aside from the seriousness of the illness he had been laid low with. Hospital, with its clean sheets, feminine touches and lack of shellfire and gunshots were quite literally what the doctor had ordered.

It wasn't a question of if Jack would recover. It wasn't even a question of when. It was more a question of what. This war wasn't nearly finished and men like Sergeant Jack Adams would still be needed.

Winter was just around the corner, and the fighting would ease for another season. It would give everyone time to recover. 1917 held no promise of anything better than the previous dreadful and costly year. Within a month the snow would be falling, the hard frost would firm the ground and transportation would be easier.

Hesketh-Prichard was about to return to England for a short spell of leave, God know he was due it. He would go back and see Colonel Alcot and his old observer Jim Cunningham. There was no one else really for him to see. He would be based at Piccadilly in the officer's club. He would call into his old office at the ministry, and then maybe do a spot of travelling. He wanted to go to Birmingham, to the gun manufacturers of the area; there were some new things he had discovered and he needed the advice of gun makers to see if they would work.

From there it was a fairly simple trip to the Alcot house, but before he went he must ask Jack if there was anything he wanted taking home, or perhaps a letter to deliver to his beloved Alice. Hex would call into the hospital himself to see Jack. He would go and see him the following day. The sniping school was closed for the next three weeks. It was as if the war was somehow on hold, it was all so very peculiar.

Flu was a killer and the weather was getting the better of a lot of men. The ones he could, he would send on leave because when they got back there were plans to move north, to Belgium and the Ypres Salient. Things would be different there. The fighting was more suited to snipers and a lot of men would need to be trained. The new school would be a sister of this one, and Hex had planned for Jack to move north to look after it once he had recovered.

There was no doubt it had been an odd month. Things within the trenches had become more balanced. The number of men lost to the German snipers had dropped by a huge amount, and the damage inflicted on the Germans had undoubtedly been significant. The Lovat scouts were bringing reports back on a daily basis about the German formations and movements. There was a definite improvement in the morale of the men.

Maybe this awful war would end soon. It was every right-minded man's greatest desire. Many had been here since the start. Three years is a long time to be away from home and it hadn't gone unnoticed that for thousands, there was no return. It was of no consequence that the Germans and French had suffered grievously, and the long lines of crosses left after a battle really didn't reflect the misery that each cross signified.

# CHAPTER 36

# Time For Change

Christmas 1916 was very cold all along the front. It was quiet everywhere and there was no killing save whatever meats were to be eaten on Christmas day.

There was a significant amount of artillery going off all along the front, but none of it was going to land anywhere that might cause injury; it was all for show. The Generals, sitting safe in their chateau, demanded the war carry on, but the officers and men out at the sharp end, on both sides, saw the season differently. So they deliberately fired the shells into a safe, unmanned area.

All along the front, British and Germans alike sang hearty hymns, each group trying to out-sing the other. The nearer the trenches were to each other, the better they seemed to get on. Even presents were thrown to opponents on each side, carvings and models, tins of bully beef and cigars all found their way into the opposite trench. Reports of men walking out into no man's land to meet their counterparts on the other side were common. It made a mockery of the war.

Jack was feeling better but he was still weak. The time he had spent in the hospital had done him a power of good and the food had been so much better than he was used to back at camp. In fairness, since he had been in the Mess, the food was better, but anything was better than 'Maconochies' and bully beef or biscuits. He had gained some of the weight he had sweated off. His uniform was still loose, but he was better.

He had no desire to go back out to the front; there was an ugly mood amongst the men this winter. The trenches were full of unease, and revolution was in the air. The French had mutinied already and all along the French line soldiers had thrown down their weapons. If news of this had got out to the Germans, it would prove catastrophic. There would be an onslaught of attacks on the trenches held by the depleted French, but they would easily be overrun.

The flu that had laid Jack out had taken its toll. Along the whole front, men had been taken ill and worse, died of influenza. The hospitals were relieved that there seemed to be little in the way of trench warfare but the beds that had been set aside for the casualties of the battlefield were now full of the casualties of nature. Jack didn't doubt the Germans were in the same situation, but it highlighted the desire for everyone to just go home.

Home. Jack thought of Alice, as he did most days, but it had been worse since the Major had brought back letters from all in Langwith. His mother had written, as indeed she often did, and so had Jim. He felt the familiar pang of loneliness that he always felt when his old friend's name was brought up. He did find a lot of comfort, however, in the fact that Jim was doing well at home.

The news about his old Captain and friend Tim was also welcome. He was home with his father, the Colonel, and doing well despite the loss of his leg. There was a letter from him as well; it thanked him for saving his life. The truth was anyone in the regiment would have done the same. He had been fitted with a false leg and was doing rather well with it, still on crutches but optimistic that within time he would be able to manage with a stick. His broken right leg had healed well and as long as he had good knee-length boots on, he had no issues with the leg whatsoever.

He also thanked him for allowing Finch to visit him and told Jack he knew that he had given up the right to the leave in favour of Finch, a favour he owed to Jack and a kindness he said he wouldn't forget. In the letter he also said that he was doing all in his power to have Albert shipped back to his homeland, but there were some issues that had to be overcome before he could ensure that would happen.

Jack was chuffed that Albert might get an early release. It would come with some promises of not returning to the war, and it turned out that Albert didn't trust the German Army not to force him back to the front line, so he was reluctant to go home until the war was over. The Colonel, in gratitude for Albert's role in saving his son, had arranged for Albert to be moved to Langwith to work on the land. It wasn't a coincidence that the land he would be working on would be Colonel Alcot's. By all accounts, Albert was doing well with his English.

There was another gratitude and gift from the Colonel as well, one that made Jack's heart swell. It was the promise of a house on the estate as a gift, without any payment for Jack if he married Alice on his return. The house would be theirs forever, signed over to them as a wedding present. Jack wanted to go home so badly but there was still no end in sight to this stupid and pointless war.

Jack thought he had seen all the best letters he could receive, but he had deliberately saved the one he wanted to read till last, the one from Alice.

Alice loved him, as indeed he loved her. It was a feeling he never thought he would be gifted with. Yes, there had been girls who he looked at when he was a lad, but never in a way that hinted at a romance. Alice had been the first girl he had kissed, truth be known the first girl who had kissed him, really. It was a sealed deal. If ever two people should be together it was he and Alice, and once this war was over, he would ask her father if they could be wed.

He would have a job, and an income and now a house. He was joyous when he thought about the future but there was this lingering doubt in the back of his mind. Death was random here, a million ways to die. One thing he did have was the job in the sniping school. It was safe, far away from the enemy artillery and even further away from the trenches.

He would be moving away to the new school within the week and had spent the past few days collecting equipment. It had all been loaded onto trucks and had gone ahead. He hadn't seen much of Flanders but had heard a lot. It was flat and wet, mud and trenches. He didn't think it would be much different than here then, either way he would find out in the next few days because his transport was due to leave tomorrow morning.

The Major would travel with him and stay with him for the first couple of days. There was talk about a promotion for Jack. The Major was trying to get him a warrant officers rank but it was difficult because he didn't belong to a unit as such so there was no establishment. The Major, however, was going to get it sorted.

It wasn't the rank Jack wanted but he did want the authority to help change things in the trenches, and being a warrant officer would definitely help with that. Still, that wasn't for Jack to worry about, not yet anyway.

He looked back and read his letter from Alice. He needed to write back to them all but for now he felt quite tired and a sleep was in order, just a nap, then he had work to do. In the distance he could hear the sound of the big guns booming, not sure which side was giving vent, but sure that a response would be forthcoming either way. It was a reminder that the war was still very much afoot.

He looked outside. It was raining again, constant and heavy, and it was sure to turn the trenches and roads into a quagmire. The journey to Flanders was going to be cold and wet, and he still had to finish his packing and write replies to the letters. It was going to be a long evening. Spring was in the air, it was April tomorrow and Jack thought briefly that maybe he was the April fool for thinking that it would ever end.

He lay back onto his bed cot, and within seconds, he was asleep. When he woke and looked at his wristwatch, the candle had burned right down, and when Jack managed to see the time he was alarmed to realise that it was three thirty in the morning. He had slept for twelve hours. He hadn't even heard the other two men who shared his room enter or put coal on the small belly fire, but it was warm in the room with a gentle cooling breeze swirling round. The rain had stopped.

He hadn't even packed his kit yet and the wagon was due to leave at eight in the morning. He didn't want to start now, as it would surely disturb the other men. He rubbed his face; he needed a shave but again that would have to wait until morning. The snoring men were strangely soporific and he settled back for another couple of hours.

The morning came and the men were roused by the call of reveille. It was six o'clock and he had two hours to wash, shave, pack and say farewell to his roommates. He did it all in an hour, and then went for a breakfast of bread and jam with a huge mug of fresh tea. The tea was odd here; it didn't have the same tang as the tea at the front, and the cook said it was the petrol that was missing. It always made Jack laugh. He never thought he would miss that taste, but maybe he did, after all.

This morning Jack felt back to his old self, and he was excited to be moving north. The weather had cleared and it was fresh but warming, the clouds were high, and in the distance he could see some aircraft. They were very high and coming from his own side so they must be ours, he thought. He would keep an eye out for them, though.

He greeted the Major and they shared a cigarette and a mug of steaming tea. Talk was easy between the two men; despite their difference in age and breeding, they liked each other and both had a huge respect for their individual skills, both unique and yet so alike.

Major Hesketh-Prichard was almost universally liked, but still some of the red tabs in headquarters either didn't agree with his methods or disliked the fact that he was able to implement them. They made it difficult for his small but crucial organisation to function, but were delighted with the results. If only the red tabs had been bright enough to realise it was a dilemma they had caused themselves.

Fortunately, some of the highest commanders thought he was doing a sterling job and supported him to the hilt. And so today saw the start of number two sniping school, and Jack was its new sniping instructor. Captain Leek would be the CO. He was one of the Lovat scouts instructors and had done fantastic work in Gallipoli. This new post was in recognition of the good work he had done at the first school in France.

It was felt that with these two men, Leek and Adams, the new school was starting from a very strong foundation. They were the best at what they did and under Hesketh-Prichard's directorship, everyone knew it would be a great success. The German snipers had been troublesome in Flanders and the British had lost a lot of the trained sharpshooters in the summer of 1916. It was a constant training programme but they had caught up in France and now it was time to take the fight back to the Germans, and Flanders was going to be the theatre for fighting.

# CHAPTER 37

# *Flanders Fields*

Ypres had been a wonderful town with an imposing town hall: the 'Cloth Hall', it had been named. It was a million tons of rubble now, as indeed was most of Ypres. Jack was amazed at the destruction. There was a market square scraped out of the detritus of the old town and a road that ran right through the middle of the town.

Looking at the cloth hall, he turned his head to the right towards the old moat that ran along the path of the old medieval town. Beyond that was Potje, and further along still, Poelcapelle. No one was lying when they said it was flat. Flattened would be more accurate. There were no buildings that were upright and not a wall had survived the onslaught of the German shelling, but this wasn't the battlefield, this was a victim. The shelling had nearly stopped now, save for the occasional shell that landed in or around the area.

Although it wasn't far in real terms to the area called the Somme, Flanders was a million miles away in attitude and intent. Of course, there had been large battles hereabouts but this part of the war was far more static than in France.

No real gains had been seen here in the past three years. Once the fighting had become static, there wasn't much change. One thing that the British were now winning was the sniper war. The Germans still had exceptional shots but things were getting more difficult for them and Jack was here to look around the trenches to see just what the situation really was.

One thing the Germans had here in abundance was the high ground, if you can call the slightest incline high. It made the trenches and ground held by the British very wet and incredibly muddy. The rain ran down the fields and settled into the British trenches making them a living quagmire. Every man and animal hated it, the thick clawing mud that made movement so very slow and laborious. Cold and exhausted, both men and mounts often died where they fell, unable to carry on.

Jack's new unit was based at Poperinge, about 8 miles to the west of Ypres. Famous for its large variety of beers, 'Pops' was relatively quiet from enemy activity but it did get its share of long-range artillery. This, in the main, was because of its strategic importance to the allies. It was like a main artery in the supply route for equipment and men bound for the salient that had been formed in previous battles.

This bulge in the enemy lines was a constant pain in the side of the dug-in Germans, causing them to keep it well manned to prevent the British from breaking out from the stalemate that was being tolerated by both sides. Each side had ambitions to ensure this situation worked to their advantage, and so a constant influx of new men was needed. 'Pops' served as a perfect staging post for the British.

Jack was working in his office when Captain Leek came in, waving his arms and shouting that the "Yanks were in". It took Jack a cup of tea and a seat for the Captain to understand what it was he was saying, but the news when it came was music to everyone's ears. The Americans had declared war on Germany. The lift that all the British soldiers had been waiting for had arrived. The anticipated resupply of men was going to be massive and with the sheer weight of numbers, surely this must be the beginning of the end for the beleaguered Germans. There was extra rum issued in celebration. The feeling in the office was one of optimism and excitement.

No one noticed the mail delivery. The 'postie' left the letters on the Captain's desk, there were none to be signed for or orders to be returned, so he left unseen. If he had known what was contained within the letters he had delivered, he might have done it differently.

Captain Leek had called for Jack to come to his office. In itself, this was not an unusual occurrence, but the sign for no one else to enter warned Jack that it wasn't a usual meeting.

The letter the Captain held in his trembling hands foretold Jack it was bad, but nothing could have prepared him for the dreadful news he was about to hear. "I'm sorry, Jack; it's about your parents. There has been a fire, and I'm afraid they have both been killed. No one could help them, it was a candle apparently, the fire. By the time people were able to get them out it was too late. I'm sorry, Jack."

Jack was numb. He felt the cruel sting of grieving tears burn his eyes. He had seen and delivered so much death in this war and he never thought it would affect him, but now there was a thumping in his chest. As he locked his fingers together around the back of his neck, he looked to the ceiling, not sure what to do or say.

The Captain poured a glass of whiskey, a large glass for each of them, and pushed one over the desk towards Jack. As he picked up the glass, tears rolled down his nose. He wasn't a fan of strong liquor like whiskey – he wasn't used to it – but he downed the amber fluid in one. He felt the burning fire of a malt whiskey on its journey south to his churning stomach.

Plans were made for Jack to get back home for the funerals.

From Poperinghe to Calais, then over the channel and a rail ticket north from London, changing at Birmingham and Derby. At the Langwith station Colonel Alcot had his car waiting to meet him with his closest friend, Jim, sitting in the passenger seat.

# CHAPTER 38

# Dark Days In Good Company

The two men hugged. Jack hadn't seen his old friend and mentor for months, since he was away himself on leave and Jim had stayed behind to help eliminate 'Wolfgang'.

Jim looked well, really well; the fresh air of the home countryside had been a blessing for his gassed and damaged lungs. He had a healthy cough but it was a small price for him to pay to live.

Jack had thought about his departed parents for the last two days, sleeping fitfully on the various modes of transport he had travelled on, and although he was tired, he was pleased Jim had met him at the station.

"Have you eaten, Jack? Alice has made you some 'snap'."

Jack smiled for the first time that week. He hadn't heard the colloquial word 'snap' – meaning food – for ages; it wasn't common in the Army, and it made him feel at home.

"No Jim, I haven't felt much like food, but I'm famished, now that I'm home."

The two men ate a thick ham and onion sandwich together, food shared between men that had shared so much more than that in the past. It was the catalyst to bind them back together as friends. It was painful for Jack, who felt guilty for not missing his friend as much as he thought he might. The truth was, he never allowed himself the pleasures or comforts of home into his wartime thoughts; it might distract him and that would be fatal.

"I miss you out there, Jim. It's not the same without you. It was tolerable when you were there old friend. Now my battle is to survive. Do we know what happened to mum and dad yet?"

Jim said the fire had started downstairs. "Set the curtains alight by the look of things. It was the smoke that killed them, Jack. They were asleep upstairs, and they never suffered. They have been moved to the chapel, the funerals are tomorrow. I hope you don't mind but Edith, Alice and the Colonel have taken care of all the details."

Jack felt a sense of belonging. It was a double-edged sword. On one side he was desperately sad that he would never be able to hold his mother or father, and yet he felt excited that he would see Alice, her family, and his friend, Jim.

He looked out of the car window. The rolling hills were showing the first signs of spring with snowdrops in the gardens. He caught the first glimpses of the big house in the distance. He knew the road so well, and round the next bend in the road he would be able to see the village.

"Can I see them, Jim? Before, well you know, tomorrow."

Jim had anticipated the request and the chapel was to be opened for him, with the vicar on call. "Aye Jack, I've asked if they will open the Chapel of Rest for you, when do you want to go?"

"This evening will do. Where are we going? Is the house gone?"

"Yes Jack, it's all gone. I have most of your stuff packed away, but it stinks of smoke. The girls have washed what they can, but it'll need plenty of fresh air to clear it. I thought we might go to my house, the spare room is made up and Alice is there, waiting for you to come home."

The house had indeed been burned to the ground. All the remaining undamaged furniture and remains of a lifetime collecting were stored in the shed under a tarpaulin, safe from the elements. Jack's whole life prior to his army career was now wrapped in a small pile of detritus. There would be time tomorrow, after the funeral, for him to sort it out. There were plenty of things to sort. He was only here for a week and he had already been gone for two days. The war would wait.

For Jack, the rest of the journey was a trip down memory lane, all happy memories, and Jack hoped that the next couple of days wouldn't change his history with this happy village. The villagers stopped what they were doing when they saw who was in the car. They stood and bowed their heads and the men removed their hats. These people, who had suffered so much loss, were his understanding family and friends. This was where his heart beat and would always stay.

They carried on past the butchers and the shops, up the street and round the bend to set up the scenic view of the row of houses that were home to the workers on the estate. Next, they went through the gated lodge house and onto the gamekeeper's cottages. There, standing at the front door, Alice waited. The weather was still cool and she had goose bumps on her arms. Her heart beat just a little faster when she saw the car round the corner. When the car stopped, Jim, the driver and Jack got out.

Alice ran toward her man with open arms, her cheeks damp with new tears. Jack looked round and was surprised that the two of them were alone. He collected her into his arms and hugged her, and as she melted into his arms, he cried. Like a child who had lost the family pet, he cried. The frustrations and emotion of a pent up war all came to him in a rush. So powerful, he sobbed, his breaths gulped in and sobbed out. He was as a broken man in her arms and they cried together.

In time he collected himself, and wiped the face of Alice. It had been a year since they had seen each other and she thought he was thin and tired and he couldn't deny either. They went inside and Jim offered him his chair. It was a humbling experience for Jack. As he hugged Edith, there was a knowing nod; just a very slight movement but it spoke volumes between the two men.

"Welcome home, love," said Edith. "We are all here for you, and you will do fine. I have water heating out in the back so you can take a bath. Alice and I will sort that, you sit here with Jim and have a catch up."

Jack sat in the chair and Jim went into the kitchen to collect a couple of mugs of hot tea. When he got back, Jack was asleep in the chair.

They left him for an hour before they reluctantly woke him. He had a lot to do tonight, and as ever, time was against them.

He bathed and shaved, his shirt was ironed, and Jim polished Jack's boots. It was nearly time for the group to go to the chapel. The Colonel had left an invitation for them to dine with him tomorrow after the funeral but they had to walk to church in an hour so they had better get a shift on. For the first time in an age, Jack felt human.

Jack's emotions were at odds with each other. The walk to the chapel was tragically sad but tinged with a guilty happiness. On his arm was the woman he loved, but he was painfully aware that she had made this walk once before to say goodbye to the husband she lost, in a service dedicated to his memory.

Now she walked with a new man, one she truly loved, now that she was older and knew what love was all about. Not the childish feelings of excitement she had cherished with Tom, but a deep seated and devoted feeling deep in her heart. There were no words to describe her feelings. Poets and bards had tried for millennia to explain in words what she felt, and she knew they were close, but still it didn't quite reach the spot.

At the door of the chapel, they met Tom Preston, the vicar of this parish. A kindly looking and peaceful man, he had the face of someone who shared in the suffering of this community. His services had been in great demand these past years, as Langwith had suffered grievously from this war. She had given her youth to the war, not knowing that those lads who went would come back different people, stained with the ravages of a barbaric war. She was a true mistress of hatred who left her scars on the very souls of the innocent. Reverend Preston had felt each loss like a strike to his heart. He had baptised nearly every one of the men lost to the war; he had been vicar here for thirty years and knew each and every one of them.

Tonight he was especially saddened. The undertakers had done a sterling job of cleaning the faces of Mister and Mrs Adams, who were regular church goers, as indeed Jack had been before he left. It was like greeting one of his own children when he shook Jack's hand, and he handed him back to Alice with a smile. As well as seeing all the hurt of a manmade disaster, he could also recognise the joy that only God could bless.

"Shall we go inside? It's getting dark out here," said the vicar. "Your mum and dad are at the Altar."

Jack went in, followed by Alice, Jim and Edith. The vicar then followed them in and closed the door. There was celestial music quietly filling the church and Jack felt the warmth of faith return to his sceptical being. Mr Evans, the organist, was hidden behind a screen at the front playing 'There is a green hill far away'. It had been one of his mother's favourite hymns, so it was very fitting.

At the front of the church were two coffins, lying side by side. As Jack walked down the aisle alone, he saw the undertaker sitting in the back, quietly waiting to put the lids on the coffins. He had given his night up to ensure that Jack Adams could say goodbye to his mum and dad, as indeed had all the other people.

Jack got to the foot of the coffins when he realised that Reverend Preston was standing before him. At the head of the two coffins there was a wreath of lilies from the florist next to Harry's butchers. Jack was moved to tears. They looked so peaceful, just as though they were asleep. Jack was no stranger to death; it was a constant companion these past two years.

It struck him that none of the dead he had seen before looked quite at rest, unlike his parents. Jack looked at the vicar as if to ask permission to touch his mother's soft face. It was cold and dry. He bent over and kissed her on the forehead and a tear fell from his eye onto her skin. A gift forever, he left it to roll down her cheek. Next, he kissed his father and said goodbye.

They all said a prayer and Jack went to each person who had stayed to give him this opportunity, and offered his thanks. It was a lovely thing for them all to do and he felt that keenly. He turned away and walked back down the church to his new family.

# CHAPTER 39

# Lay Me Down To Sleep

The morning sun was the first Jack knew of the start of the day. Today was going to be tough. It had taken Jack a couple of minutes to remember where he was, at Jim's house. There was nothing familiar here; the bed had been soft and the sheets stiff with starch. It was quiet; birdsong was about the only sound Jack could hear. After saying goodnight to Alice, he had walked back to Jim's. It wasn't far, but on the way he had passed the burnt-out shell of his home; even now you could still smell the smoke from the burned timbers.

Jack looked at the time on his watch: it was nearly six, and he thought maybe he should wait until he heard someone move in the house. He needn't have worried. There was a gentle tap at the door and Jim brought him a fresh brew of tea, hot and sweet. Jack looked at his old friend and wondered how he managed with his broken lungs. They hadn't really talked much about the war, there hadn't been time yet, but today was going to be a struggle and a long one at that.

The funeral was planned to be at ten thirty. There was to be no procession, as the bodies were in the church already, laid on ice to keep them cool. The first warmth of the spring was starting to encourage life to start all around. The irony wasn't wasted on Jack. After the service, there would be a buffet laid out in the Sunday school. It was yet another gesture that caught Jack off guard. Jack had seen to it that Jim wasn't out of pocket; he had plenty of money with no opportunity to spend it in France and Flanders was bare of shops. Besides, there wasn't anything he needed apart from the occasional writing materials, cigarettes and boot polish.

Then after lunch, Jack was going back to see Alice's parents at the shop before dinner at the big house and he was looking forward to meeting Tim after his return home. Yes, it was going to be a full day, and it all felt so surreal.

Jack sat up in bed and drank his tea, chatting to Jim about how things had changed out on the front, his meeting with Albert, and Tim's rescue, but they were all sketchy, void of detail. Jim told Jack he was doing well. In fact, the Army had said he might be able to return to real line jobs such as stores and supply but the Colonel had quashed it and demanded he stay. He had done his bit, and he was getting too old for this entire war lark, was what the Colonel had said. Jim knew it to be right and Edith was delighted. Anyway, the war would be over soon now that the Americans had joined in. Jack couldn't disagree and hoped it was soon; he had no desire to go back, not to that war, not to any war.

At breakfast Edith was as mischievous as ever, trying to lighten the mood, speaking of the lovely Alice and how she was a 'perfect match for Jack'. Jim scowled at her to leave the lad alone but Jack could see the smile in Jim's eyes. It was all harmless fun and it did lighten the mood, and Jack found himself smiling as well. He ate a fine breakfast, the first time in ages that he had fresh eggs and bacon with thick sausages and real bread and butter with homemade jam. All in all Jack felt, well, at home.

He washed and changed, ready for church. It was only a short walk and now the morning mist was lifting, it was pleasant walking. In the distance he could hear a bell; it was the school hand bell ringing to call the faithful to the church. It was time to say goodbye to two of their own. Jack felt the cold grip of trepidation run along his spine; he had felt this before but never here, this was fear he shouldn't ever have felt at home. Jim in his best Sunday suit and Edith in her black dress, Jack in his best uniform, clean and pressed, boots shiny, they made a handsome sight.

Outside the church stood Reverend Preston. He walked towards Jack and held out his hand, and Jack was surprised how warm and soft the skin was. It was a friend's handshake, not formal or even firm but gentle and kind. Jack stood and talked to the vicar for a second or two whilst Jim and Edith went inside to take their seats.

Jack could hear the soft melody of a hymn playing and it comforted him to think there was someone inside to share this day.

The vicar coughed and said they were ready.

Jack opened the church door, amazed at the sight that met him. The church was packed full, with people standing along the back with no seats left in the pews. It made him feel weak and he put his hand out to grab a handhold. Standing back upright, he looked down the aisle to his mum and dad. The coffins had been sealed and cleaned and each sat on a trolley covered in a white sheet. Flowers adorned the trolley. To the left stood the choir.

Jack couldn't believe how many of the townsfolk were there. As he walked to the front people caught his eye, smiled and nodded. This tragedy had hit everyone hard, and the ladies were tearful, dabbing at their eyes. The men – what men were there – held their loved one's arms to offer support.

At the front in the very first pew were Jim, Edith and Alice. One row back stood the Colonel, along with Tim and Alice's parents. Jack tried to look strong but he knew he was shaking. All the church was full of people who had known Jack's family forever; he looked along the line and saw face after face of people he hadn't seen for years.

He took his place and the vicar started the service with kind words, but the spear to Jack's heart was the first hymn. The organ played those first notes and the choir broke into one voice, singing 'Abide with me'. Alice reached out to take Jack's trembling hand.

After the service and internment, Jack and the vicar stood at the entrance to the churchyard to say thanks to each person who had been to the service. Jack shook every hand; it was a shared moment and all the mourners took the opportunity to tell Jack how proud they were with his war record and medals. His parents were very proud of their son as well. He heard it time and again but they didn't really know what he did in the war and he was happy that they didn't.

At the end of the line, after shaking what seemed like a hundred hands, Jack took one more offered hand, and when he looked up he froze. It was the same blue eyes he had seen before, first time in a shell hole, and the last to say goodbye. Albert stood proud in front of him, nodding in respect. Jack was pleased to see him standing there. Of course, it was a work day here, not a weekend, and the day to day work out in the fields had to carry on. Albert was with an escort but he seemed like a nice bloke and gave Albert some space to offer his condolences.

"I am sorry to learn about your parents," he said in a heavy accent. "I am happy to meet with you again, Jack." He gave Jack a letter which was sealed, and when Jack went to open it, Albert closed his hands over Jack's. "Open it later; it is secret for you."

Jack thought it was peculiar but put the letter in his pocket. He shook Albert's hand again and with that, he was gone, back with the escort.

# CHAPTER 40

## Out Of The Ashes

After the buffet, once the crowds thinned out, Jack stood at the foot of the now 'Adams' family plot. He was alone with Alice. Jim and Edith had gone home and Harry Barber and his wife had gone back to the shop to make some tea and change clothes. Alice and Jack were to follow presently. Before he left his mum and dad to eternal rest, he wanted some peace, some time alone with Alice.

She had been wonderful today; she seemed to sense when he needed some support and when to let him go, it was uncanny. As they walked to the gate one last time, he turned to look at the church, such a sad place today. Over the last four years, it had born more sorrow than it was meant to in a lifetime, becoming the scene of both sorrow and hope. Tears enough to wash the windows, he thought, he had contributed his own today.

He looked at Alice and it dawned on him that he'd never told her how he really felt. He took hold of her hand to say thank you for helping him through the day and said instead, "Alice, I love you". She blushed as did he. "Thank you so very much for being here today and for helping sort all this out."

She took his other hand and clasped them with hers to her bosom. Face to face, looking into those troubled eyes, she kissed him.

"I love you too, Jack Adams, Lord help me for it but there it is. Now, mum and dad will be wondering where we've gone; we should go, and maybe come back tomorrow before you have to go back."

Go back: those very words pulled on his heart. He didn't want to go back, he was no coward but God knows he didn't want to go back to war. He would, of course, as it was his duty, but before he went he had something to do. They walked back to the village and to Harry's. Looking at his watch he had about three hours with them before he had to go and change for dinner with the Colonel tonight. He was looking forward to the next few hours, and once again he felt the cold chill of fear run down his spine.

Back home, Alice ran upstairs to change out of her black dress and shawl. Her mother was already up there, waiting to help and brush out her long hair.

Downstairs, Jack was pacing. Harry noticed he was fractious and said for him to come and sit down and have a smoke; it would help him calm his nerves. Jack asked if he could talk to Harry, man to man.

Harry looked a little surprised, but stood and pulled down his waistcoat over his hips.

"Aye lad, you can always talk to me as an equal."

"Sir, it's not as an equal I want to talk to you, it's as Alice's father. Harry, I want to ask if you would grant me permission to ask Alice to be my wife."

Harry stood as straight as any Sergeant Major, bolt upright. He looked Jack straight in the eyes.

"You want to marry our Alice?" There was a quiver in his voice.

"Yes sir, I know the timing is poor, but I was standing at

the church today and realised that with all my heart, she's the one I love. Above all else, it's Alice that I want, sir."

"Have you spoken to Alice about this, Jack? Have you asked her?"

"No sir, and I won't if you don't give us your blessing. I know she has been hurt before by this war, and I will understand if you say no, but please sir, say yes."

"Jack, lad, she is my only child, she has indeed been badly roughed up by this blood bath of a war. Son, if it's my blessing you seek, you have it. That lass has been better since you took an interest in her; there's some of the old lass back in her. Good God in heaven Jack, yes sir, you have my blessing and I'm as proud as a father could be. I wish yours were here to share a drink with us. But when the hell are you planning on asking her? Her mum will kill me if I don't tell her, and you don't have much time. And I've told you before, it's Harry to you, Jack, not 'sir'."

"I'll ask her tonight if that's acceptable to you, sir, er, Harry?"

Both men laughed out loud. Harry took Jack's offered hand. It was a firm, reliable handshake. Harry put his left hand on Jack's shoulder, and for the second time in a day he had tears in his eyes.

"You two will make a fine pair. A good long life is my wish for you, blessed with children of your own. I'll be proud to call you my son-in-law Jack Adams, proud as punch."

The ladies came down the stairs and found the two men chatting like washer women. There was a sense of happiness in the air and Alice couldn't quite decide if she was imagining it but she thought her dad's eyes were wet again, for the second time in a day.

# CHAPTER 41

# Dinner For Eight

Jack arranged to pick Alice up at seven o'clock; it was a short walk to the big house and dinner was being served at eight.

Back at Jim's house, there were some personal things that Jack wanted to deal with. There were few possessions of Jack's parents left, with most either being destroyed in the fire or, indeed, in the putting out of the fire. There was never much, anyway; his life had always been a simple one with little in the way of material goods.

Jim had a box of small family artefacts he had collected from the burned buildings, including his father's bicycle and his mother's wash tub, both of which had been stored in the shed, but there was a box that held everything personal to Jack and his family. A safe box, it was tough and robust so hadn't been damaged, and within it were all the things his parents held dear.

Jim had placed the box in Jack's room. It wasn't particularly big or heavy and it sat on the table in front of the window. Jack opened it to look at the lifelong collection of precious family keepsakes, possibly worthless to anyone outside of this room.

There was his father's fob watch and chain which had been his father's father's, and it was clearly old and well loved. It was worn on Sundays for church but rarely had Jack seen it worn anywhere else. There was a lock of hair from Jack's head from when he was a baby, neatly sewn together and placed in a locket that his mother had worn around her slender neck. There was Jack's Medal, which looked out of place, all new and shiny. There was some money as well: about thirty pounds, not a fortune but more than enough to pay for everything today.

Then there, in the corner, was the jewel in the crown: his mother's wedding ring. She had to remove it years ago because her fingers swelled so much it didn't fit her. Fearful of losing it, she had placed it here in her treasure trove. She didn't need a ring to show her commitment to her husband, she often said.

Jack sat quietly and thought about the day that had just been. The world had gone mad. There was a war raging over there in France and he was sitting here with a wound no bullet could inflict. His whole world was here in his hands, but so was his future. Just a tiny gold ring, worn thin with age, but with it he hoped that his whole world might change. With this ring, he would become the man his parents wanted him to be, a husband – and if God allowed it – a father. He felt sure he was doing the right thing but wondered if he should talk to Jim before he proposed to Alice.

There was a knock on his room door. It was Edith and Jim, smart in their Sunday best and changed out of their funeral clothes.

"Are you ready, Jack?" asked Jim. "It's time we were going; we don't want to be late."

Jack looked up at them both, such dear friends. For the first time, Jack was glad Jim had been wounded; he shouldn't be at war, he was a good man, God fearing and honest. With his beloved Edith by his side, Jack thought this was what married life should be. He hoped he would one day be able to be like them.

"Aye, I'm ready. It's been quite a day."

He slipped the ring into his pocket and noticed the letter Albert had passed him at the graveyard. He quickly opened it, cross with himself that he could have forgotten, that someone had taken the time and effort to write him a note and he hadn't read it. It was in German. Jack was puzzled. He folded it over in his pocket; he would find someone to read it later when he got back to Flanders.

He ran a comb through his hair, along with some Brylcreem, polished his shoes on his trouser leg, had a look in the mirror, and then left for the most important night of his life.

The house was magnificent; it hadn't changed one bit. Jack walked with Alice on his arm, with Jim and Edith alongside.

From the window of his study, Colonel Alcot watched the two men with their ladies walk up the driveway. He felt an immense sense of pride in the pair of them.

There was a knock at the door, it was Tim. Dashingly handsome, he stood with his sticks. He said he had the best leg money could buy and looking at him standing there, the Colonel believed it was worth every penny they had spent. Oh, the Army had done splendid things, saved his life indeed, but the wooden legs they offered were basic and heavy with large leather straps going up and over the shoulder to help keep the leg in position. The other leg had healed well; in fact, there was nothing really to see. But the scars on the inside, well, the Colonel knew the lad had them; he heard him cry out at night, and it was a cry of desperation and fear. Good job the lad had good breeding. He was tough and carried his wounds like an Englishman should. It was going to be a devil of a job to find him a good wife now he had a peg leg, but there were hundreds of men with false legs and besides, the lad had class and there was a queue of delightful young fillies just waiting for the right man.

"Our guests are here, Father. I can't tell you how much I'm looking forward to tonight. Thank you for doing this; it means a great deal to me to be able to thank Jack personally." Apart from the funeral today, this would be the only time Tim had seen Jack since that night. The night he had carried him away from all the pain and dread of the trenches, the night Jack had saved his life.

When he entered the room, Jack wiped his hand down his trousers to make sure it was clean. Tim walked over to them and spoke first. Jack was glad he did because he wasn't sure what to say or indeed how to say it.

"Jack, good to see you, you look well, and ah hello again Miss Barber." It was the first awkward moment; Tim didn't really know what to call Alice – was she Mrs Kelly or Miss Barber? He coughed with an embarrassed nod.

"I'm terribly sorry, I didn't mean to cause any offence. Is it OK if I just call you Alice?"

It was the first time anyone had even made an effort to think what to call her. Alice was touched that Tim Alcot might be embarrassed and quickly said, "Please, just Alice." It made everyone happier.

Dinner was a simple meal by the standards Colonel Alcot was used to, but it was a feast for his guests. Mrs Millward had excelled and the spring lamb was served with a full variety of fresh garden vegetables the like of which Jack hadn't seen for years.

The conversation seemed to centre on Jack and the stories of the war. How had he come to shoot down an enemy aeroplane? He told them the story of how he had avoided the shelling by falling into the well.

How had he captured Albert? And was 'Wolfgang' as good as people said he was? Jack told the stories, managing to miss out the more gruesome details. Jim was fascinated and didn't miss a thing. He knew Jack was missing much of the detail to spare the ladies.

The next question was the most difficult: the Colonel asked about Captain Alcot's rescue. This one was very difficult to dress up. The murderous Hauptman Berger was well cast as the villain, with Jack the hero. Tim was clearly fascinated, as he had no memories of any of the rescue. He, of course, was cast as the victim.

"But what role did Albert have in it? And this fellow, Finch, what did he do? Brave man that he was." The Colonel hardly drew breath. He was firing question after question, and Jack was like a good opening batsman, playing it back with a very straight bat. Jack looked at his Captain; he had a sad face all of a sudden. Jack knew about Finch and the Captain. It was a forbidden love but the rules had all changed with this war; there seemed to be no rules anymore.

"Finch is a brave man, sir. He helped carry the Captain here and kept him from bleeding too much on the way back. This was after he had cut all the wire from around him."

"Was," said Colonel Alcot. "Was... he was killed about a month ago, damn shame I never got to thank him personally, damn shame."

"Oh Lord, I didn't know," said Jack. He looked at the Captain who responded with a knowing nod.

"Anyway, it can't be helped, and Jack, remember that house I offered you, well you will need somewhere to go now. It is a tragic shame about your parents; they were fine people and they were very proud of you, as indeed we all are. The house is yours; it's not a mansion but I'm sure you will be happy there. We need to make an honest man of you, though, no man of mine can be seen living on his own now, can he?"

"No sir," said Jack.

When was the right time to ask? He didn't want to scare Alice off.

As time slipped by, no one noticed the late hour. Although widowed, Alice had readopted her habits from before she had married and afforded her parents the courtesy of being home at a sensible hour. She caught Jack's eye. She loved him so much and was loath to end what had been a superb evening. She had seen a side of Jack she had never seen before and she loved the way he laughed with Jim. They were more like brothers than friends and the Colonel was like a father to them both. It was easy to forget that it was only today that Jack's parents had been laid to rest.

Jack looked at his beloved lady and realised instantly the advantage he had be given. He was desperately trying to find an opportunity to ask Alice his question and he saw that opportunity might be realised if he now made his excuses to walk her home. The Colonel wouldn't hear of it and sent for his car to take her home. Jack arranged to come back tomorrow to discuss the house. He felt humbled by the offer; he had sought no reward other than the life of a man he had known most of his life.

The motorcar pulled up at the front door. "Your carriage awaits ma'am," said Tim, laughing. He had delighted in seeing his friend and hero Jack, the man who had saved him and protected his secret. There was much to like about Jack Adams.

Jack shook Tim's hand; he would forever be 'his Captain'. Then he remembered the note Albert had passed to him in the Churchyard.

"Sir, can I ask a favour? Albert gave me this letter today, it caught me by surprise to see him, to be honest." He reached into his pocket and handed it over to Tim. "It's in German, sir, and I don't speak a word really, certainly don't read any. I wondered if you might be so kind as to read it to me tomorrow, I'm sure it's just his condolences, and that's a nice thing for him to do. I would like to write a reply if I can, tomorrow if that's OK with you." Tim took the letter and said he would be delighted to help.

Polite handshakes for the men and a kiss on the cheek for the ladies, Jack was getting better at the finer things in life.

Jim said he would be home presently and that if Jack got back before him, he should turn in for the night.

Jack ran to the motorcar. Once in the motor, the driver smiled and Jack asked if it was possible for them to go via the lake. The driver obliged without further question. Both Alice and Jack had fond memories of the lake and boat house; they had stopped there once, before the war when they had first started walking out together.

Sheltering from the rain together, it was in many ways the first time they had seen each other in any kind of romantic form. Neither had said anything at the time – it was far too familiar – but they both felt it, and they both had remembered it.

When they arrived, the moon was half lighting the boathouse, and the lights from the motor ensured that the path was lit. It was so quiet.

There in the half light, Jack kissed Alice with all the love a man can muster, not a passionate kiss but warm and loving. With that, he knelt down and asked Alice if she would marry him. A week ago he was in mud but it was the mud of Flanders, full of death and doubt. The mud he was kneeling in now was full of hope.

Alice was stunned. She couldn't believe her good fortune. These words had been whispered in her dreams for over a year.

"Of course I will, Jack, you have no idea how I've longed to hear you say those words. Now get up you daft bugger, I spent hours cleaning those trousers."

They both hugged, and laughed and then hugged again. The drive back to the Barber household was only a short way. For Jack and Alice, it seemed a lifetime. Alice had an old worn ring on her finger, and the new owner was happier than a princess with new glass slippers.

Back at the house, the party had all but finished. Jim and Edith had taken their leave after Jim had one of his frequent coughing fits. Both Tim and the Colonel were sympathetic and no one minded when Jim left for the bathroom to lose the beautiful dinner they had just so enjoyed.

The Colonel and Tim sat in the sitting room in large green chesterfield settees smoking cigars and enjoying a brandy, when Tim felt the letter Jack had given him before he left.

He opened the letter with a sword-shaped letter opener and, placing his brandy and cigar on the table, he moved into the light to read it. It took him a couple of times to understand the contents but what it said made Tim take a sharp intake of breath. He read it again then said to his father, "This is a letter from the German to Jack, father, you need to hear this. Dear God, you need to hear this."

# CHAPTER 42

# The Note

*My good friend,*

*Please excuse my writing and the unfortunate manner of your receiving this letter. I am very sad that your parents have died in such a tragic accident and I apologise for not being able to tell you the news that is in this letter in person but my English is still very poor. I have much to thank you for, Jack; I am quite safe here in England and Herr Colonel is being very fair with me as is his son, Herr Capitain. Things in my homeland are very dark, and like you, I too have had grief to bear as my sonne, Hans, has been killed in France. He was just 17 and had no right to be fighting but he was proud and headstrong like his father and the war has a thirst for our young.*

*I am an old mann and should have died out in the battlefields, not my young sonne.*

*This war has taken so many of our countrymen on both sides and I have heard tell that there might be a way to shorten the war quickly.*

*I am sharing my accommodation with several other fellow prisoners. Not all are quite as happy with their situation as I, and they are full of boast and bluster about how we will win this conflict and be home, but I can see no end to the misery.*

*I was listening to a Hauptman last week that has heard there is to be a visit of the peacock leaders of our armies, General Ludendorff and his senior officer Hindenburg. He is a head sure and arrogant officer who knows little of the sacrifice we have endured. It is his practice to walk along the trench parapets with his feathered hat to show his disdain for the British, but like the coward that he is, he only does this in the communication trenches, safe behind the German lines and safe from men like you and I, or so he thinks. I have the dates and times he will visit and the exact location in Mons (not far behind the German lines). Jack. I could and would be shot if what I tell you ever became known and I trust you to understand that I have no desire for this war; all I want is to return home to my Frau. The sooner we can rid the world of these men such as Berger and his like, the sooner we can all return to peace. I am assuming you will get one of your friends to read this letter for you, please pass my best wishes and respects to your Capitain and Finch.*

*Gods luck to you 'Jack' remember to keep your bullets dry and may God return you to your homeland and loved ones soon.*

*I remain your friend despite the circumstances of our meeting; in a peaceful world I would have liked your company.*

*Albert Hagerman*

# CHAPTER 43

## Time To Return

Jack had two more days to sort out all his affairs. The money he had from his father's safe box would cover the cost of the funerals and any sundries such as food and drinks. The Colonel had stood the cost and Jack wanted to repay him as soon as possible. Initially, he had thought he would have to pay from his own savings and had no concerns about doing that. There was plenty of money available to him in his savings book, but it would have had to be transferred to the Colonel once he got back. But having the cash there made it all easier as he didn't want to be indebted to anyone; everyone had shown such kindness, he felt he should make sure there was nothing outstanding on his return to the front.

Harry was his usual cheerful self, and was busy telling anyone and everyone who would listen about the engagement. Alice was with her mother, away today shopping. Jack had arranged to meet her tonight. It would be their last night together, well, evening, and the night belonged to celibacy and sobriety.

Jim was still drunk. Edith was busy washing and 'doing' around the house.

Today Jack had business with the Colonel. He wanted to look at his new house, and he wasn't even sure which one it was. He had almost forgotten about the letter he had handed over to Tim; the night had held a happiness that belonged to the young and the drinking, and talking had taken the whole Barber family into the early morning.

Plans had to be made and the ladies were going to make them. Any money Jack had left after settling his debts today he would hand over to Alice to fund the planned wedding. Obviously, that would have to wait till until he got back, but it seemed the war would be over soon, now that the Americans had joined in. It should be over by Christmas, but they had all heard that before.

Jack enjoyed the walk to the big house this morning; he was looking forward to telling his employer about the engagement. He had borrowed some of Jim's better clothes, as all his had been destroyed in the fire. Besides, they wouldn't fit him any longer despite what Alice thought. He was a much bigger man after his time away. Not fat; fit and lean, but more of him.

He strode confidently up the gravelled driveway, whistling as he walked. Today was the start of his new life; he had lost everything and yesterday he laid his old life to rest, but it had also been the catalyst for this new life, a life planned with Alice.

Jack watched as a rabbit hopped away into the undergrowth. It reminded him that summer wasn't far away, and he wondered if the rain had stopped over the channel; he had never seen it rain like that anywhere here before. He thought France and Europe must always be wet. Not worth the cost of the many lives and friends he had lost. It was the first time he had thought about his role in the war for a few days. Those few days had been peaceful, but as much as

Jack didn't want to return to the fighting, he had to go back tomorrow evening to catch the late train to the coast, and the first ship he could board to get back two days from now.

As he approached the steps that led to the front door, he set off to the side, not so much the tradesman's entrance but more for the casual visitor. Jack was more comfortable going in the tradesman's, it was where he belonged.

Jack saw that there was another motorcar parked on the drive, one he hadn't seen before, and as he started to walk round the side of the house someone called him from the front door. Jack turned round to see Tim waving him to come in the front entrance. In all the time Jack had been coming to the big house, he had never been in the front entrance, and now this morning he was about to go in for the second time in two days. How strange, he thought, and skipped up the stone stairs to the door.

Tim waited for him. He had a serious look on his face and Jack was instantly aware that he had seen that face before, back in France when Captain Alcot was worried or frightened, which was most of the time, in fact. Tim offered a hand and Jack shook it as he removed his borrowed cap and wiped his boots on the mat.

"Jack, we have a visitor."

"Oh sorry, sir. I'll come back later, I didn't realise."

"No, Jack, it's you he needs to see, he's in the study with father. It's that letter Albert gave you."

"He isn't in trouble, is he? Should I have refused his letter?" Jack was slightly concerned; he didn't want to get Albert into trouble in any way.

"No, Jack, he isn't in trouble, no one is. Come in and let us explain."

In the study there stood two men, the Colonel and another man, tall and thin, elegant even.

"Ah Jack, come in," said the Colonel. "This is Brigadier General Julian Rosewood, he's from Headquarters."

Jack stood to attention and felt instantly uncomfortable "Sir."

"Relax, Adams. I'm sure you're as shocked as I was, Gerald. You had better explain what we have been discussing, and you might want to get the lad a drink; he looks like he's seen a ghost."

Tim was asked to sit down; his leg was very sore today. He had been on it quite a lot yesterday so it ached like blazes today.

"Maybe you would like to explain to Warrant Officer Adams what the letter said?"

"Warrant Officer? Sir, I'm only a Sergeant. I'm sorry, there must have been a misunderstanding."

The look the General gave Jack said differently. "Mr Adams, I rarely make mistakes, and when I do, no one tells me I have. As of this morning you are a Warrant Officer, and when this meeting has finished you might want to go and tell your new fiancée the good news that you will be here for a couple of weeks longer. Oh, don't be surprised that I know; the Colonel here was always dreadful at keeping secrets. He's told me the good news, let me be the first to congratulate you. By all accounts you deserve a bit of good news, I hear it's all been a bit dire. Condolences for your loss, damn shame, losing one's parents like that. Now, Captain, are you going to take all day to explain to the man how we know?"

Tim stuttered and explained that Harry had sent a note with the meat delivery first thing this morning announcing

213

the news of the engagement. He offered his congratulations, as did the Colonel.

The General stood smoking a pipe and nodded his impatience. He understood that Adams was the best there was at what he did, indeed he had been informed by Hesketh-Prichard at the club only a few weeks ago what a sterling job Adams had been doing, but now there was a new game afoot, and Adams might be the key to ending the war up to a year before it might grind to a natural and ultimately pathetic end. He coughed. It was enough.

"Jack, the letter Hagerman gave you is dynamite. I have written it out in English so you can read it. We called the General as soon as we read it; really, it's an important thing. Read it."

Jack relaxed and read the letter. It was a nice letter and Jack was saddened that Albert had lost his son. This war had indeed taken its toll; Jack didn't even know Albert had a son of fighting age. But what was all this stuff about feathers and Ludendorff? Jack wasn't even sure who Ludendorff was but it was obvious he was important. But this didn't feel like sniping, this felt like an assassination mission. Jack read it again and placed it back on the desk.

"Sit down Adams," said the General. "What do you think, can you nail the bugger?"

"Well, sir, do we have a map of the area? How far away is he going to be? But in short, yes sir, I can." Jack didn't want to sound cocky but he was sure he could hit a target if he only could see it. He was just wondering about the 'not far behind the enemy lines' bit.

He would have preferred it to be 'not far from the British lines' but that wasn't likely really, was it?

# CHAPTER 44

# Target Ludendorff

The 'mission' was going to be more than challenging, and although it wasn't a suicide mission, it was without doubt very dangerous. This time it couldn't be done by a single sniper; it would need a team, at least an observer and sniper.

There were plenty of things to plan, and having the backing of General Rosewood was an enormous help. He had sent a message back to Belgium and arranged that Warrant Officer Jack Adams would be seconded to a headquarters unit in Aldershot.

This mission was classified as 'Top Secret' and this was in no small part due to the fact that Jack would be working with an ex POW.

Following the disclosure of the contents of the letter, it was felt that two main questions needed to be answered. The first question was: is the information reliable? And the second question was: if the information was correct and reliable, how could the British take advantage of it?

Jack said he would like to meet with Albert; it would give him a chance to talk about the letter and also give him the opportunity to pass on his condolences for Albert's loss. It took less than an hour for Albert to be sitting in the Colonel's office. Jack hadn't even had the chance to go and tell Jim or Alice that he was staying for another two weeks or so.

General Rosewood, the Colonel and Jack were sitting waiting when Albert was escorted into the office by two military policemen. They both looked burly and spiteful until they saw the General, when suddenly their attitude changed dramatically and they seemed much less keen to push their ward around. Why would a General want to meet a Hun here? Neither of them had the balls to ask, though.

Typical, thought Jack. He had seen their type before and guessed that neither of them had ever seen the front or even left the country. Those that had been had a different view of prisoners, a kind of empathy, born out of knowing what they had been through in the trenches.

Albert saluted the General before he removed his hat. As a prisoner of war, he needn't do either but he was respectful. Jack shook Albert's hand and it helped calm him. The Colonel asked them to come to the dining room, as there was more room and seats for all there.

They all sat round the large table and tea was requested. Mrs Millward was in her element; she had never been this close to a Hun, or a hero and especially a General. She was quite looking forward to the women's meeting in the church hall so she could boast. She wasn't a boast by nature but this was an exception.

The Colonel saw the mischief in her eye in an instant and pulled her to one side to explain the importance of her silence. She agreed, of course; she had been with the family for years and had been well looked after, even enjoying the Colonel's special attention now and again. All in all, she would rather not disappoint the family she called her own.

Tim was acting as a translator. Albert's English was very good – he had made a super effort to try to learn it in the time he had been here in England – but no amount of good learning or goodwill would be enough to discuss today's events.

With tea served, the General was trying his best not to intimidate anyone, and in fairness, he was doing a very good job of it. He was a good commander, one of the younger ones that the British Army had turned to now that the 'Old and Bold' that had been the British Army's commanders had been retired, killed or replaced. Julian Rosewood had an uncanny knack of understanding a situation and taking advantage of opportunities that came his way. He very much viewed this as an opportunity: the chance to kill one of the top commanders of the great German empire would shake the belief of the Germans to the bone. No longer would they feel that they were invincible or untouchable.

The chances were that the only two men in the world who could carry out this mission were sitting here, right in front of him. All he had to do now was find a way to ensure this mission succeeded, and if possible get the men he sent to do it back safely. In an ideal world, that's what would happen, but if push came to shove, killing Ludendorff was more important than getting the two men back. He didn't tell anyone that part of his private thoughts, though.

Before any of this could happen, he needed more information from Hagerman, and so rather than force it out of him, as he was quite capable of doing, he would ask.

He seemed like an affable chap and before very long Rosewood had forgotten that Hagerman was German, or at least that he was supposed to be the enemy. He was at ease with Adams, that was a sure sign, and there was an understanding between them, an understanding of a fellow warrior that previously he had only seen in men who felt they were equals.

Albert was asked how he knew that the information was correct, and no one expected the answer he gave. It made all the men look first at Albert and then at each other. It was one of those moments when no one was sure what to say next.

The reason that Albert knew that Ludendorff was going to be there at a particular day was due to a medal presentation. As part of that presentation, there was a special award for a father and son, whom had both given their lives for the great cause of Imperial Conquest. That father and son were Albert and Hans Hagerman, and they had been awarded the Iron Cross class one.

This was a special event because neither man had been awarded the class two medal prior to the highest award, the class one. Even in death, Germany was trying to use the Hagerman family, and set them as an example for greatness.

The German Army had decided to ignore the fact that Albert wasn't actually dead. It served their purpose for him to be dead, so he was dead, despite a letter to the Red Cross from their British counterparts stating otherwise.

Monica Hagerman, Albert's wife, had written to Albert asking what it was all about. She was a grieving mother, already broken hearted by the news that her beloved husband had been killed and then her belief in God had been reincarnated by the news that Albert was, in fact, a prisoner and not dead. When she had received the letter from the Rotes Kreuz stating that Albert was in England as a POW, her heart was mended.

Hans had been a kind boy but full of the national fervour, and as soon as he could, he slipped away and signed the pledge to join the Army. He was gone within a week and she had lost both the men she loved to this glorious war. Glorious only to the living or the ignorant, not the mourners or wounded.

The local priest had visited Monica; he had the news in a telegram that Hans, her only son, had died a hero's death. There was no further information until the local newspaper had called to see her. They came to inform her that her family were being celebrated as heroes for the nation in this grand gesture from command on high.

The information she had was that Albert was dead, but she knew this to be untrue, as she had letters each week from him. When she questioned the authorities, she was told categorically that it was a rouse used by the British to break the hearts of the fine German women: the letters were fake.

So the game was afoot. The German authorities were happy for Albert to be dead. Monica knew that he wasn't. The letters she had received from him had been personal with nuances that he alone would know and say. In her heart she knew he was alive, but she was also wise enough and cynical enough to know there was no sense in telling anyone else the facts.

Monica had already been rewarded for her husband's sacrifice with a small but welcome war pension, and now she was set to receive more reward for her son's sacrifice. From a financial point of view, it was cheap propaganda. Photographs taken of the false headstones showing the names of Albert and Hans would be used in the newspapers all over Germany. It would drive recruitment in a country where there were few left to recruit.

The Germans were living in uncertain times. Shortages in food and clothing were a serious problem. The one thing that wasn't in short supply was the lie and bluster of the national leadership. In their eyes, the Germans were fighting a noble and just war with terrific heroism and successes all along the line.

The daily telegrams to the recently bereaved said otherwise.

# CHAPTER 45

# Reunited

General Rosewood sat and listened. He was as shocked as the rest but needed to put over a suggestion. He had already planned it in his head – what he was going to say and offer –but having seen the two men together he was sure his task would be a lot easier than he had initially imagined.

"Albert, I have an offer for you. I will understand if you decline it but I think you'll find it an agreeable arrangement."

All the men looked, first at Rosewood and then at Albert.

"I want you to go with Adams here, and help with this mission. You have already shown me that you have no love for these blighters and in return, when you get back, I'll ensure you are returned back to your family in Germany as an early repatriation: 'wounded and unfit to continue as a prisoner of war'. The war will be over for you and you will be home. Does that sound like an interesting proposition? You don't have to agree, of course, and I won't make you. If you refuse you'll just go back to the camp. You have already done us a great service, and I'm sure it wasn't your intention for all this to happen, but you can't put the genie back in the bottle, what is done is done. It will be easier if you help us, but if you don't, we will do it anyway. What do you say?"

Albert thought about it for a minute before nodding. He was clearly thinking things through in his head because he was shaking and nodding as though having a conversation with himself. The final head movement was a nod.

"I will help you, Herr General. Jack here is a fine shot but he will find it difficult behind the German lines. I have some ideas that might help. You are right, in what you say. I have no feelings for this pig who orders our men into certain death, and the war will be over soon, everyone knows that is true. With the Americans, well now, the advantage is with the British. Let us hasten the end of this war as quickly as we can. It is not just my wish to go home but I am sure everyone on both sides would like that."

The men around the table nodded in agreement as Albert spoke. Every now and again, he would struggle with a word and Tim would help but all in all, Jack was impressed by the very good English that was spoken and he was glad to have some help on this mission because he didn't really know what it involved yet.

There were plans to be made, and things to be set in motion. The General called an end to the meeting and said he would be in touch. It was agreed that it was perhaps best if Albert didn't go back to the camp and Colonel Alcot said there was a room available in the stable block, usually reserved for the groomsman, but he was away in the war so it had been cleared. Albert gave his word to be honourable and his guard was dismissed back to camp alone, with a story that the prisoner was being transferred to Aldershot camp for his own safety. The camp commandant would be spoken to.

If Albert had any reservations about the task ahead, they were laid to rest when he had learned that he would be working with Jack. He held Jack in the highest esteem, both as a man and especially as a sniper. He had no doubt the mission would be a success. Although it didn't sit easily with him that he would be going to war against his old comrades, it was a means to an end. The ridiculous men in charge, those men at the very top of the command chain, had let him and his son down, and it was now their turn to pay. It was their turn to suffer.

Jack had news to give as well. He left feeling more worried about the future than he had been when he arrived, but more than anything else, he was relieved. He had been promoted, so there was some good news, and he had a bit more time with Alice, and there couldn't have been any better news than that.

The room was now quiet, the meeting done. General Rosewood finished his pipe and banged out the ash in the fireplace. "Well Gerald, the die is cast. What do you think, will it work?"

"General Rosewood, I'll lay you a wager, they'll get the job done. I don't know how, but I'm sure they will."

"Good, good, now I need to be getting back. You know. Gerald, this war has cost a lot of families, none more so than yours. You should be very proud of that man of yours. I don't know about the Germans, but he scares the hell out of me."

# CHAPTER 46

# Off To Aldershot

The train arrived at North Camp station, lost in the cloud of steam that embraced the carriage like a shroud; the smell of smoke filled the air and soot settled on all the surfaces, including Jack and Albert.

There was a Sergeant waiting for the two odd companions. Jack still had his old Sergeant's chevrons sewn neatly to his arm, and Albert had a clean uniform and didn't look out of place in a station full of soldiers. The Sergeant thought Albert was French and Jack couldn't see any reason to change his perception.

North Camp was located just to the south of Farnborough. As the three men walked out of the station, Jack could see that there were wooden buildings, row upon row of them but they weren't heading towards any of them. It gave Jack a clue as to how big a garrison town was; he had never seen a peacetime army camp, and this was as near as he would get to one.

On the road outside the station stood a lorry. The Sergeant jumped into the cab and Jack and Albert climbed onto the back under the canvas roof and sat on the wooden benches. The drive to their new offices only took fifteen minutes and the truck rattled and crashed along a rutted track. The truck came to a standstill and the engine coughed and spluttered then begrudgingly stopped.

The two men looked outside and saw where they were going to be working for the foreseeable future: it all looked grand.

The two men were busy chatting when they were yelled at from a doorway.

"You two men there, move your arses and run over here now!"

Jack looked round. Surely the man wasn't shouting at them? They had just arrived, but there wasn't anyone else so Jack pointed at himself and looked towards the crazed man in the doorway. "Me?"

"Yes you, get here or I'll have you locked up in the guardroom!"

Jack nudged Albert and they walked over to the red-faced man who was shouting.

"You don't walk here, you march, now swing your arms and march like soldiers."

Jack could feel the blood in his veins boil; who the hell was this man shouting at them? As Jack closed in on him he noticed the man was a Sergeant Major, a warrant officer like himself.

"Are you talking to me Sergeant Major? Because if you are, you might want to lower your voice, and my colleague here doesn't understand a word you're saying."

The red-faced warrant officer was incandescent with rage. His face was contorted and spit was foaming on his lips. "How dare you! How dare you talk to me like that? Do you know who I am? I'm the Sergeant Major."

Jack was in his element. He had seen idiots like this many times in France, and although he knew he was in the wrong because he didn't have his correct rank on his own uniform, he was going to enjoy educating this jumped up tyrant as to the real facts.

"Hello, I'm Warrant Officer Jack Adams, and this is Albert Hagerman, he's a German. Are we going to be sharing a billet?"

The colour drained from the Sergeant Major's face. The bully had been faced.

"Warrant Officer, you have Sergeant's stripes on, why are you incorrectly dressed?"

Jack said as calmly as he could, "What's your name? And if you raise your voice to me again I'll knock you on your arse. If you doubt who or what I am, call General Rosewood in Headquarters; he will vouch for me. Now please step aside and let us enter." Jack's voice was as cold as ice, and he held the Sergeant Major's eye with his.

The man stepped out of the way and Jack and Albert walked into the corridor that led to the various offices, all empty.

"Shall we start this chat again? I'm Jack, now what's your name? There's no need for us to argue."

"I'm sorry," said the now quietened man. "I was expecting you tomorrow and when you turned up in the wrong uniform with a Froggy, it, well, threw me a bit."

"German, he's German not French and he carries the same rank as me. I'm guessing you haven't been over the channel, have you?" It was obvious he hadn't ever seen a German uniform, and Albert was in his best one, so he can't have been in the front line.

"No, I was injured before we got sent over. I've been here for three years, and I have no desire to go, either."

"Thought not," said Jack, the disgust barely hidden in his voice.

"Do we have an office, or a room we can use?"

"Yes, it's over the bridge on the other side of the canal, your accommodation is there as well. The mess room is on this side. Where is your gear?"

Jack said he didn't have any, and any equipment should already be there. He was handed the keys to his new offices and the two men took the short walk to the bridge. Once over, they saw for the first time the newly built, half-brick and half-wooden block of buildings that were going to be home for the time being.

When they got inside, all the gear they could have ever wanted was laid out on tables. General Rosewood had been as good as his word. There was even a telephone. They had maps, photographs and street guides to the towns that Albert had said they would need to go through.

It was time for them to start planning their mission. There would only be the two of them, and laid in the corner of a room were two beds. That made it easier because they didn't need to go outside at all for now. Later they would try to arrange a trip to the 'long range' at Bisley. The shooting range was only about ten miles away and Jack needed to fire some rounds at targets. On the long range, he could fire as far as a thousand yards, and that, for anyone, was a long shot.

The only thing missing were the rifles; they would be in the armoury along with all the ammunition he needed. Also, he had arranged for the German Zeiss sniper scope to be fitted to his rifle. It was much better than the one he had been using before, and when he had looked down the scope attached to Albert's rifle all those months ago he was determined to try to acquire one for himself. Once again, he was pleased General Rosewood had been as good as his word.

Within the hour, the two men had everything in their hut, rifles and sights included. There was tea on the boil. Oddly, Albert had acquired quite a taste for tea since he had been captured. He liked his sweet and without milk, while Jack liked his white with no sugar. It highlighted that the two men had different tastes but they were of one mind when it came to shooting. It was a deadly and lethal partnership.

Despite the late June sun, there wasn't much the two men could do outside so they opened the maps to plot a route from Ypres to Poelcappelle, then onto their final destination, Roulers.

They laid out the maps and pinned them on to the table to stop them rolling back inside themselves. It was only now that Jack realised the gravity of the situation; Roulers wasn't just over the German lines, it was miles behind the line. It was also a major German supply and holding route so there would be plenty of Germans to avoid before and after the shot. Jack was very glad that Albert had decided he wanted to do this because there was no chance that Jack could have done this without him.

They had three weeks before the presentation day. Three weeks to plan the mission, move location, get into the right place and take the shot. After that, only God knew what would happen. Bizarrely, Jack wasn't worried about after the mission; he didn't really think much about it. Three weeks and it would all be over: Albert would go back to Germany a free man, and Jack would, he assumed, go back to 'Pops' to carry on with the school. No one had said what would happen after, so he made his own plans, in his head.

CHAPTER 47

# Train Hard, Shoot Easy

The following days were spent looking at photos of the area and comparing them to the maps.

There was a welcome break for the two men when they went onto the range to practise and zero their weapons. Both Jack and Albert had sniper rifles and Jack carried a revolver as opposed to Albert who carried his Luger pistol. It was important for the plan that both were familiar with their weapons, but it was more important that they knew where the bullets landed on a target at various distances.

Neither was quite sure where they would be when the shot was to take place. It was impossible to carry out any 'on ground reconnaissance' and neither of the men had actually been to Roulers, but they were sure that if they arrived safely they would, between them, find a spot that would afford them the opportunity to take a shot.

Out on the range, both men felt at home. Down in the butts, there was a man who would mark the target when they shot. He wasn't sure who they were or indeed why they were shooting but he knew very quickly that they were marksmen. Bullet after bullet hit the bullseye. Judging by the time lapse between the bang and the hit he guessed they were shooting from the back points on the range. He didn't know that they were shooting from a hundred yards further back than the furthest firing points, way back in the trees, over eight hundred yards away.

Jack was astounded at how good the German Zeiss optics were. The rubber eyepiece fitted his eye perfectly, and the view was crystal clear. They had been mounted on his rifle especially and the armourer had done a perfect job. So good, in fact, that it would be an easy mistake to think they were made for the Lee Enfield that fitted so snugly into Jack's shoulder. Albert had his 'Mauser' rifle and he was every bit as accurate as Jack: he never missed.

There was a friendly banter and rivalry between the two, and Jack was constantly surprised at how good Albert's English was becoming. He was able now to hold a conversation, with only the occasional stop when he had to think about the right word. The men had formed more than a bond between colleagues, they had become as friends.

The next day saw a step up in preparation for the two would-be assassins. A number of mannequins had been acquired that were sturdy and about four foot high, and each one was mounted on a pole to a height of about six foot. Once sunk into the ground, the two of them paced out the approximate distance. The targets looked tiny from 800 yards. The object of today's lesson was to see just how much the bullet dropped over that long distance.

Neither man was used to shooting at extreme range like this, but it would be a great asset if they trained at distance and then didn't need to shoot that far. It was a far breezier day today, and with a brisk breeze from left to right, it made the shot even more of a challenge. Jack was amused that they were both having so much fun just training.

The following day they were up early to be on the range by 08:00. A breakfast of tea and toast was enjoyed, and a jam sandwich was all they had to take on the range with them. Jack had a flask of hot tea and some hard biscuits, and both men had a water bottle full as the weather was getting warmer; they needed to drink plenty out in the open.

The sun was already higher than the butts and so wasn't in their eyes. The dummies were stuck into the sand and the pair walked back down the range. There was a small group of men waiting for them when they arrived at their firing point, and amongst them were General Rosewood and his team. They were all armed with service binoculars and they made various comments about how small the targets were at this distance.

Jack stood to attention and saluted, while Albert shuffled his feet together and bowed his head in respect. The General reciprocated and the atmosphere returned to being fairly relaxed. The General lit up his pipe with a long match and puffed. The sweet smelling smoke of hand rubbed tobacco filled the morning air.

"There is a lot of ground between us and that dummy, Adams."

"Yes sir," replied Jack, "about 800 yards."

"You think it's going to be that far then, looking at your maps and the like? Do you think you can hit it at that range?"

"Oh, hitting it isn't the problem sir, it's killing it that's proving harder."

The group laughed at Jack's quip but Jack didn't quite understand the joke.

"What do you mean, 'Killing it'? It's a damn dummy!"

"Sorry sir, I meant hitting it in the right place to kill it. Too low and the blighter will just be wounded, and we can't guarantee hitting him in the head, so it has to be in the chest, sir, and that's why we are trying the dummy, sir. It will give us a better idea as to his size at range, sir."

"Ah, I see," said Rosewood. "Well carry on, I'll be interested to see if all this effort is worth it."

Jack checked the range finder: they were at the 700 yards marker. He climbed down in the shooting pit, and Albert went into the pit next to him, about five yards to his left. Jack rolled some cotton wool and dampened it with some spit. He then made it into a small ball and pushed it into his ears, with Albert doing the same. The onlookers would put their fingers in their ears.

Jack loaded his rifle and cocked it ready to fire. He looked down the Zeiss sight and smiled again at the clarity with which he could see the target. It always made him smile; he still hadn't got used to it.

He looked to the treetops to help gauge the wind, took a deep breath, and slowly let it out. He did that three times. On the third breath out he stopped and held his breath, just whilst he squeezed the trigger. There was a sharp crack and the rifle barley moved in his hand. It was nearly three seconds before there was a splash of sand behind the mannequin.

Under the dummy, all those yards away, safe in the depths of the butts, a young corporal looked up at the target. He was armed with a snooker cue and fixed on the tip was a small white disk about the size of penny. The idea was to put the disk over the entry hole so the two men could see it from their firing position. In the days he had been here, they hadn't missed their regular targets once. It looked like today was going to be the same. He slid his cue up into the air and placed the white disk over the hole. It was about three inches to the right of the centre line, and about four inches higher than the midline, just above the right nipple.

Jack cursed; for him it was miles off target. Albert laughed and shook his head at Jack's annoyance. The General nodded his head and puffed away at his pipe, amazed at the shot. Even with his binoculars he struggled to see the target, let alone the white disk.

Next, it was Albert's turn. Jack shouted a few slight alterations to assist him and Albert closed both eyes as he too slowed his breathing. Once he was ready, he squeezed his trigger and again there was a loud crack in the morning quiet. Three seconds later a new hole appeared in the target smack bang in the middle of the target's chest, about two inches lower than Jack's shot: this target was dead.

Jack's next shot was perfect, less than an inch below Albert's shot, but he was cross with himself because he wouldn't be getting two shots in a couple of weeks. He might not get any, but at best he would only get one.

Albert fired again, and ironically mirrored Jack's first shot, this time to the left. Once more the disk went over the hole, and once more the corporal shook his head in amazement. These two jokers were deadly. He lit a cigarette and waited for the two of them to come and look at their work. He raised the safety flag just to ensure they didn't shoot him, then he lifted the mannequin down. He was stunned at the results.

He wasn't quite expecting the whole of the command staff to turn up and was glad he had his hat on when they did. He saluted, first the Captain, then the Major. He had never seen a General and didn't recognise the rank studs in his uniform, but he had seen red tabs before and knew they were very important, so he saluted him as well.

"Yes, yes, carry on Corporal," said the Major. Jack could see the young corporal's discomfort so sent him on "an errand" to save him from further embarrassment. Albert knew what Jack had done, as did the General. It was one of the reasons why Jack was so liked. It was his humility.

"Good shooting, Adams. I'd say this bugger is dead," said Rosewood.

"Yes sir, he is for sure, but not the first time, well not definitely. All the other shots would have killed him, sir, but I'm not convinced this first one would. I'll have another crack in a bit when the wind changes a tad. There's no point in shooting him again now. He's dead."

"Well," said the General. "We will let you get on with it. I have to say, Adams, you are a hell of a shot, as is your German friend. I'll admit I was a tad worried it might be impossible, but I'll eat my words here and now. That's the damndest shooting I've ever seen."

Jack stood to salute the officers, but realised he didn't have his hat on so he just stood to attention and bid the General goodbye. Then Rosewood did the strangest thing: he walked over to Jack and shook his hand.

The next few days were spent repeating the exercise over and over again, as there was no room for error. Any and every mistake in judgement, at any distance, was corrected and practised again.

At the end of the first week the scores were equal: both men had hit the target exactly the same amount. There was room for entertainment, but even that was competitive. They tried Jack's old favourite next, adult hide and seek. The rules were simple: neither man could move more than fifty yards from the other, and each man in turn had ten minutes to dress in the camouflage they felt was appropriate for the surrounding area. It was astonishing just how undetectable each man could make themselves.

However, there was a problem with the game. The environment in which they were practising was different from the place they were going, and at the end of the week the two of them went to an old demolition site to see if they could adapt their chameleon-like skills to the urban environment, just in case. They needn't have worried, as within minutes they were able to hide with remarkable efficiency. No one further than ten feet away would be able to see either of them.

The time passed quickly, and soon it was time to cross the channel. Once they had packed everything away and cleaned the accommodation block, there was nothing to show they had been there at all. The key was left in the guardroom for the Sergeant Major. Jack didn't really want to meet him again, because he might say something to cause offence, or worse.

Then it was off to Southampton and a crossing on a Navy boat bound for Calais. On the boat, the two men shared a moment of uncomfortable fear. Each had his own reason. One was hoping to go back home but was getting further away by the second, the other hoping there was a home to go back to in Germany.

By nightfall they would have arrived in port, then the long journey by London Bus from the docks to the railway station and from there a train to Poperinghe. They would spend the next day discussing things with Captain Leek.

They couldn't actually discuss what they were doing, and it might be a bit awkward with Albert, but they would sort things out. Most people thought Albert was French so they hadn't encountered any problems on their journey so far. Things might be slightly more difficult on the French side but both men knew that their plan would require them to change roles soon.

Once they had crossed into the German lines it would be Jack who would become the 'prisoner' and Albert the man who would keep him alive in a very hostile world.

# CHAPTER 48

# Return To War

The camp at 'Pops' was just the same as when he had left. His office had changed though, as there was a new man sitting behind the desk. Sergeant Bob Preston had taken over the role when Jack had returned to 'Home Service'. Jack hadn't realised he had been transferred to another service, but not wanting to appear stupid, he played along.

All they were here for really was some fresh supplies. Tomorrow they would get to Ypres and from there the more dangerous advance into first Potyze and then over the German lines and onto Frezenberg, about two and a half miles further on. From there it was a six-mile or so walk to Passchendaele before the final five-mile walk to Roulers.

It was expected that there would be chaos on the German side because only last month the battle for Messines had finished with significant advances for the British, and the whole area was busy with casualties and clearing roads and tracks. There had been some huge mines exploded, and listening to Captain Leek brought back painful memories of July 1916 and the disastrous day at the Somme. All that had seemed a lifetime ago, until now. Jack could remember the mine and all those lads running onto a hail of bullets whilst he sat there, helpless, but worse than that, unable to be of any help whatsoever. He shook his head and tried to concentrate.

Today's date was the 6<sup>th</sup> July and the weather was trying to brighten up. It was very warm but the sun was reluctant to show; it was as though even the summer had given up on this war. It was a sad fact that men had come to look at omens just as had their forbearers in battles and wars long since finished.

Captain Leek was quite keen to know when the secret mission was due to finish and Jack heard a small alarm ringing in his head. He couldn't tell the Captain what he was here to do but he could say it would be over in a couple of weeks. He asked why it was important.

Captain Leek was in a quandary. He liked Jack but couldn't risk telling him anything about the proposed attack due to take place on or about the second week in July. As always, there would be an artillery barrage to try to soften up the Germans before the main attack went in. He wanted to warn Jack to make sure that whatever it was he was doing was over and finished before the 12<sup>th</sup> July. Being anywhere near the German held ground around Passchendaele would not be a healthy place to be. He couldn't tell Jack any more, partly because he didn't really know much more, but if Jack was caught and he had any information that might prove useful to the Germans, they would surely kill him trying to find out what he knew.

Jack sat and listened. If he had understood everything, the bombardment was due to commence the day after the shot. It wasn't close to where they were planning to be, but it would make getting back much, much harder.

In effect, and to summarise their position, they had just 6 days to be back here. Less than one week to change the course of the war. If they were successful, the Germans would lose heart and with the Americans about ready to join in the war, the final push must surely be just around the corner. One way or another the war must be finished by Christmas, but Jack had heard that before.

It all started tomorrow, but before that there was kit to check, ammunition to pack, and weapons to clean, at least the inside of them. Tomorrow they would start out and it should be no more than three days to get to Roulers, the target. Ludendorff would be in that town on the 10$^{th}$ of July and the two men wanted to be on site and in position the day before. They had identified a church from the pictures they had from before the war. It was only five hundred yards from the ceremony, a range they were very comfortable with. From that range they wouldn't miss, but the problem was getting away.

Five hundred yards was close, so the camouflage had to be superb, and within the backpacks both men carried were various items to aid with the dark arts of adult hide and seek. Jack felt the familiar knot of tension tighten within his stomach. The last time he felt like this was only a few weeks ago, when he had asked Alice to marry him.

Albert was quiet, scared even. He had thought this through a hundred times. He wanted to go home to Monica; God knows she had suffered more than most. He had felt the pain of losing Hans as any father would, but a mother's loss was so much harder, and he felt the guilt of being the cause of so much grief himself.

He had shot many, many men and some of them would have been about Hans's age. He had caused the pain but the leaders of his lost cause were the real villains. He was determined to finish this mission but he had a subplot, known only to him: he was going to get Jack Adams home, back to his loved ones.

He had a plan forming in his head but he didn't know what fate was going to present once he had been responsible for the assassination of the chief of the General Staff. That self-same man who had blood on his hands, the blood of hundreds of thousands of his countrymen, the blood of his son, and if necessary, the blood of Albert Hagerman. After all, Albert was already dead according to the German high command.

It seemed strange that there was already a headstone just a few miles away with his name on it, and that next to it was the headstone of his son. No father should have to endure the loss of a son, especially when that son was too young to be in the war and certainly too young to fall, dead and unfound.

# CHAPTER 49

# The Road To Hell

The next morning the two men bid their farewells to friends and foes alike. It only took them a short time to find a lift to Ypres. Traffic was a virtual constant between Ypres and Poperinghe and there was always room for a couple of foot soldiers, even if one looked remarkably like a Frenchman. From Ypres, it was time to take to the road on foot.

From the wreck of a town that was Ypres, they stayed on the only major road out, one which ran north east over the river and that served as a moat in ancient times, and then continued out into the countryside. The long roads were still busy with transport to the front line, and presently they came to the tiny village of Potyze. Studded here and there were the farms; on the right there was 'Lancer farm' and then 'Hussar farm' further on the right. On the left were the remains of the Château that housed the medical aid post.

Further up the road they came across the first of the mass graves, dug in an attempt to give the fallen a safe haven in the shadow of the fallen trees, and just far enough away from the aid post to be sensitive to the scared and nervous.

A fallen tree marked every thirty yards along the road. It was a sad reflection of a time when the roads had been lined with tall, proud trees. Now these trees lay broken and shattered, victims of an industrial killing machine. Artillery shells fell indiscriminately, no target in mind, just random destruction. It served as a reminder that the killing hadn't finished.

They hadn't got too far along the road before a concerned sentry stopped them. "Whoa there lads, where you going? The German lines are just up that road and they have a hunger for both British and French, and you two look like lunch."

Jack had planned for the Germans stopping them but hadn't even considered the British stopping him. He took the soldier to the side of the road. He couldn't tell him what they were doing, and he wouldn't be believed even if he did, so he made it up as he went along and hoped the lad wouldn't think he was mad, or worse, a deserter.

"See that man? He is a German sniper. I'm Warrant Officer Jack Adams and I caught him, but he has just heard that his son has been killed. We think it might be a human kindness to let him go home and say his goodbyes. We will be back in a couple of days, so be a sport and let us through."

"Lost his son, eh, sir? It's a proper bastard, this war. You come back this way, sir, and call out the name, "Davy Jones". That way you shouldn't get shot. It's the password we have made up for the week."

Jack said his thanks and with no more fuss, the two men dropped into the ditch at the side of the road. From here on in, it was going to be wet and uncomfortable.

Jack passed his rifle over to Albert along with most of the other equipment; from here on, Jack was Albert's prisoner. Both men made sure they were mudded, just to ensure that they looked like they belonged out here in the mud.

The cover story was simple. Albert was to appear to have been wounded (shell-shocked would be best as there was no obvious injury), Jack was his prisoner and they had to return to Roulers. The prisoner had new information about the next attack and he needed to be delivered to headquarters. It wasn't much of a story but it was as likely as any other and there was an element of truth to the whole lie.

Night was closing in; it was time to rest up. Up ahead was a perfect culvert. Dry and clean, it was a drain under the main road. There was no traffic on this road any longer. Just up the line lay Frezenberg and the German lines. Tonight was the last in no man's land; tomorrow the gamekeeper became poacher, and as every poacher knew, to catch the biggest game you had to go into the lion's den.

Once they had settled into the makeshift den, they opened their packs and pulled out a blanket each. Jack had a small surprise for Albert. He pulled out a small hip flask he had filled with Albert's favourite tipple. The sweet Kirsch tasted like nectar, and it brought a smile to Albert's dirty, tired face. The two men shared a sandwich of corned beef; rations would be short from now on because toileting was now an issue and these two men were professionals. From tomorrow they would need to be, but for now, it was time to get some kip.

There was no real hurry in the morning because they really wanted to be mobile in the daylight. If anyone were to see them it would be more easily explained in daylight. Night time made soldiers nervous and trigger-happy. Dawn was about the worst time because they could see you to shoot you, and at dawn everyone was tired and more likely to shoot first and ask questions later.

It was best for them to be obvious and not skulk in the shadows.

Albert had to present himself as the returning warrior, confident and relieved to be back on his own side. It was the only way to stay safe but there were no guarantees. From here on in, they would have to play it by ear.

Overnight, there was the usual shelling but it was far overhead and posed no danger to them. First light was early; it was light by 4 a.m. Breakfast was a simple drink of water and some hard tack with a piece of cheese. Once they were ready, they had to make a move. Both men were nervous and keen to get going. It was the waiting that made them nervous and they knew that, once underway, they would feel more in charge of their destiny.

For Jack, the thought of having no weapon at all on his person was daunting, as from here on in Albert had to carry both rifles and Jack the backpack. Within an hour of waking, they were on their way to Frezenberg and into the lion's den.

They felt it prudent to stay hidden for the first couple of miles, just to make sure they weren't a soft target for either side's snipers; they knew there would be some and once they had gone further down the ditch and dyke system they felt it safe to emerge above terra firma.

They didn't talk much. Frezenberg was about two miles away but they had to get to Passchendaele by nightfall some six miles further, plenty of time for two men walking but they had no idea what they would encounter, if indeed they encountered anything.

They needn't have worried; there were very few people around at all and none that showed them any interest. The summer sun was hot and by the time they reached

Passchendaele they had finished all their water. It was 5 p.m. when Albert saw a German soldier close enough to speak to. All day they had seen soldiers but they'd all been in the distance, or on the back of horse drawn carts on the road. Although they had had some enquiring looks, no one had stopped or even shouted at them. It was clear the German communication was in a mess following the recent battles. The soldiers looked tired and in a state of shock. They certainly didn't look in a state to fight.

Albert approached the man who was standing by the remains of a shop in the small village of Passchendaele. Once, it had been a butchers, now it was empty, and like the rest of the village, intact and relatively undamaged. It seemed an obvious place to set up a rest station. Inside, the meat hooks still hung on the metal lintels. Where there were once hinds of beef and pork, now they were filled with equipment hung there by tired and weary soldiers, each trying to get some rest in a warm and safe building. The road was busy with troops moving up to the front, all too busy to talk to a stranger, especially a stranger with a British prisoner.

Albert walked to the water bowser and went to fill his canteens, and a big Sergeant, who had a bandage around an old wound in his arm, stopped him. The blood had soaked the bandage and had set hard as it dried.

"What do you think you are doing, old man? This is water for the German Army, not the British." He nodded his disapproval towards Jack.

"We all need water, Sergeant, even prisoners. We have a long walk back to headquarters and both our canteens are empty." Albert went to fill the water bottles but again the Sergeant stopped him, this time grabbing Albert's arm.

"I said no water for the pig!"

Albert looked at the hatred in the Sergeant's eyes; his own blue eyes took on a familiar dead look.

With cold loathing, he spoke very quietly. "Look down, arselecht, to where your balls are at the moment, and you will see that the blade just about to geld you is quicker than you. Now let go of my arm or I will stick you right here and now." He pushed the razor sharp blade a little harder and felt the cloth of the Sergeant's uniform give as the knife slid onto his scrotum.

"One more word, or even a squeal, and I'll gut you. Now step away and let me get my water. Then I'll be on my way, and you might be able to father another child, but be sure, if you say one more word, you will die right here."

The Sergeant looked into Albert's cold, sinister eyes and knew, without any doubt, that this man shouldn't be trifled with, nor crossed; he could tell Albert was a killer. He stepped aside. This man must be mad, driven beyond the brink by the shelling, he had seen it many times before. He convinced himself that it was best to leave him be, and he walked into the shop.

Albert filled both bottles with water. It was warm but clean and both men had a long drink from the bottle before he filled them back to the brim. Passchendaele was only a short stop, and within an hour they had carried on towards Roulers, some 5 miles further up the road.

On the walk, they tended to walk side by side. They talked calmly about all the things they missed and home. To anyone looking on, they would have appeared as friends. They had never talked about what they did before they actually met on that fateful day in the shell hole. There seemed little to say;

they each knew what the other had done and the reputation each had.

Fate was a strange ringmaster; it was fate that had led them to this path. Albert knew that he wouldn't be walking back this way. If he lived, and he quite doubted he would, he would head back home to Monica. His service done, no debt to pay, he wondered if there would be a happy home now that Hans was dead.

He never even got the chance to say goodbye to his son, it was this unknown feeling that was within him. An amalgam of grief and rage, with more than a pinch of loathing, which allowed him to believe he would make the mistake that ultimately would cost him his life. He had a job to do before anything like the luxury of death.

Like the vermin that had been Hauptman Berger, the high command had little or no respect for the ordinary soldier. One day there would be a revolution, and on that day, the workers would be freed. His job was to ensure Jack got into a position to kill as many of the imperial command as possible, but then he had to try to get him back to his own people.

The time he had spent with the English had been, on the whole, a good and happy time. He had seen the way the common folk were, and they were the same as he.

# CHAPTER 50

# Roulers

It seemed unlikely that two armed men – one from the German side and an Englishman in full uniform – could just walk into a major military encampment. Such was the chaos on the streets, but more the disinterest in anything other than personal survival.

Albert and Jack had arrived at the outskirts of Roulers by nightfall. Tired and hungry, dirty and thirsty, they fell into an old farmhouse outbuilding about half a mile from the town. In the near distance they could hear a train, it was puffing steam and the occasional toot of its whistle was shrill but still pleasant to hear. There were very few trains in the area and this one must have been a military supply train, dumping equipment at a yard a few miles away.

The two men rummaged around the old pigsty, long since vacated by any pigs that had lived here. The smell was better than they first imagined and with a few sweeps of a boot, the floor was ready for the men to sleep.

Overhead, there was the sound of artillery, and this time Jack knew it was German, on its way to the British lines. He had heard the sound of shelling for years and yet, tonight, it seemed more disturbing. It was a mournful sound. Soporific yet tragic, death and destruction was flying overhead and nothing could stop it.

For a moment, Jack was totally unattached from reality. He never heard the footsteps of the men at the doorway, he had assumed it was Albert coming back from taking a pee outside. He was brought back to earth instantly by a blow to his kidney and a scream of "Hands up!"

The initial kick was rapidly followed by several others, all painful, but none quite as painful as the one that connected directly with his balls.

There was yelling, but it was all in German and Jack didn't understand any words apart from "Hands Up". He rolled into a ball on the floor, with his hands over his head and face as the blows continued to rain down on him. Within a second or two they had stopped, and Jack dared to take a look at his assailants.

He was horrified to see it was the Sergeant from way back in Passchendaele, this time with three men he hadn't ever seen. They were laughing and whilst one spat on Jack, the other undid his fly buttons to relieve himself. Jack was disgusted as the warm urine splashed his face and head. The Sergeant laughed louder, and as he did, his companions joined in. Jack felt the rage rise in him. This was no way to take a prisoner, and what had they done with Albert?

As the last stream of urine was forced out, there was a cough and a gurgling sound from the man shaking his manhood. The cough became a wheeze, and as Jack looked up, he could see the first four inches of a bayonet protruding from the German's stomach. Then there was a pistol shot, quickly followed by two more. There was a louder rifle shot and the dying man with the protruding bayonet was blown off the blade by a bullet. Blood splattered onto Jack's face as he looked on the scene of carnage.

Inside the sty were three dead Germans, two with headshots from very close range and a third with a large hole in his back from the rifle bullet. There was a click, clack as a rifle bolt was worked and then another shot. This one was into the back of the running soldier who was about thirty yards away. It was the Sergeant who was running, but not any longer. The bullet hit him in the neck and threw him forwards onto the floor. He was also dead. It all took less than a minute.

Albert stood at the doorway, the smell of cordite filling the small room and mingling with the smell of fresh blood. Jack felt quite nauseous.

"Jack, are you hurt?" asked Albert

"No, I don't think so. Well, not badly. What the hell was all that about?"

"They obviously followed us, I am so sorry. I was taking a crap, I didn't even see them coming."

"Jesus Christ, Albert. I'm glad we are on the same side." He looked down to see the three dead Germans, and the efficiency with which they had been dispatched made Jack wonder. He wondered if he could have done that, as it was close and personal. Killing with a bayonet was normally preceded by rage and fury, but as Jack looked at Albert, he was sure he could see him smile.

"I couldn't let them kill you, Jack. You are my friend, and besides, it was me they were after; that Sergeant was trouble right back at the water bowser. He was stupid to follow us, he should have just walked away as I asked him."

"We need to hide the bodies," said Jack. "They'll be found and then there will be trouble for us."

They collected the bodies and dragged them to the building, where each was stripped. Then, they found various bits and pieces of redundant farm equipment scavenged from the area and tied them to their feet, before Albert stabbed the bayonet into the four bodies' chests so that they'd sink and not bloat up, or float up to the surface in the warm water.

Once they had finished this grizzly chore, the bodies were thrown into the small lake that lay just behind the farm. They quickly sank below the surface, never to be seen again. Just some more names lost in the war effort. They were glad of the night's darkness; it helped hide the deeds of the killers.

Apart from stumbling around outside, and making more noise than they liked, they were comfortable with what had to be done, and got on with it. When they had finished, they were hot and sweating from the hard work of moving the bodies and equipment. The Sergeant was about the same size as Jack so they kept his uniform but had a small fire with the rest.

There in the corner were the water bottles, food and ammunition. All liberated from the dead, and now pressed into service to feed the living. There was sausage and cold potatoes, but it felt like a feast to the two hungry men.

By the time they had finished, they both felt drained. The long walks in the hot daylight hours had been tiring, but the adrenaline and exertion of the last couple of hours had left them feeling shattered. They had cleared away the mess from the pigsty and managed to find the original door for the sty building standing up against the back wall. It just dropped back onto the hinge brackets and was fully working in seconds. Now they could close themselves in and feel even safer.

Whilst disposing of the bodies they had found some bales of straw left over from some cavalry troop or horse and cart. Either way, it was enough to make a decent bed on the floor and within a few minutes, with the door locked from the inside, they were sound asleep.

Jack was woken the next morning by the sound of aircraft overhead. The aeroplanes were quite low, and the high-pitched noise of the propellers grabbing at the morning air was in stark contrast to the quiet of the night. Albert was sitting by the window, smoking a pipe of tobacco.

He was reflecting on the previous night and the fact that he had no problems killing men from his own side. It wasn't the first time he had considered his apparent lack of allegiance to his countrymen. He was more concerned with the man he had become rather than feeling remorse for the people he had killed. He reflected on the fact that this war had changed him as a man. Prior to the war, he hadn't killed anything more problematic than a hog or boar. Now, killing had become easy; there were few feelings at all, let alone remorse. He wondered if he would ever be able to recover and vowed that once this war was finished, he would never lift a weapon again.

He had been watching over his new friend, asleep and restful. Today was a difficult day because they had to find the church, and once inside, get to the top of the tower. From there, they would have a perfect view of the area where Ludendorff would be making his pathetic gesture.

Jack yawned, looked at his watch, and was surprised to see it was gone nine o'clock. The warm July sun was already getting high in the sky and it was nearly time for them to move on. Today was really about doing reconnaissance; having a map was one thing but seeing it for real was different again.

Before they left, they both agreed that they needed to check the area for any sign of last night's fracas. They checked all the ground they had been over and found nothing. If anyone missed the German soldiers and came looking, they would find nothing here.

Jack changed into the dead German's uniform. He knew that he had crossed a line. If he were caught now, he would be shot – there would be no question – but he knew he was going to be shot if he was caught, no matter what he was wearing. They packed Jack's uniform into the backpacks and set off. If stopped, they would have to pretend Jack was dumb with shock and let Albert do the talking. Once again, Jack's fate was in the hands of his German friend.

Breakfast was the remains of the supplies from last night: cold sausage and stale bread, followed by strong, black coffee. Rations were scarce and the added bonus of the acquired food was welcome. It had come at a high price for those who had brought them. Breakfast finished, it was time for one last smoke before they left.

In the distance they could see the tower of the town hall. Magnificent and massive, it was the perfect place for a sniper, perhaps too perfect.

Only time would tell.

# CHAPTER 51

# Up In The Tower

It surprised Jack that there were so many different units moving around Roulers, and none paid the two men any attention.

It took them only an hour to reach the Market Square, at the end of which stood the magnificent building that was the town hall. The belfry was huge.

Albert sat on the kerb at the side of the road and at the edge of the square. It was really quite hot now. Hundreds of soldiers walked past them, all looking weary and unhappy. Gone were the days of bravado, replaced with a reality of death and mayhem.

It was unnervingly quiet without the constant booming of the artillery. Albert asked a couple of stragglers what was happening, only to be told they were going back to the front early because an attack was due. The artillery was saving their ammunition. The attack, when it came, was going to be met with equal fire and fury. The German army might be tired and weary, but they were a proud nation and they truly believed that they would be victorious. It quite unsettled Albert.

Albert kicked Jack's foot and the act was on: Jack acted dumb, a distant stare without focus helping to complete the picture.

The pair walked towards the towering hall, and at the steps they looked up at the tower. It stretched up towards the sky. It would indeed be perfect. All they had to do now was climb the stairs. They had thirty-six hours to be in place and ready. Plenty of time, really. They took the first step heavenward.

The massive doors were unlocked and ajar and as they stepped in, the world went dark. Apart from the beautiful windows, still intact and complete, there was no other artificial light to be seen. It took a few minutes for their eyes to adjust to the dimness inside, but when they did, it was breath-taking.

Albert walked round and tried the different doors. Each time he opened the wrong one he cursed. Behind one, the clerk of the hall was sitting eating his lunch, reluctant to abandon his position of dubious authority. He stood to greet them, and seemed pleased, rather than annoyed, that someone was even vaguely interested in his building.

Albert said he and his wounded colleague were on their way back to the hospital and needed a rest from the summer sun. He was happy when the clerk confirmed that the hospital was about 5 kilometres further back. Albert said there would be time later for them to retire back to the hospital, but for now, did he mind if they looked around? The lunching official was happy to leave them to their own devices. Everything of value had been removed before the town had been fully occupied by the advancing German Army.

Albert apologised for disturbing lunch and took his leave. The next door was a stairway, a long stone spiral that rose skywards. Slipping through the door, they started their ascent. Up and up, round and round, the tight spiral made

255

their legs burn with the effort. They passed the first floor entrance and continued climbing for a further three levels until they came to the belfry, empty of the majestic bells, long since removed.

The shutters on each wall were old and mainly riddled with worm; they easily allowed for a slat to be removed so the men could look out over Roulers. They had a commanding view of the market place and the ceremonial square that had been fashioned for the coming presentation. Inside the room, dark and stiflingly hot, were piles of linen rolls all scattered like jumble. A handy bed for later, but there was little sign of any occupation, or indeed any visitor for many months, if not years. All apart from the birds who had nested and had chicks. Here, both birds and the two men felt safe.

Jack prized one shutter from each window, allowing plenty of light to seep into the darkness. With this light, they could see that far from being abandoned, it had been home to at least a dozen men in the past. Their names were carved into the scaffold for the bells. Dates ranged from 1914 to only a few weeks ago. This was a disturbing revelation, not least because if anyone should find them, or come back to claim their space, they wouldn't be allowed to give the mission away. There was only one way to ensure that.

Having removed one high shutter from all the windows, Jack proceeded to remove two lower shutters on the west wall window. This offered a grand view, and at the right height for the snipers when lying prone. Albert dragged some linen rugs over to the floor under the shutter. Within minutes, the two men had made a fantastic shoot spot, and all the equipment, rifles, scopes, ammunition and rations were laid out ready for either cleaning or eating and drinking.

Albert had blocked the door so no one could enter. It was indeed all they had hoped it would be; the view was awesome and from the east window they could see the train line with steam trains on the line as far away as the eye could see.

Apart from the fleas in the linen and the lice in their uniform that were now going mad to feed on the hot and sweaty bodies of the two men, things couldn't have worked out much better.

Jack stripped down to his pants and Albert followed suit. By removing the shutters, they had inadvertently allowed a cooling breeze to blow through the room, a fortunate mistake that afforded them a simple luxury: fresh cool air. The dust, on the other hand, wasn't welcome, and there was plenty of it now that it had been disturbed. Both men had to cover their faces so as not to cough and make any undue noise. In time, the dust would settle or be blown away, but for now it was a nuisance and nothing more. The danger would be if they lit a match, and Jack pointed this out to Albert who agreed instantly with a realising nod of his head. No fags or pipe then.

They took sips of the warm water in their bottles, and nibbled on hard biscuits whilst they cleaned the two rifles, and the optics on the scopes and long eyeglass. Once all was ready, they dared to take a look through the telescope at the area they needed to see. They estimated the range to be no more than 400 yards, easily within a comfortable range for either sniper; with or without scopes they would both be able to hit a saucer from that range. Over the afternoon they had moved more of the linen rolls nearer the shutters to help form a platform for the shooter to lie on, so no rifle barrel would protrude outside the window.

The distance from the window to the platform was only two feet, but it would ensure that, in the chaos following the shot, no one on the ground would be able to see where the shot had come from. It was a sign of the thoroughness of the two men.

Once they had both had a good look around, they sat under the window ledge with the cooling breeze playing across their wet faces. It wasn't long before they dozed off. The complete madness of what they were doing together was lost on them. No one would ever believe that two men, at the height of their military prowess and from opposite sides, could conspire to attempt to assassinate the High Commander of an Army, deep behind enemy lines and with little or no prospect of escape. It was madness. The madness of sane men driven beyond what was considered normal in any other time but a war, but here they were nonetheless.

They slept the sleep of righteous men, men who truly believed they had right on their side. Tomorrow would see the culmination of a plan that had started with a note of condolence to a man who had lost so much, from a man who felt he had lost everything. But it was more than grief that bonded these two men: it was affection and friendship, as well as a shared desire by each to ensure the other man survived the mission.

When they awoke, the day was nearly finished. The war, on the other hand, continued unabated. The shelling had started again.

There was very little left to do apart from wait, and that was easy to do, so they waited.

# CHAPTER 52

# The Long shot

The sun broke through the shutters and sent a sliver of light along the dusty floor. This slice of light grew longer and brighter, lighting the room. The day had begun.

Jack looked at his watch: it was half past five, and the parade was due at ten.

Breakfast was simple and ablutions were basic but the tension was already building. Albert was awake and washed, cleaning his beloved rifle once more before cleaning each single bullet. Unusual for soldiers but not for either sniper, each bullet was cleaned as thoroughly as the rifle; oiled with the last of the moisture of oil on the pull through cloth, every bullet was treated with the same care and attention. Attention to detail was the difference between life and death, and although by oiling the bullet, it did give off a slight smoke from the muzzle of the barrel, today's mission was well hidden and no one would know or see the slightest puff of blue oil smoke. Out in the field, you just wouldn't do it.

Outside, there was more activity than they had witnessed the previous day, but that was to be expected. Today was special; it wasn't every day the Commander-in-Chief visited.

Albert had mixed feelings about the day. His only son was being remembered today, albeit in death. He was also being remembered himself. It suited the command for Albert to be dead even though they had been told he wasn't.

The irony wasn't lost on him. Today was a means to an end, and although he really had no pride in what he was doing, he did have hope. The hope that by killing Ludendorff, the German war effort would lose impetus. It was all but finished anyway.

Down in the square, a band started to blow, not tuneful but individual instruments clearing the passages. It was nearly time.

The band stopped their racket, as did the artillery, and all was quiet outside. As Jack looked down his sniper scope, Albert used the telescope. The view was clear and sharp. The band started to play again, this time together. It was quite loud and it showed to both that the wind was blowing towards them. This was easily confirmed by looking at the flags which had been erected around the top of the makeshift cemetery. Through the telescope, Albert could see the two headstones standing side by side. He knew his name was on one and on the other was Hans. He felt overwhelmed by grief and felt the back of his throat burn as he tried to hold on to his emotion.

Jack climbed onto his makeshift platform and settled his Lee Enfield onto a roll, acting as a rest to ensure he was as steady as a rock when he squeezed the trigger. He checked his watch: it was quarter to ten.

Looking down through his sight, he could see that a parade had formed, and it was clear that the men below were as smart as they could be. There was a lot of spit and polish and everything looked brand new. Albert said it was a medal presentation for the brave, and then there would be a solemn moment as the father and son were remembered as giving the supreme sacrifice.

Albert nudged Jack and told him it was time. At the far end of the parade, a fine carriage had arrived. The band struck a fine tune, and then it stopped suddenly. Within a few seconds, it struck up again, and this time it played the National anthem of Germany. Albert looked shocked. Jack stared at him and wondered what could possibly be causing Albert to look so unsettled. Albert peered hard through his telescope.

"Jack, it's not Ludendorff; the bastard isn't here. It's the Kaiser, shit! It's the Kaiser!"

Jack looked hard at the distant walking figure which was surrounded by an entourage of sycophants. There, right in the middle, stood a man he instantly recognised. He looked just like his own King George.

He realised instantly that there could be no shot. It would be a catastrophe to shoot the Emperor. Such an act would inflame the war effort, not end it. Jack thought what he would do if someone shot the King. He couldn't comprehend what the results would be. Right or wrong, every man loved his King, or indeed his Emperor. It would be both stupid and suicidal to take that shot. All the training, all the effort, everything had been for nothing.

Jack was desperately trying to get his head and thoughts together. He had put his rifle down, he knew he couldn't shoot the Kaiser, but what happened now? Did he just try to make his way back to the British lines on his own, or would Albert want to join him, or go home to Monica?

Albert was just about to put down his telescope when something caught his eagle eye in the distance. He looked and fine-tuned the scope to help him clearly see what he was looking at. Seeing it and not quite believing what he saw, he looked down and cleaned his eyes before looking again, his blood turning to ice.

There in the distance, about 400 yards beyond the Kaiser, was a mortar and a team of four men. The mortar was out of place; hidden as it was in a backstreet, it certainly didn't belong there, but what terrified Albert was the fact that the mortar was aimed at the Royal party.

"Jack, look at that. What do you think it is? Beyond the square, about 400 yards." He passed the telescope over to Jack who, lying down, had a perfect view.

"Where am I looking, Albert?" He glanced along the line being pointed out by Albert's outstretched arm. He saw it straight away and looked at Albert.

"That's a mortar. Bugger, there's a mortar pointing right at us?" He hadn't even considered that it might not be them as the target.

"Jack, you fool! It's not us, no one knows we're even here! It's the presentation party. They must be trying to assassinate the commander. Surely they can't know it's the Kaiser. How would they know such a thing? Jack, we cannot allow them to kill the Kaiser. It will be a disaster! It has to be the Bolsheviks, Jack."

News of the revolution in Russia in the February had spread like wildfire amongst all sides. It was well understood that all the fighting men had had enough. Indeed, just the month before the French had seen deadly reprisals for mutiny in the trenches, with firing squads serving out the punishments for the leaders. Surely the same must be true in the German trenches. There was disquiet in the British lines, so why not the Germans?

"Jesus, Albert. That has to be at least 800 yards, and with the wind, nearer 900. That's a very long shot, but what choice do we have?"

Looking back at the mortar crew, it was obvious that they were preparing to fire.

"Let's try anyway, you take the one on the left," said Jack, and both men took up their weapons. The process of the shot had begun.

Taking two long, slow breaths in and out, Jack was in the moment. His total concentration was on the shot he was about to take. He aimed about two inches above the target and slightly to the right to compensate for the steady breeze.

He squeezed the trigger gently, then there was a deafening boom from next to him and he let his finger tighten fully, his rifle jumping back into his shoulder instantly. Within a second, two bullets were on their way.

It seemed like an age before Jack was able to look down the telescope to see if they had managed to hit their targets. In the distance, two men lay dreadfully wounded. The one on the left had been caught in the stomach and was writhing around on the floor, whilst the one on the right had been hit higher in the chest and was motionless. Two hits, not bad, but the next two were as committed to their cause as the first and had picked up the shell ready to drop it into the barrel of the mortar.

Jack's next shot was away in a flash but missed. As he fired, so did Albert, who managed to hit the mortar and send it spinning round, which at worst bought them some time to have a third shot. It was whilst aiming the third shot that the door erupted inwards.

There were just too many of them to fight. There was a scuffle, and for the second time in a week, Jack was on the floor, being beaten and kicked. He looked up to see Albert being hit with the butt of a rifle, and as he looked away he saw, just for an instant, the edge of a rifle stock.

Then, with a huge bang, it all went dark.

# CHAPTER 53

# Caught

When Jack awoke he was covered in blood, his blood. He had a large gash above his left eyebrow that clearly needed stitching, and a sharp pain in his side. When he felt down it was also covered in blood, and there was a neat slit in his vest where a bayonet had paused, albeit briefly, whilst the blade slid deep into his side.

He was outside. The sun was beating down and as soon as his captors saw him open his eyes, more kicks followed until he nearly passed out again. Only a lone voice stopped the pain. It wasn't Albert.

Albert lay at Jack's side, his hands tied and blood covering his head. Like Jack, he had taken a dreadful beating, and like Jack, his captors had thrown him down the stone spiral staircase. Unlike Jack, he hadn't had the good fortune to be unconscious. He had felt his ribs break as he bounced down and only the last almighty bang to his head from a stone step had made him senseless, but not pain free. He groaned in agony; his right arm was clearly broken as was his collarbone. His face was swollen and blooded, his nose broken and a large laceration behind his ear showed where the rifle had hit him.

"Halt!" screamed the officer. "The next man to strike either of those men will be shot and I'll do the fucking shooting, now stop." There was an edge to this man's voice that cut through commands. It was from an educated but streetwise man. A man who didn't need to try to be authoritative as it came naturally.

Jack couldn't understand a word, of course, but Albert was trying to speak, and as the officer knelt over him, he wiped Albert's mouth with a wet handkerchief. Albert – who was still in most of his uniform – was obviously a German but Jack – who was wearing only his underwear – wasn't, and he hadn't spoken a word since he had been hit. No one realised he was English until they had found his folded uniform in a German backpack.

"Get these men some medical aid immediately; there's more to this than meets the eye. So tell me again, sir. These men went upstairs two days ago but they were both German and one was wounded, are you sure?"

The town hall clerk nodded. "Yes that is correct, one was mad. I thought you should know that they were deserters hiding away."

"These men, they are not deserters, they are something else, and if these idiots stop trying to kill them for one minute, I'm sure they will have a fascinating story to tell." The officer helped Albert to a chair; he looked as though he was dying.

"My name is Albert Hagerman, and my friend is Jack Adams. He is British and trying to help me get home." Albert was in great pain but as determined as ever to save Jack's skin one last time.

"We caught some Bolshevik deserters four days ago back at a farm on the way here. I can tell you where it is roughly but they are dead so they won't be able to help you. We were resting for the night and they attacked us, but before we killed them they told us about a plot to kill Ludendorff and the Kaiser today."

Albert was making the whole thing up as he went along but it was very convincing and the officer was enthralled.

Albert went on. "We didn't know where they were going to shoot from but they were all bombardiers so we knew it was a mortar. The tower was the best place to see from, did we stop them? Your men came in before we had finished. If you look at the headstones the Kaiser was to bless, you will find my name. The one next to it was my son, Hans. My friend here was just trying to get me back to right a wrong, as you can see I'm not dead yet, but it won't be long. Don't let him die. Please don't let him die; he is a good man, brave and honest. Jack Adams, that's his name." Albert coughed as a pain racked through him. At last, he closed his eyes and passed out.

The officer was asked to move by the medical bearers. Jack had a wound-dressing put on his side; it was bleeding very badly and the blade had obviously severed a large blood vessel. He was drifting in and out of consciousness, and despite the warm summer sun he was cold.

With all of his resolve, he reached over to his friend Albert and took his hand. He squeezed, and was rewarded by feeling Albert return his gesture. Both men were near to death, and yet even in the desperate fight to stay alive, they had thoughts about the other. The officer saw this moment of kindness and drew his pistol to help them on their way to peace.

# CHAPTER 54

# Hospital

Jack sat in the hospital bed. He had undergone surgery the day before and his side was very sore. He was still woozy from the gas they had anaesthetised him with, but he was alive. His eye was bruised and caked in dry blood but it was under a bandage and the bleeding had stopped. The long cut above his eyebrow had been sutured neatly, but it would leave a scar.

As he sat there, he felt alone; the ward was full but everyone else was German and he couldn't understand anything that was spoken, although he did understand that he was now a prisoner himself. The war was over for Jack and he felt a strange sense of relief that he wouldn't be called upon to kill again.

A young German officer walked down the ward with the doctor and a nurse. As Jack looked down the long ward, the sun was shining onto the back of the three and there was a fug of cigarette smoke hanging in the roof space. In the distance, Jack could hear the constant explosions of shellfire. It was coming from the direction of Passchendaele.

The group stopped at Jack's bed. The doctor looked at the charts on the end of the bed and nodded. The young officer said, in a perfect English accent, "You're awake, good, I'm glad to see that. My name is Hauptman Smit and I am here to find out what you were doing in Roulers, Mr Adams."

Jack blinked his eyes and swallowed. His mouth was dry and the nurse offered him a drink of water. "My name is Warrant Officer Jack Adams. Sir, can you tell me what has happened to my friend Albert Hagerman please?"

"Yes, of course, you must be wondering what has happened to him. He is fine, in fact you can see him from here if you look." He pointed to the other side of the ward. There, about ten beds away, lay Albert, his head in a bandage and his arm in a sling, asleep.

Jack let out a huge sigh of relief, which was quickly noted by the Hauptman.

"You are good friends, yes I understand. Hagerman has told me everything and I can assure you, you will not be harmed. On the contrary, once you have recovered you will be sent back to your own side as a mark of respect from the Kaiser. We found the mortar and the men responsible for the attempt on the life of the Emperor. You had killed two of them and we caught a further two who confessed to being Bolshevik sympathisers. You are to be congratulated, Warrant Officer Adams, we owe you a great debt of honour."

Jack was stunned. He hadn't got a clue what this man was on about but he seemed quite happy. Jack and Albert had agreed to say nothing if captured so what the hell had Albert told them? It seemed to Jack that the Hauptman had a story in his head that meant Jack wasn't going to be shot as a spy or sniper and the fact that he could see Albert meant they hadn't shot him, either. It was all a bit confusing and Jack did wonder if the anaesthetic had fully worn off.

The next day, Albert explained the lie to Jack. "It just seemed like a good idea at the time," said Albert. "The truth, it seems, was harder to believe than the lie so they are all quite happy to believe the tale we have spun. They are sending me home to recover, Jack. I've been told I won't be able to fight anymore so the war is over for me. You are going back to your side this week as well, with a letter from the Kaiser no less, to ask that in honour of your bravery and as a gentleman, you won't be asked to fight anymore either, and that on your return to England you are to be released from service. You have been granted a full pardon and a medal from the Kaiser, Jack. For us it is over. It's time for us to go home, Jack."

Jack helped Albert fill a pipe with tobacco. He didn't feel like a fag, but there was one so he took it, and with the same match he lit first the cigarette, and then the pipe for Albert. Albert took the offered pipe and had a couple of puffs. His ribs still hurt like hell, but he coughed more if he didn't have a pipe.

Jack lay back on his pillow and took a long drag from the cigarette. The two men blew a long plume of smoke into the air and watched as it mixed into a long swirl.

They looked at each other and smiled.

It was over.

# Epilogue

Jack sat on a huge tree trunk. It had been blown over in the strong winds of winter. He had finished work for the day; the pens had plenty of food and the new pheasants were well settled. The weather in the summer of 1922 had been kind.

There had been changes, of course, there had to be. Some of the changes had been very painful, like the suicide of Tim Alcot in 1919. It had hit the Colonel hard to find him hanging in the barn. He had returned from the war a broken man. He never really recovered from first losing his leg, and then losing his lover. Jack had known about Tim's secret but never let on.

Jim had done well. He drank too much for Jack's liking, but Jack understood and it didn't get in the way. Edith said she didn't mind Jim having a drink, and that was good enough for Jack.

There had been some significant changes for Jack, more than most, he thought. He had married Alice in 1918, six months after being released from the hospital in Buxton. His wounds had healed well, and although he sported a long, thin scar on his eye which Alice called his 'German duelling scar', he had little time to dwell on what had happened since the birth of the twins. They were 4 years old now, the boy named Albert and the girl Elizabeth after Alice's mother, who was now with God. She died of Spanish flu in 1919 whilst the twins were just babies.

He had thanked the Lord for his mercy in a church, at the funeral of his mentor and friend, Hesketh-Prichard. To Jack, he was a hero, but it appeared that to the rest of the world it hadn't taken long to forget the great man; there wasn't anyone from the military there to pay their respects.

Big Albert wrote letters each month to Jack. It was a constant comfort to him that his old sparring partner and friend had survived to go home to a loving wife. Monica had waited, and never believed that God would take both her men. Jack knew that a letter was waiting on the mantelpiece behind the clock for when he got home later. He had seen the postman out and about and he had told him there was a letter from Germany.

As estate grounds manager, Jack held a good position on the estate. The Colonel had made good his promise to look after the men he employed who had gone to war. Jim had his old job back, and as ever, Jack carried more of his job than he should have shouldered, but he never minded. Jack felt he was blessed. He had great friends, men who had shared the same things in a stupid war, but never felt the need to talk about it.

As Jack approached the house, he waved to Alice from the paddock. She was hanging the washing out. It was all she seemed to do these days, but Jack knew she did so much more. He watched as Albert hid, a children's game of hide and seek, and he knew that Lizzy would have her work cut out to find him; he had his father's talent.

Back at the house, he washed his hot face and hair in the sink at the back yard. Alice pumped the hand pump and cold, fresh water gushed over his head. It was good to be alive.

The letter was where he expected it to be. He sat in his chair with a fresh cup of tea and a huge jam sandwich on a side plate. He kissed Alice and told her, as he did every day, that he loved her.

It was, indeed, good to be alive.

# The Letter

*My Dear friend Jack,*

*I hope this letter finds you in good health. We have enjoyed a hot summer so far and the woods are busy with hunters so I am kept busy also.*

*I trust that Alice and the children are doing well. I have sent a wooden carving by parcel for the children's birthday. I hope it arrives in time but the postal system here is not as reliable as it was in the past. I am hoping that one day I might be able to come to England and see my English family and old friends.*

*I have news from Germany for you. I have been employed as shoot major and town mayor since Helmut Plekt died last year. It does mean I have to attend various shooting parties but none will be as exciting as the ones we used to do together eh?*

*Monica is in (how did you say it?) rude health despite the dreadful shortages we still have to bear. I have heard that things are getting better since the Nazi party have started in the south but things there worry me Jack. There is violence on a regular occurrence, there is much shame felt by the men who came back, and I fear many of them are still looking for a fight. Did they not get enough between 1914 and 1918?*

*We are lucky here in the area, we have many jobs in the fields and woods but in the towns and districts things are looking sour.*

*One day you might be needed again to shoot the leader of the Nazi party for I fear they have war on their minds. One such man is in the paper here, he is getting a name for himself as being a troublemaker, like us he was in the war, and his name is Adolf Hitler.*

*I will say my goodbyes to you Jack.*

*Your friend always*

*Albert Hagerman.*